Warlocks of Evergreen

Warlocks of Evergreen

The Evergreen Journals Book I

T. I. DUNSTERVILLE

ISBN-13: 9780692682500
ISBN-10: 0692682503
Library of Congress Control Number: 2016905734
T. Dunsterville, Evansville, IN

Basking in its solar fire,
The slumbering planet crawls with incessant life.
Awake not to ire,
The behemoth that knows you well.
Tread softly the skin of a world,
And learn its language before it awakes.
By Dasimbe Halcon

Table of Contents

MAP I (South): Olin and Phoenix to Osa Marsh

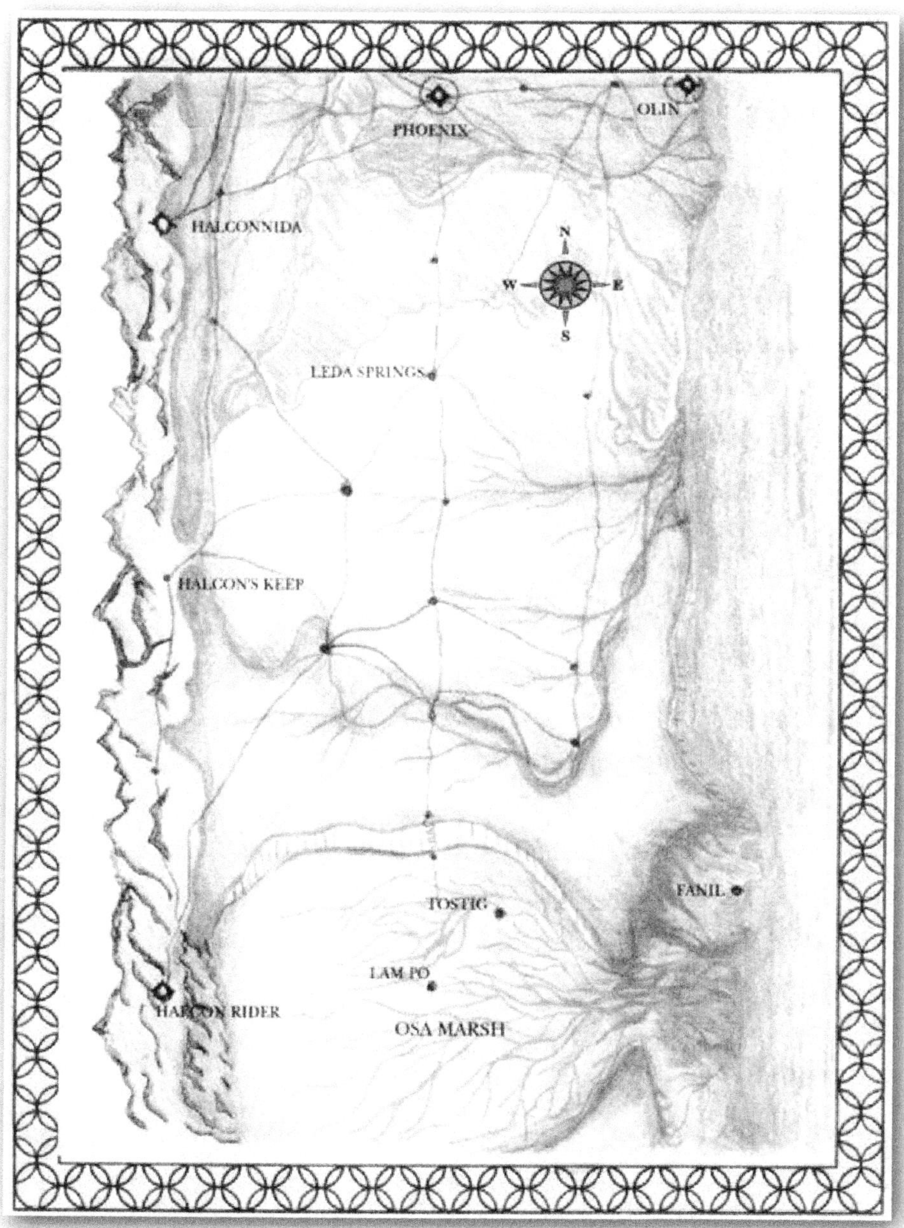

MAP II (North): Olin and Phoenix to the Northern Forest

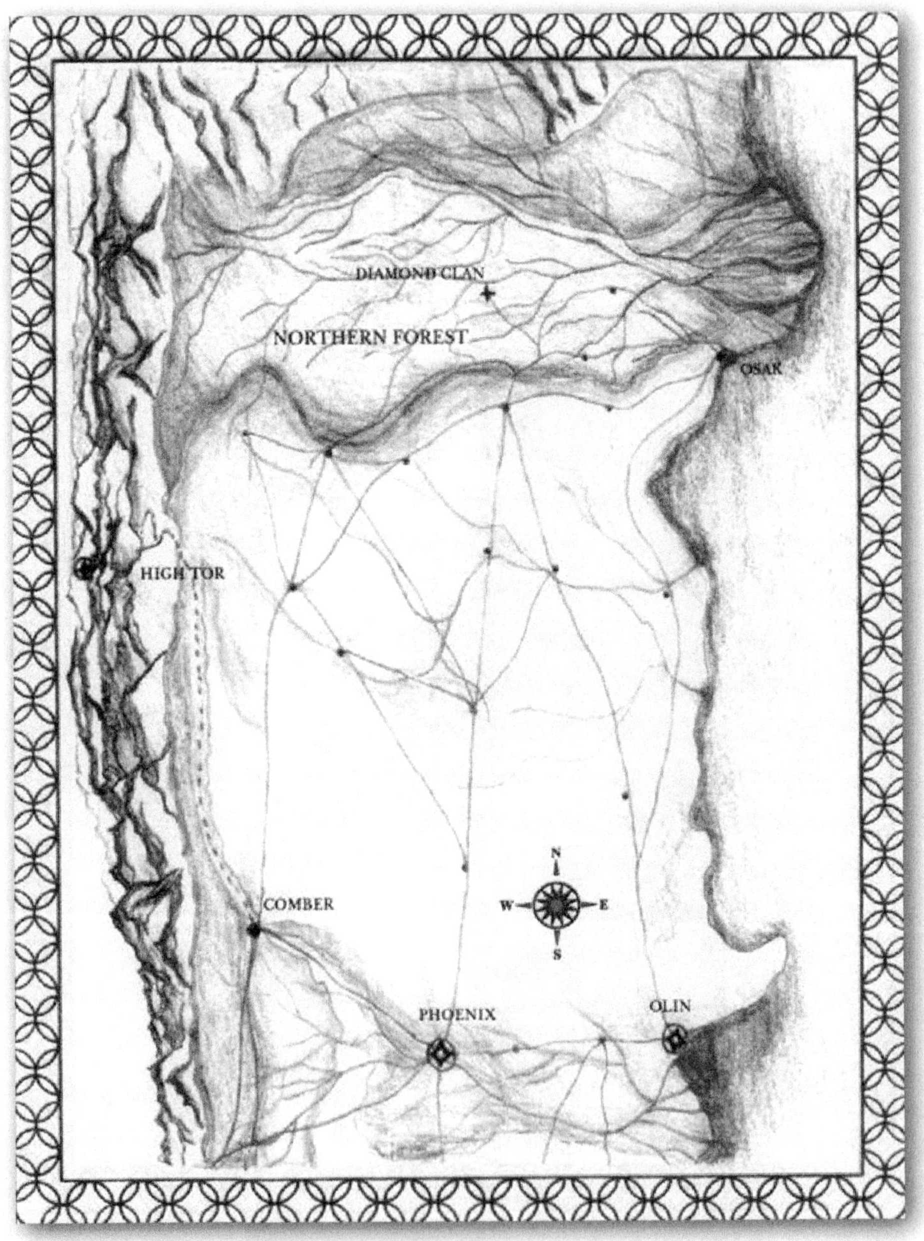

Prologue

Dasimbe Halcon

What will these men and women think of my world, a planet that is alive and speaks to you, not in words but in images and visions laced with emotion and intent, even to the choice of a mate, I thought as I sat in the viewing chair with my hands clasped loosely in my lap. Although a film of sweat coated my palms, I remained calm and determined, shoulders relaxed, as members of the Galactic Federal Union's governing council appeared in their own viewing chairs. Some had dressed simply in GFU uniforms, as I had, while others wore elaborate and (to me) exotic attire. We met in a holographic setting, yet featureless backgrounds gave no hint as to the nature of each man or woman's home world, and I held my curiosity, excitement, and any concerns behind a suitably restrained smile. Then, when the last member's image had materialized, the head councilor said, "CIAM, start recording." He paused before his gaze rested on me. "With all one hundred twenty-one members of the Galactic Federal Union council present, I introduce you to our guest, Dasimbe Halcon. She has requested our attention regarding the planet Evergreen and its quarantine. Representative Halcon, are you aware that this session is being recorded by CIAM, the Central Information Assessment Module?"

I nodded. "I am aware of the recording."

"Then you may proceed," he said. He gave no nod in return.

I took a breath and began my carefully honed argument. "Honorable members of the Galactic Federal Union, as the half-breed daughter of a human sorcerer and a sea sprite of the planet Evergreen, I have been chosen to represent both its human and indigenous species in our protest of the continuing quarantine.

"I understand that sentience of planetary magnitude is rare, an enigma that challenges humankind's conception of life and intelligence, and that many in the GFU question Evergreen's intentions toward humanity. Also, the genetic changes and the unique mental talents that have evolved among the planet's population are feared by some and desired by many. I understand this too. Yet we on Evergreen believe the planet poses no threat to humanity and that this fear is unwarranted.

"I am not alone in my plea that the GFU consider repealing the quarantine. Many of the residents who share my love and knowledge of Evergreen have granted access to their personal memory journals to provide you with a better understanding of the relationship between our planet and its human inhabitants. Thus, I ask that you join in our memory transference."

Then I reclined the viewing chair, and its transference shield flowed to cover my body, covering my eyes and plugging my ears. Each council member mirrored my actions. When the transference drugs took hold, I slipped into a structured dream, a remembrance of my past and the pasts of others.

What follow are those of our recollections that were transferred to the councilors.

Halcon Rider

Stephen Scott—Summer 1835 AB

I slipped through the shadows, a wraith wreathed in a summer night's sweltering darkness. The smaller moon, Silver, in its dark phase, shed no light on the slumbering city, but only half an hour remained before the larger, full-faced Copper, would rise to cast its golden glow. In my minor shape-change, I appeared fully human, yet in this city, even a human abroad in the deep of night would be suspect.

An irritating tickle of sweat threaded down my back as I paused at a corner near the apartment I shared with my foster brother, Karl. Using mind search, I felt for guards hidden up and down the street.

Damn, too many, I thought and glanced up at the apartment's dark, lifeless windows—dead sentinels that revealed nothing. A quick mental scan of the interior revealed no human presence. This gave credence to the rumor that Karl had been taken by Paul Rider's men. I shivered at the thought and then pushed it aside to consider my options.

I decided the best chance to enter the apartment undetected would be from the rear, where an absence of streetlights and an abundance of trees cloaked the yards and back alley. I melted further into the shadows and edged down the street.

Unfortunately, more of Rider's men guarded the alley, and they held flickering torches. I debated using an invisibility ward, but broadcasting that much mental energy would risk Rider's detection. Erecting a milder confusion ward, I switched to night vision and disappeared into the shadows of the alley. The humans saw nothing as I passed.

I opened a gate, its well-oiled hinge giving me silent entry into the high-walled pocket of darkness behind my apartment. Concealed from prying eyes, I canceled the confusion ward. Remembering the long unused and noisy backdoor lock, I considered shape changing into the guise of a large cat. In that form, I could easily slink under the trees and climb to the second floor. I decided against it. The larger expense of energy would definitely disclose my presence to Rider and the few half breeds he retained. I returned my attention to the alley and Rider's men, each silent in his own pool of torch-cast light. None seemed to register my presence. Only a distant dog's barking joined the incessant burr of insects to bother the night.

Retaining night vision, I reset the confusion ward and loped off into the dark toward the large tree whose sturdy branch extended beneath my bedroom windowsill.

I climbed a route I had previously scouted for escape rather than entry and soon slithered through the window into my abandoned, dusty bedroom. Scanning the shadows, I noted a few things I would take on my way out, then crept toward the deeper darkness of the hall. I held my breath and stepped into the gloom, listening for any creaking floorboard. Nothing in the apartment stirred except me. The air hung heavy with silence and summer heat—no scent of life remained. Sweat coated my palms as I released a breath and started down the hall toward the slightly lighter rectangle of Karl's bedroom doorway.

I entered his room, as abandoned and lifeless as the rest of the apartment, and my dread became reality in the dust carpeting the floor and coating the furniture. Nothing had been touched in weeks. The room reeked of Karl long gone.

I clenched my fists, fingernails biting into palms. How long since Karl had been taken? Was he imprisoned with my foster parents and sister? All signs had indicated this desolation, yet I had hoped—

Grief and bitter disappointment flared, and pent-up anger against Paul Rider flamed into rage.

Smothering the urge to howl, I hissed through gritted teeth and flung up a ward to screen this mental broadcast of emotion from Rider and his half-breed lackeys. I struggled to subdue my feelings and, in the space of several deep breaths, brought the seething mess under rigid control. Only a slight tremble remained, and my eyes stung.

I took another deep breath and scanned the room for any secreted message. I found none, but my attention caught on a model sailing ship partially hidden in a shadowy corner shelf. Karl had built the ship after our last family vacation on the Babel Straight. I reached for the ship and its sunny memories but held them for only a moment. The memories hurt. Stowing the ship in my backpack, I left the room.

I reentered my own room and grabbed the few remaining personal items. Picking up a small recent family portrait, I gripped the frame in tight fingers and scanned each face in turn.

Samuel and Donna Barns, my foster parents, stood together. Until their incarceration, they had spent every workday at the Barns Foundry where Karl and I had worked as managers. I stood beside Karl, his eternal grin eclipsing my smile. At thirty, we were the same age and the best of friends. Twenty-three-year-old Jasmine sat in front. I smiled briefly as I recalled how a younger Jasmine had followed Karl and me everywhere. Although I still thought of her as a child, for the past two years she had been engaged to a Meridian named Xanth. Karl had been engaged to Xanth's sister, Celdony. I remembered Jasmine's tears and Karl's anger when the Meridian community fled South Halcon to escape Paul Rider's abominations. Were it not for Samuel and Donna, Karl and Jasmine would have followed.

Cliff stood to the other side of Karl, his smile as spare as my own. Two years my senior and a member of South Halcon's border patrol, he roamed who knew where. Again suppressing threatening emotions, I hastily shoved the painting into my pack and climbed out the window.

Leaving the alley the same way I had entered, I again adopted human guise and kept to the shadows as I walked to my contact point in Halcon Rider. My footsteps sounded hollow in the shroud of silence enveloping nearly empty streets. Only a few years before, the commercial district's nights had been brightly lit and boisterous times. Now shops closed early, the population thinned by conscription and a nebulous fear of Rider's soldiers. The soldiers seldom stopped anyone yet remained a constant reminder of the violence used against half breeds, nonhumans, or anyone obviously opposed to Rider's "cleansing" of the human species.

I slowed my pace and opened my thoughts to pick up mental impressions from my foster family. Within limits, sensitivity to family and friends guided a mental opening with little detectable use of talent.

There! Catching a thread of their dreams, my focus flew to the old jail near the city center. I sensed the walls and guards surrounding them, and although their troubled dreams held despondency and an underlying fear at being imprisoned, they remained unharmed, and no immediate threat loomed beyond incarceration. With a sigh of relief, I closed the link, but frustration remained—it would be impossible to aid their escape without putting them in danger or revealing my identity as a half breed.

A restaurant loomed, one our family had frequented with friends, and familiar odors lingering from the evening brought bittersweet memories of camaraderie and better times. Two doors farther along I pushed memories aside as I entered the Anvil Tavern.

Peering into the gloom, I spotted my contact at a table against the wall halfway down the room. Mason Hill used a mild confusion ward, like I did, to screen his blue skin and unusual eyes from the human population. Only our immediate friends, families, and foster families knew our true identity and appearance.

"Stephen," he greeted me and nodded slightly but did not smile.

I nodded in reply as I slid into the opposite chair. He signaled a waiter who hurried forward to take my order.

"The same," I said, pointing to Mason's beer. The waiter departed into the shadows. The huge and poorly lit room, although not as full as it could be, remained busy enough to screen private conversation. Overhead fans struggled to stir humid, odorous air and added their swish to the drone of voices and clink of mugs and bottles.

"I just came from my apartment," I said.

My gaze fixed on Mason. His eyes held mine, steady but compassionate. "I'm sorry, Stephen. We had no idea they were going to take Karl, or we would have gotten him out of the city. He's being held with the rest of your foster family."

"I know, and I hope that because they're not half breeds, they'll be OK."

He sipped his beer and frowned. "Their only crime was in owning something Paul Rider wanted. Now he has the foundry, I doubt he'll harm them, but they may be imprisoned for some time."

"And Samuel and Donna openly spoke against him. They'll never leave that prison." My anger rose again.

The waiter returned to place a beer in front of me and then scurried off to serve another customer. I clenched the stein.

"Steady," Mason said and sent a mental touch of calming influence in my direction.

My stranglehold on the stein eased as tense muscles relaxed, and I again gained control of my feelings. I nodded in appreciation. "Thanks. Do you know what Rider's plans are?"

He leaned forward, elbows on the table. "We do now. He's just declared war on North Halcon. Benjamin cut his visit short and returned to Halconnida when the news went out. I doubt he'll return."

The declaration of war did not surprise me. I smiled, albeit wryly, glad that my true brothers, Benjamin and Daniel, who were also scouts, would be out of the mess South Halcon had turned into. Benjamin had returned to represent us in Halconnida, and Daniel usually traveled incognito from Halconnida through the whole eastern region to Olin on the coast.

"How about your foster brother, Cliff? Did you find him?" Mason asked.

I had gone to inform Cliff that he now served in the army of a man who had incarcerated his family. I had not found him, and now I knew why.

"No, too much troop movement."

Mason shook his head, his eyes filled with concern. "Will you be all right working here?"

I pondered his question, which was valid enough considering my feelings. "If you're asking if I can control my emotions enough to function without endangering myself, I think so. Either way, I'm not leaving until the GFU calls us in."

He nodded. We both knew that with only two of us in the city, and no Guide Scout covering the rest of South Halcon, information on Rider's activities would be scarce—and vital. Nevertheless, at some point, the Galactic Federal Union would pull us from Halcon Rider. Although we knew how to defend ourselves, Guide Scouts were never intended to be soldiers.

I stared into my drink, thoughts roiling. Although several of my true brothers and sisters ranged across Evergreen, purposely fostering peace between the species, it had come to this—one man had taken over a city, then a country, and now he prepared to spread war, hatred, and genocide elsewhere. I shuddered at the thought.

Mason scanned the room while sipping his beer to see if we had attracted any undue attention. The patrons remained engrossed in their own beers and conversations.

"Mason," I said, catching his attention. "How far do you think Rider intends to spread this war and his sick, warped idea of civilization?"

His face hardened, eyes reflecting the bleakness in my own. He shook his head. "Who knows? But I fear attacking North Halcon will not satisfy him for long."

Ｐ Ｈ Ｏ Ｅ Ｎ Ｉ Ｘ

Dasimbe Halcon—Summer 1835 AB

I jerked awake, heart thudding and body tangled in sweat-soaked sheets. Apprehension followed me from sleep with the remnants of a dream, yet I remembered few specific images, only vivid emotions. Grief, I had felt that, and anger. I shivered, and my pulse slowed as I tried to recall more, but obscure thoughts flitted and faded as I sought them and left nothing except dour dread.

I stirred myself to stretch. The dawn light had changed from pearl gray to molten gold, and although shadows still clung to the room's edges and amid the dried plants hung from poles across the ceiling, the night's chill was quickly dissipating into summer's heat. Shoving the damp sheets aside, I sat up, swung my feet to the bedside rug, and stretched again, trying to ease tight muscles and shake off any lingering uneasiness, but my skin crawled with the feel of it.

"Damn, what was in that dream?" I muttered as I rose and headed for the shower, hoping to drown my agitation in running water, but it remained to prickle my skin as I toweled dry.

After donning a sleeveless tunic and shorts and hastily braiding my hair, I hurried through still cool and shadowy granite halls to join my older sister, Cierva, for breakfast and to tell her of my dream and its strange effect. Our parents would have already eaten and left for an early council session.

Cierva, as lightly clad as I, stood by the south-facing dining room window, feeding crumbs to a green-scaled mite perched on the ledge. Its tiny

7

scales glinted faintly, first green and then gold, in the shaded morning light as it hopped about avoiding her touch while pecking at what she offered. Piping its distinctive call, it flew away when she turned to greet me.

"Good morning, Sim. Can you pack with this dreadful foreboding hanging over us?" She absentmindedly brushed the remaining crumbs from the sill.

Foreboding! Was that what I felt? The unpleasant feeling went right to my bones. I grimaced but continued across the room to pull morning bread from its bin.

"I can work, but what's causing this?" I answered. "And how do you know what foreboding feels like?" In my agitation, I neglected to return her greeting.

"I don't know what's causing it," she said as she joined me in the kitchen and pulled iced juice from the cooler. "But whatever it is, we have to finish packing. We leave for Olin in two days." She poured juice into two glasses. "As for knowing the feeling—do you remember when Mother and I attended the weavers' gathering in Olin last spring?"

I nodded and bit into my bread. She handed me a glass of juice and joined me at the table.

"Then you'll remember that a storm brewed later than usual, well beyond the normal storm season. Fortunately, everyone along the coast and those aboard ships felt foreboding long before the storm. If not for that warning, lives would have been lost."

"I remember the story, but isn't that a kind of foreknowledge?"

She shook her head. "Not quite. It's a vague warning of things to come rather than specific images or ideas. And it always feels awful."

A warning! I felt that, but what about the intense grief and anger I had sensed on waking? The emotions had felt so real, and the vague thoughts and images that had faded leaving dread anticipation—were they only a nightmare? I grimaced again as I sipped the juice. I ate only a few bites of morning bread before we left for the living area to start packing.

The residential wing of Phoenix's huge administrative complex stood on a rise above the Comber River. Colossal blue-green marazul trees shaded the building in feathery darkness, yet ceiling fans struggled, and by midmorning, the combination of heat and packing left us dripping with perspiration.

A voice interrupted our labor. "Hello. I see you're busy." Gloria Sanchez stood by the door. Her dark eyes, normally twinkling, held a somber cast. "Can you come by tonight? We should visit every night before you leave for Olin." She frowned. "After that, I'll probably die of boredom."

"We'll try to," Cierva answered as she wrapped a large shell in soft cloth.

"If we have any energy left," I added.

Gloria pouted. "Well, see that you do." Then she waved and turned to go. "I have a class. I'll see you later."

I wondered if Gloria, a budding sorcerer from North Halcon, felt the same foreboding as Cierva and I. Would she recognize the feeling—or know what caused it?

We continued working, and by noon, the plains surrounding Phoenix shimmered under a haze of heat and dust. Tired and edgy from the foreboding, I sighed with relief when Cierva closed the lid on the last box, brushed aside the wisps of hair clinging to her damp forehead and said, "This room is finished. I think we deserve a break."

I nodded and flicked a lock from my own brow before whacking a nail into the box's lid.

While she prepared a noon meal, I left the residential wing and descended toward the diplomatic offices on the second floor near the city council chambers to inform my parents of our progress.

My human father, Ciervo Halcon, a sorcerer from the mountainous North Halcon, represented the city of Halconnida to both Phoenix and Olin while my mother, Dalia O'Meral, a sea sprite from Olin, represented her people to Phoenix. Attending council meetings and social functions in both cities, they monitored any change that might affect trade or relations between the human and sea-sprite communities.

Meanwhile, Cierva and I bobbed between the two cultures, never feeling wholly of one or the other. Although we found friends among those who like us lived the nomadic life of diplomats' children, Cierva was the only person I knew who shared my half-breed heritage. Mixed-species unions and their offspring were rare, and although I felt no animosity from either species, as I came of age, I felt our differences more acutely.

I arrived in the corridor outside my parents' office as my father handed a coin to an administrative page in exchange for a wire message. The young page bobbed his head and smiled before scurrying off, sleeve ribbons fluttering, to deliver the remaining letters in his pouch. He seemed oblivious to the heat. My father smiled after him before turning to gesture me into the antechamber adjoining the office.

"A message from Halconnida," he said to my mother, who stood by a small table where a plate of meat rolls, a dish of fruit, and a jug of iced cider awaited them. Looking as cool and comfortable as always, Mother wore a sleeveless sea-sprite shift of pale iridescent fire that glowed in contrast to Father's white trousers and shirt, which were adorned only with the mountain folk's colorful embroidery on collar and cuffs. Behind Mother, a shimmering sea-sprite tapestry scented the air with the smell of sea grass as it moved in a breeze from one small window. Muted voices mingled with the clip-clop of horses' hooves and the rumble of wagon wheels to filter in from Phoenix's streets.

Mother smiled as she sat down and gestured Father to the table's other chair. "Ciervo, let the bad news wait for a moment while we eat."

Frowning, Father dropped the envelope to the table and took his seat.

I gaped at the envelope as a chill ran down my spine and wondered, as always, at Mother's calmness in the face of adversity or bad news—and bad news it was; we all felt it. The missive lay on the table like an evil talisman, its mysterious intent reaching out to ensnare us.

"Do you plan on joining us, Dasimbe?" Mother asked.

Despite the unusual ambiance exuding from the message and my curiosity, I looked up and smiled. "Thank you, Mother, but I'm having lunch with Cierva. We just finished packing the main room."

"Very good, and thank you both," she said before she sent me off with my curiosity intact, the envelope remaining unopened on the table as I departed.

Cierva's north-facing room felt reasonably comfortable. Although a jumble of packing boxes cluttered the floor, small tapestries she had woven from the silky threads of sea grass still hung by the window, and a richly hued spread of Phoenix cotton covered the bed. We lolled across that while we ate our midday meal.

"I think I know the source of the foreboding. It's in a message from Halconnida," I said before biting into a red pear, its juice gushing into my mouth. "But I didn't get to read it," I mumbled and then continued to eat as I waited for Cierva's response.

At first she only nodded, saying nothing as a small frown creased her brow. What could be said when the message's contents remained a mystery?

She ate a handful of nuts and then sighed and rolled onto her back to stare at the ceiling. She grimaced. "Let's forget about the foreboding for a moment. I'd rather talk about something more pleasant, like Olin." Her face brightened. "Harrin and Jalin expect me to join the council next year as a junior member."

Although a budding weaver, Cierva enjoyed debates with her sea-sprite mentors and aspired to become a diplomat like our parents. Meanwhile, I flirted with ideas of travel and adventure that had nothing to do with my training as an apothecary.

"I wish I could see more of Evergreen," I said as I discarded the pear core and reached for a handful of nuts. "I'd go from city to city meeting all sorts of people and writing their stories. That's a diplomat of sorts."

Cierva laughed and then lightly chided, "You're only seventeen. I hope you plan on finishing your training as an apothecary first. I know you enjoy it."

I scowled in her direction. "Of course, and I do love my work, but sometimes I feel like doing something more exciting."

Nevertheless, I valued my medicinal training and varied education. Besides classroom studies, I attended council sessions. I knew enough to follow the sessions and record salient points, although Cierva had more interest in these things than I. She had been attending council meetings on a regular basis for two years, while my training in council had just begun.

By giving Cierva and me an opportunity to study matters of government and diplomacy, as well as a trade, my parents encouraged us to follow in their footsteps, hoping to foster a growing bond between the human and sea-sprite communities.

Twenty-year-old Cierva enjoyed her weaving and appeared well on the way to becoming one of Olin's master weavers, like our mother. She also shared Mother's cool reserve and quiet beauty, with heavy black hair, silver-gray eyes, and the iridescent skin and slender stature of a sea sprite. Except for my iridescent complexion, I took after our father, with bright, red-gold hair and green eyes that reflected a less sedate personality. While Cierva dreamed of putting her budding diplomatic skills to the test, I wanted adventure. My parents seemed pleased with her choices, and they waited for me to grow up.

After our break, I went to my own room, where pale walls highlighted the aromatic medicinal plants strung on poles across the ceiling. A ceiling fan stirred the plants to lightly scent the air, giving an illusion of freshness to the summer heat. I hoped the electricity would not give out, as it often did. Although the building's granite walls kept the shaded room comparatively cool, the fan labored, and a sheen of dust and perspiration from the morning's work coated my skin. I went to shower.

When I returned to my room, I gathered my brush and comb and relaxed in the recess of a shadowy, stone window seat to dry and comb out my hair. The faint scents of potted wisteria, mimosa, and jasmine drifted in on a light, dry breeze as I gazed on the rooftop oasis belonging to the family who lived below our third-floor apartment. A marmalade cat dozed on a cushion beneath a striped awning surrounded by fruit trees in wooden tubs. Flowers of pink, salmon, red, orange, and yellow cascaded over pots set against sun-drenched, whitewashed walls. At the roof's edge, a wall of dark-fringed marazuls towered to arch overhead, screening the view of the river and plains beyond. The splash of fountains in the courtyard beneath the marazuls tinkled above the background noise generated by Phoenix's busy streets on the far side of the building.

Despite my peaceful surroundings, foreboding intruded, an irritating prod to do something—but what? I frowned and contemplated a visit to our own garden but decided against climbing the spiral stairs to a rooftop that baked in noonday heat. Better to stay in the relative cool of my room and try another form of escape.

Lowering my comb and closing my eyes to the view, I envisioned Olin perched on its cliff high above a sparkling, sunlit sea. I imagined a sea bird's piercing cry rising above the sound of surf crashing into rock and felt for the brisk scent of brine. With a salt tang on my tongue, I reached for the rhythmic sound of the sea lapping nearby beaches, and then the ocean slid over my skin in a cool caress as I submerged beneath its waves. As my fantasy enveloped me, the feeling of disquiet hovered tenaciously—and the scene suddenly changed.

I stood on an icy parapet as a winter storm raged, sleet-drenched winds tearing at my hair as the stones shivered beneath my feet. The air thundered with the voice of a swollen, angry ocean flinging itself against the cliffs below Olin's seawall. I grasped at the rime-covered stone, and then I saw him, a few feet away, a figure swathed in darkness, sleet, and mist, radiating an awesome mental power reaching out and out—

A knocking interrupted the vision.

"Sim, Father will be waiting." Cierva stood by my open door, reminding me it was time for our lessons in the use of our mental talent.

"I'm coming," I said and shook myself out of the dream to leave my window aerie and cross the room. "Cierva, I just had the strangest vision. I was watching someone sending from Olin's cliff top wall during a winter storm. To send from outside in a storm! How crazy is that? I couldn't see who, but the send was unbelievably strong."

"Foreknowledge?" she asked.

"Sending outside in a storm?" I frowned at the thought and shook my head.

Cierva shook her head also and then started down the hall. "We had better go."

We walked through the administration building's wide halls with their familiar hum of everyday activities: pages with arm ribbons streaming as they ran their errands, city councilors and representatives from outlying towns hurrying to attend afternoon meetings, and the never-ending petitioners waiting to present their questions or grievances. Through the crowd, I glimpsed Gloria's handsome older brother, Manuel, as he spoke with his friends. I liked his laugh and wondered what it would be like to know him better. However, as Cierva and I continued on, smiling at all those we passed, I remained acutely aware that he, like all the humans around us, felt nothing amiss. Cierva and I kept our foreboding, and our mental abilities, to ourselves. Although many in Phoenix knew our father was a skilled mountain sorcerer and held him in awe, they, including the other Halcon mountain sorcerers, knew little of our mother's sea-sprite talents and nothing of what Cierva and I could do. The humans of Phoenix and the surrounding plains displayed no talent and seemed to have little interest in such things.

Cierva and I made our way to the building's core where huge octagonal rooms housed the main council chambers. There we descended below ground to the subbasement and entered the cavernous, ward-shielded, octagonal room used for talent training. The remaining rooms at this level were for storage. Our classroom, fully two stories deep, held shadowy corners, but beautiful, dimly glittering sea sprite tapestries graced the walls, perfuming the air with the scent of sea grass. Worn carpets, a few tables, chairs, and shelves scarcely furnished the enormous space. A great hearth opened on one side of the room to augment the poor heating in winter, and high above our heads, numerous small windows let in air and daylight. Dust motes drifted down in sunbeams that barely touched the top of the glimmering tapestries.

Father awaited us, an agitated presence filling the room. A tall man with red-gold hair shot with silver, his green eyes flashed fire.

Cierva and I paused respectfully at the entrance, waiting for his direction. He had always commanded respect, winning the loyalty of those who worked with him from the time he led North Halcon's border guard as a young man. He carried his responsibility as an ambassador with equal ease. I was intensely proud to be his daughter.

He gestured for Cierva and me to sit without a customary greeting. This did not augur well for future events. I went to my seat across from Cierva and quickly sat down.

Father, seemingly lost in thought, paced once across the floor before he too sat down.

"Sim, Cia," he finally greeted us, and before we could reply, he said, "I have bad news. The local conflict in South Halcon has escalated to include the whole southern region, and now—" He paused and sucked in a breath. "The south has declared war on North Halcon." He frowned and shook his head, his eyes sparking in agitation. "What can the idiots be thinking of?" he muttered.

I felt a jolt of memory. Something in the dream! But before I even gasped, Father continued. "I'm needed to help train a larger force for North Halcon's defense. If the conflict continues, I'm to command a division of the army, which means I won't be going with you to Olin, and our family may be split up for some time."

He stopped, his face registering a struggle of emotions before he said, "I'm sorry. We won't be having lessons today. I leave for Halconnida tomorrow, and you will return to Olin with your mother as planned."

He looked for our response, but Cierva and I sat in stunned silence trying to comprehend what this meant to us.

Worry for my father swallowed the memory of my dream. Although vaguely aware that South Halcon had internal problems, and that the threat of violence kept humans in the Halcon Mountains in constant mediation, this turn of events shocked me. Skirmishes and border disputes among the mountain people flared up with regularity but had never led to outright war. Now our father planned on going into the middle of it. He had often returned to Halconnida for diplomatic reasons but never when there was danger or for any length of time. Now I feared for his safety.

"We'll do as you say," Cierva finally responded in a whisper. I nodded in numb assent, feeling as if everything secure and familiar in my world had been shaken apart.

He excused us from the room.

For the rest of that day, shock, disbelief, and anger warred within me as Cierva and I finished preparing to leave for Olin. We said little, too consumed by our feelings to communicate easily, but we each knew how the other felt.

The next morning, those leaving for Halconnida because of the newly declared war gathered under the building's front portico to say good-bye to those who were staying behind, and that group of traveling merchants and diplomats from North Halcon included Gloria's family. My parents had already said their good-byes, and Mother remained composed, but I could feel Cierva's distress as if it were my own.

Gloria approached us. "I'll miss you." Her voice cracked.

"And we'll miss you," I said and hugged her. My fear for her safety added to my fear for my father.

Having said his official good-byes, Father approached Cierva and me. He hugged us both. My eyes blurred and burned with unshed tears as he embraced me.

After releasing me, he turned to my mother. They clasped hands in a silent farewell before he turned and mounted his horse. Then he and his fellow travelers rode out from under the portico and into Phoenix's streets.

My hands clenched into fists, and fingernails bit into palms as I watched him go.

"South Halcon," I said. "How could they do this? What's wrong with them?"

"Sim," Cierva said, and she reached for me.

I released a fist to grasp her hand, and we clung together, watching until the retinue disappeared from view.

* * *

The next day, Mother, Cierva, and I left Phoenix, heading east into the morning sun with two heavily laden wagons. I experienced none of my normal anticipation on leaving for Olin. Instead, sorrow and anger left a sour taste in my mouth. I shifted in my saddle and looked back toward Phoenix, but resignation took hold as we descended a wooded slope and thick-leafed oaks hid the city from view.

I turned back toward the east and, despite the day's blossoming heat, shivered in apprehension. A warning of things to come coiled in my mind like a serpent. The foreboding had not abated.

OLIN
Dasimbe Halcon—Winter 1835 AB

*A coral jewel on the ocean's shore, Olin glows, a bright
backdrop to the colored sails of ships and fishing boats
that ply the bay in summer. In winter, storms cast
towering waves against the cliffs below the city, yet warm
halls resound with song and laughter, and tales are told
while the storm waves dance. Then, when the sky is dark
and violent, Olin is filled with the sea sprites' light.*

— *ENTRY IN DASIMBE HALCON'S JOURNAL*

Four months had passed since our arrival in Olin, and the year had
slipped deep into its winter-storm season. All along the coast, the dark
underbelly of a tempest tore the ocean into great sprays of spume, and the
sound of waves pounding on rock reverberated into the furthest reaches of
the city. On a cliff above the frothing sea, a mist-shrouded Olin spiraled
inland and downhill in dim coral rings toward the southwest and the sheltered docks. On an island in the center of the bay, a tall, mother-of-pearl
tower shimmered through intermittent curtains of sleet.

On the highest edge of the cliff, the city spiked into storm-watch parapets and towers, and despite the waves thundering below, I walked a curved
parapet high above the seething sea. The storm suited my restlessness, and
although I was snug enough in boots and a waterproof woolen cape, my

face stung from sleet whipped by a gale that wound my cape into a shroud and coated my lips with brine. Fingers of icy wind teased a red-gold lock of hair loose from its restraint, the only color in a world turned gray by the storm and the coming of night. The bright strand snaked across my eyes. I pushed it back beneath my hood in agitation and continued walking, thoughts of Gloria, my father, and the war in the Halcon Mountains foremost in my mind.

I knew fighting continued along the border between North and South Halcon while the inner cities remained untouched because Gloria and I had written long missives back and forth over the months. She wrote of daily events and of her fear for her parents being near the war zone. Her parents and Manuel had traveled on from Halconnida to their home near the border town of Halcon's Keep, while Gloria and her younger brother, Raul, lodged with cousins in Halconnida. I also wrote to my father, who had little time between training new recruits for anything more than a short reply, but he also assured me that Halconnida remained safe. While thankful for this, I remained despondent. I missed my father, and worse, the foreboding never abated. It shadowed my days and followed me into sleep. My training as an apothecary, frequent joyful gatherings in Olin's great hall, and my awareness that Cierva felt the same daily foreboding did nothing to ease my growing frustration. I wanted to go somewhere and do something. I wanted to hug my father.

Meanwhile, the residents of Olin seemed uninterested in the war, even in council meetings, and that puzzled me. The sea sprites thrived on news and gossip. Was the war of no consequence to them?

For the first time in my life, I felt trapped in Olin, and I hated the feeling. I also hated the fact that Mother's ties to the sea kept us from joining my father in his distant mountain home. Sea sprites could travel only a short distance from the ocean before their physical health and mental faculties declined, and Phoenix seemed the natural limit. Although Mother handled the separation without comment, I felt her frustration as keenly as my own. Cierva, despite the foreboding, remained calm and seemed a better companion to our mother than I with my constant agitation, so before night added its darkness to the storm, I left the warmth inside Olin to walk the parapets alone.

Head bent against the chill, biting wind, I trod carefully on the ice-rimed stone, still lost in thought, my hood pulled close. Then a sudden, fragmented wave of alien thoughts and images tumbled into my mind—and my own thoughts splintered into chaos.

I stumbled on the wind-torn walkway and reached a hand to steady myself against the slick stone balustrade. Trembling, I flung up a guard to dampen my reception and attempted to clear my mind as I peered through the mist and darkness. Immersed in thoughts of the war, I had failed to notice a lone figure facing inland, his back toward the angry sea. My pulse raced, and although shielded, I felt his presence as if he were blood kin or a half breed. Had he not been sending inland with such incredible strength and intensity, he would have registered my presence immediately.

Amazed at the strength of his talent, I froze into stillness and then gasped as recognition hit and sharpened into shock. My nostrils flared, and I trembled. This is real, I thought in fear. It's really happening. The strange vision of someone obscured by a storm's darkness, sleet, and sea spray—

I took a deep breath and shook my head slightly, trying to think through my fear. Thoughts clicked into place, and I remembered that the sea sprites' talent naturally guarded the city from any malicious intent. They would have registered him and his send as they did all that went on around them. Laughing at myself, my fear dissipated. That he stood in the main structure of Olin meant they considered him a friend, but who was he?

I attempted to assess him. The figure was male, although his cloak and hood hid that fact from eyes if not from mind, and he still sent inland to some distant receiver. Warily, I moved closer, but curiosity overcame caution as I drew near, and I dropped my guard to carefully open on the edge of his send, invading his privacy.

A sharp dagger of pain lanced between my eyes. With a hissing gasp, I staggered as the howling wind, stinging sleet, thundering ocean, and shivering stone all receded beneath a knot of blinding pain, and I sank to my knees on the parapet.

A mental probe feathered the edge of my thoughts as I fought the pain. Not a deep probe, yet it sickened me. I knew I probably deserved the abhorrent probe and cursed myself for having invaded his send. I peered up through tearing eyes to see a hooded shape looking down at me. The probe vanished, but the pain remained.

"From the Halcons," his comment resonated in send. *"Why are you in Olin, child of the mountains?"*

I felt no condemnation in his formal question, only curiosity, and realized that thoughts of the war in the mountains had left the most recent trace in my mind.

Because the storm made oral conversation impossible, I fought the pain and rising nausea to send him an answer and asserted my right to be in the city.

"I'm a child of sea-sprite blood also."

I felt his breath of surprise echo through my mind and wondered if he had heard of my family. Despite the pain, I faced him with pride and perhaps defiance.

Then he pushed back his hood.

I gasped. *Not human!* Strands of damp, black hair loosed from a ponytail trailed against blue skin on high, sharply defined cheekbones. Darker blue lips, although fully human, were set in a firm line. And his eyes! Totally black and glittering with swirling shards of light, they were utterly alien and strangely beautiful.

He went down on one knee and grasped my gloved hands. Tingling warmth emanated from his fingers into mine and coursed through my hands, arms, and body until I felt warmed throughout, and the agony of throbbing pain disappeared from my head as if it had never existed.

A surge of bonding followed. To my surprise, I felt kinship obligation and the sense of fates entwining, something I had never experienced outside my family.

"Who are you?" I sent in amazement. *"And what are you?"*

He continued to gaze at me and frowned, a line of darker blue briefly crossing his brow. *"Much like you it seems,"* he whispered in my mind and then asked, *"Is Ciervo Halcon your father?"*

My pulse quickened as I answered, "*Yes. Do you know him?*" Perhaps this man had been to Halconnida and recently seen my father.

He only nodded and then looked toward the tower door opening onto the parapet.

"*Let's get out of this storm,*" he prompted before I could ask another question.

He stood, drawing me up with him, and then released my hands. Warmth vanished along with his touch, and the chill of the storm again swirled around me. Towering over me, taller than any human or sea sprite, he gestured me forward. Eager to hear news of my father, I headed for the tower door.

We entered the tower and descended into Olin's neat spiral of coral halls. Moist air held the scent of sea and sand. Snug and pink-hued like the inside of a shell, the halls, living areas, communal gathering areas, administrative rooms, and council chambers remained well lit with steady glow lights, unlike Phoenix in winter with its drafty buildings and flickering electric lights. Most rooms clustered around courtyard gardens, and at Olin's heart nestled a great hall with an adjacent kitchen. The weaving halls and dyeing yards, docks and fish market, inns, taverns, and stables, and a huge central market extended out from the main spiral in separate loops.

I knew the man beside me was no merchant staying in an inn because he stood within the main spiral. Before I could ask what business he had with the sea folk, I received a send from my mother.

"*Dasimbe, please bring him to my room. I felt his send and know he intends to speak with me.*"

The stranger had heard Mother's open send and nodded, so I led the way through curving pink halls to our family's rooms, the muted thrum of the sea accompanying us as we burrowed deeper within the coral coil. The stranger remained silent. Although burning with curiosity, I felt too reticent to ask questions. He would only have to repeat himself when we stood before my mother, and in truth, I found his countenance daunting.

I knocked when we arrived outside Mother's room, and we entered upon her summons. Cia sat beside Mother at a large loom, her pale eyes widening in curiosity. Mother, expecting us, had put her shuttle aside.

I closed the door, but to save the carpets from damp, we remained in the entryway, dripping moisture from our capes onto the coral floor. I introduced my mother, my sister, and myself before asking the stranger, "Who are you, where do you come from, and why were you sending from outside in this weather?" I griped the edge of my cape, impatient to hear his answer.

He smiled, seeming amused by my questions. "My name is Daniel Scott. My home is in the mountains beyond North Halcon, but my recent travels took me through Halconnida. I know your husband, ma'am," he addressed my mother, "and plan to return to Halconnida immediately. I leave in the morning. As for my sending from the parapets"—he turned toward me—"I enjoy the privacy of a storm. I'm sure your interruption was unintentional."

The mention of my father and Halconnida overcame the sting of his comment, but his answers did nothing to relieve my curiosity. I had never heard the name Scott, but the name Daniel was common enough in Phoenix, and neither name gave any real clue to his identity. His appearance still demanded an explanation, as did his height and clothing.

He had loosened his cloak on entering the room, and I could see some of what he wore beneath. His clothes appeared similar to that of most humans, except for the lack of color. The black cape, coat, trousers, and boots seemed overly severe, even stark compared to the plains peoples' earthy browns, greens, and rusts. I could see no ornamentation. My father's people, the mountain folk, wore colorfully embroidered garments, and even their farmers managed some bright stitchery. Against the sea folk's light, bright, shimmering fabrics, the solid black appeared entirely alien. His leather trousers, tucked into high leather boots, were garments worn for riding. Wearing leather for comfort and durability indicated someone who spent much of his time on horseback. This was no tradesman or farmer.

I shivered in excitement. The blue skin on high, sharp cheekbones and the black eyes filled with glittering, swirling sparks bothered some memory. An obscure reference in one of my father's more unbelievable tales told of a tall, blue-skinned race that dwelt high in the mountains beyond North

Halcon. Seldom seen and rumored to have powerful talents, warlocks were a people out of legend.

I stared at the stranger. Had the legend come to life? Although I sensed him as a half breed of some kind, he reeked of talent far beyond what I knew. If he were a warlock, it would explain his powerful send.

During his introduction, I felt the stranger open his thoughts to my mother by lowering a shield as strong as any sea sprite's, leaving her free to search his mind. I marveled again at the strength of his talent.

Meanwhile, he assessed us each in turn. A smile softened his severe features, and his glittering eyes danced with warmth—or mirth.

His focus returned to my mother. If he knew the sea sprites, he knew my mother already understood his intent from the gist of his send, without invading it as I had done.

Seeming satisfied with what she found in her search, Mother stirred and smiled in return, but her silver gray eyes were serious. She arose from behind the loom and approached us. Cia remained seated, watching and listening.

"Please be seated, and let Dasimbe take your cape."

Mother gestured Daniel to her small sitting area where red and gold cushions covered ledges cut into the coral that comprised the floor and walls.

As he unclasped and handed me his cloak, I caught a flash of silver on his collar and focused, glimpsing three silver stars before he turned away. Watching as he took a seat, I eyed his tall, rangy form, lithe as a sea sprite and yet broad shouldered and flowing with underlying strength. Were warlocks warriors as well as mages?

I hung up the cloaks and helped Cia put away her weaving tools while Mother let down window coverings over a wintry night held at bay by mental force shields. The gold-threaded red shades added an appearance of warmth to the slightly chill room. My attention remained on the stranger. He seemed relaxed, at ease in his surroundings.

The blinds down, Mother took a seat opposite his before addressing Cia and me. "I need to speak with this man alone." She paused a fraction before continuing. "He can be trusted, and we have news of the war to discuss."

I felt an instant flash of disappointment—but Cia had started toward the door, and after a moment's hesitation, I followed.

The stranger posed no danger to Mother, for she had a sea sprite's formidable talent and could easily link to others of her kind. She, like all the sea people, based her trust on an accurate sense of others' thoughts and feelings. The sea sprites could be unnerving at times with their uncanny knowledge, as was this stranger with his extraordinary talent.

"Why aren't we allowed to hear his news?" I grumbled immediately upon leaving the room. "What are they keeping from us? What shouldn't we hear?"

"I can't imagine. The war is still confined to the border regions. How serious can it be?" Cierva answered.

"Then why can't we listen in?"

She shook her head and frowned. "I don't know, but there's something about this war we aren't being told, and the sea sprites are avoiding any mention of it. Still, we may be able to find out something. The sprites always know what's happening across Evergreen. Perhaps if we join together in an unfocused open, we'll catch some clue to what's going on."

Her suggestion surprised me, and I hesitated briefly before nodding assent. Although we had never attempted an unfocused open before, we knew it could be done, and Cierva was right about the sprites. They knew what went on across Evergreen but kept what they knew to themselves. Cierva and I could open our minds to Olin, as I had done with the stranger's send but without invading any private message. Perhaps a stray broadcast of thought would give us a few answers to our questions.

We retreated to Cierva's room, and after clearing the bed of a small loom, several skeins of yarn in different weights and textures, and numerous textile drawings, we sat down, took a deep breath, and linked hands.

"I hope this works," I said as we closed our eyes, and then I cleared my mind.

We had often used send and open, yet never took an open for granted. Using mental guards learned in years of practice, we proceeded carefully, for the thoughts and flashes of feeling that flowed in an open could be dangerous to the receiver. To catch an evil thought or to feel someone's pain or anger made it (to some extent) your own. Opening with a known sender helped minimize uncomfortable surprises. An unfocused open offered no such protection. I remembered my reckless open on Daniel's send and cringed.

It was a needless worry. The sea sprites' emotions were muted, as if shielded in some fashion, and we found nothing pertaining to the war in the thoughts flowing throughout Olin. It seemed that aside from our family's personal interest in the war, the sea sprites gave no heed to the humans and their war in the Halcons. This could be the truth, and our mother's thoughts remained shielded for diplomatic reasons. I felt a rare alienation creep through me and fought it. We closed our open in frustration.

After the abortive attempt at an open, I left for my own room, lowered the shades, and discarded my heavy pants and sweater for lighter, red-gold pants and a long-sleeved, calf-length tunic. I hastily pinned up my hair, and then Cierva and I hurried to Olin's huge main hall. It would be a social slight to not attend a gathering of sea sprites, and our mother expected us to be there. Despite the disappointing open and my excitement over meeting the stranger, I remembered to grab a notepad and pen. I recorded sea-sprite stories as I heard them, and the evening festivities always included at least one tale.

Cierva and I entered the enormous hall where archways led to porches and outdoor courtyards around the perimeter of the circular room. The mind-shielded archways were otherwise open to the storm. A large and shallow stone bowl in the room's sunken center served as a hearth. Although the sea sprites never felt the cold and needed no heating systems, they enjoyed the aroma of sweetly scented wood, and the warmth sufficed for any humans in their midst.

The firelight flickered across curved and carved walls inlayed with blue-green nacre. Seaweed and fish seemed to flow and undulate upward, between the archways, never quite reaching their goal hidden in the lighter green nacre glittering above. Beneath this spectacular display, multicolored cushions surrounded low tables laden with fish, mollusks, shrimp, crab, lobster, and steamed sea plants, accompanied by dark-green wild rice, and warm spiced fruit drinks. A low buzz of laughter and conversation permeated the hall as we found our cushions. Mother and the blue-skinned stranger arrived soon after and took cushions directly opposite ours.

We greeted each other, and as I glanced at Daniel, I felt a strong attraction add to my simmering curiosity. I peered at him through lowered eyelashes, reassessing him, and wondered if Cia felt as I did.

Despite the beauty of his chiseled features and unusual eyes, his countenance seemed cold until he smiled, and the silver stars on his collar, possibly an insignia or rank of some kind, did nothing to relieve the severe impression made by his clothing.

I sighed in frustration. I had so many questions but knew I would get few answers in this noisy gathering of sea sprites. The sprites seemed to take his presence as a matter of course and made no requests for the story of his journeys, most unusual for this inquisitive and story-loving people.

The hall filled, and sea-sprite musicians gathered in the open area surrounding the fire bowl. As they settled to finger tall frond-shaped harps and deep-bowled drums, a pleasing background melody built and resonated through the hall, the tempo increasing as voices joined the music. Pale images formed in the air to ripple with the merry tune. Ships with brightly hued sails tore through summer waves, sending sheets of foam and glittering droplets into a hazy sun. The sound of snapping sails mingled with song and music. A salt-laden breeze blew through the room, misting my skin. When the music reached a crescendo, the images burst into sparkling motes that showered down and vanished along with the song. The shimmering display had captured my attention and, for a moment, eased my fascination with Daniel.

Harpists continued playing in the background as a tall, gray-haired sprite named Biscane stood to receive cheers from the crowd before reciting a favorite tale of the people. I picked up my pen and notepad.

"This is a true tale of Olin," he began in the traditional opening, "and it tells how Olin came to deal with the intrusion of donkeys.

"As we all know, Olin is a city of sweet laughter and the sounds of the sea. The sighing wind, the rhythm of the ocean waves, and the cry of the sea gulls greet us each morning, and we sing at any given chance. When the winter storms come, we continue to sing, laugh, and dream of our distant homes under the sea. This is Olin as it has always been.

"When humans first came to trade, they came on horseback with a few packs, or perhaps even a packhorse. However, as any wise child of today knows, after humans came, donkeys appeared.

"One bright, sparkling day, the air of Olin was rent with a sound that stopped the people dead in their tracks. A kind of horrible laughter grated terribly upon their ears. Those nearest the offender could see the source of such abuse but could not quite place what it was. That it was a pack animal belonging to the rather rotund, well-to-do merchant beside it was obvious. Nevertheless, the animal would have to go.

"A collective mental link guided the task of removing the offensive animal with diplomacy. The merchant was approached about the eating habits of such a marvelous creature. Everyone appeared wide-eyed with curiosity and admiration, and thus the merchant was glad to tell them what they wished.

"'Why, carrots and hay are that glutton's favorites,' he said as he finished unloading his packs and looked for the hostler to take his horse and donkey.

"'Sir, might I be so bold as to ask a special request of you?' a watcher stood forward to ask.

"'Ask away, my man.'

"'I own a stable outside the last city wall, which takes the overflow when the others are full. At this time I have plenty of room and would consider it a great honor if you would allow me to stable your animal.'

"'That is some distance to pick him up again.'

"'True, but he is such a grand animal that I would stable him for nothing. It would be a great honor,' he repeated.

"The merchant seemed suspicious at this but the animal was already being tempted away by the lure of carrots proffered by the eager crowd.

"'He will be perfectly safe, I assure you, and you will never find him better cared for. The whole city will guarantee it.'

"To this, the crowd voiced their agreement, and as it was such a bargain, the merchant relented. 'Very well then, I will pick him up two days from now, when I have finished my business.' After receiving directions to the stable, he went inside the inn.

"Never was an animal better cared for or so well fed. When the merchant came to pick him up, he was amazed at his well-groomed animal. He transferred his goods from the cart he had rented to carry them from the city to his donkey and went happily on his way.

"From that day forward, all donkeys have been kept outside the city at that very same stable. The city itself pays for their keep, and you will never find a better stable anywhere in the land. Anyone who has a dispute with the cost to the city is of course welcome to live outside Olin with the donkeys, but I, for one, know when I'm better off."

The simple tale ended, and Biscane bowed to cheers and applause from the crowd.

As I put down my pen, Daniel Scott leaned across the table to catch my attention.

"What have you written?"

I stilled, mesmerized by his smile and unusual eyes with their lights now sparking rather than swirling against the black. A thousand thoughts crossed my mind in an instant, yet I remembered to smile in return and answer his question. "I've recorded the story. It's a hobby of mine."

He nodded. "Sea-sprite tales would come in handy on long nights away from home, especially if you added in the imaging." Then he turned to say good night to my mother before he stood and excused himself from the gathering.

Thwarted in my hope to question him in return and in no mood to socialize, I soon said good night to my mother, as did Cierva. We retired to Cierva's room to sit on her bed and go over the day's events.

As she warmed a teapot, I broached the topic of most interest to me. "Cia, do you remember Father's tales of warlocks? By the looks of this stranger, Daniel, he's one of those." I shivered in excitement and hugged my knees. "And I know that he's a half breed of some sort. Do you remember anything about those stories?"

"Probably not any more than you do, except that they're very skilled in their talents. I wonder why he's in Olin."

"So do I. Something to do with the war I bet, but what's he doing so far from the mountains?"

She only shook her head and seemed lost in thought as she poured tea into mugs.

My feelings about the stranger confused me. "Cia, I know he's really different, but I find him attractive."

Her eyebrows rose, and she chuckled. "He is attractive, but your feelings about him may be nothing more than the allure of the unknown." She handed me my tea. "Sleep on it, and see how you feel in the morning."

I nodded but suspected sleep might not come easily.

After finishing my tea, I said good night and left for my own room. Despite fatigue, I found it difficult to sleep as thoughts of the stranger and my father intruded. How did they know each other, and when would my father face the enemy, if at all? Was it possible South Halcon's army would soon be driven back within its border? With question crowding upon question, I decided to query Daniel Scott early in the morning before he became engaged elsewhere.

I arose an hour before daybreak and opened in a quick search for a touch of the warlock's thoughts. Then I threw on clothing and hurried down through the now dimly lit and quiet city to the outer edge of the main coil. In the predawn, mist-shrouded stable courtyard, Daniel prepared his mount and packhorse for their journey. His black clothing and horse stood in stark relief against the yard's pale and faintly gleaming crushed-shell surface. The night's storm had abated, but high surf still thundered in the background, and tendrils of fog wreathed around the coral walls to mingle with our cloudy breath. I pulled my cloak tighter against the bitter cold.

He turned from the horses as I approached. I took a deep breath and asked my first question. "Good morning. Are you going through Phoenix to Halconnida?"

He nodded with a smile. "Would you like me to take a message to your father?"

Again, his half smile and glittering eyes captured me as much as the question, but I knew I did not want to send a message. I wanted to join my father in Halconnida.

"No, no message," I replied, shaking my head.

He only nodded before turning again to tighten the pack straps.

I stared at his back, and my built-up frustration grew into an anger that burned away the morning's chill, but anger against whom or what? Soon this stranger would leave Olin, and it would be too late to ask questions. He would be on his way while I still waited for news of my father and the war, and I would receive precious little of that.

I envied this man's freedom to go to my father while I remained in Olin. I longed to travel across Evergreen as I wished. Even so, I surprised myself when I voiced my desire. "I want to go with you to Phoenix, to Halconnida, to see my father."

The stranger's hands stilled on the pack straps. Without turning he asked, "Would your mother agree to you leaving Olin?"

His question surprised me and gave no clue as to what he thought of my request. I had expected him to say no. I shivered in the cold as I thought about what my mother might say. She knew about my restlessness but could not have guessed I would want to leave Olin with a stranger. Yet aside from this man, would anyone be traveling all the way from Olin to Halconnida? This seemed the ideal chance to go to my father.

"I'll ask her," I said and hurried across the yard to enter Olin before he changed his mind.

I approached my mother in trepidation and excitement, fearing her refusal, but she only nodded and seemed prepared for me to leave. Even Cia, after a moment's astonishment, seemed to accept it, but I could feel her dismay.

I felt a twinge of uneasiness when no argument greeted my proposal. Flushed with excitement and a tinge of fear, I hurried to my room. My life was about to change again, yet unlike the change forced upon me in Phoenix, this leap from the familiar and safe came by choice. I pushed aside the fear and started to pack.

I stuffed as many medicinal plants and unguents as I could into a specially pocketed satchel. I hated to leave any of the valuable pharmaceuticals behind. In another bag, I packed trail clothing, toiletries, and only one tunic and matching pants. With shaking hands, I bound my long hair up into braids around my head and donned well-worn travel leathers. Around my waist, under my shirt, I strapped a money belt holding all of my meager wealth, payment I had earned as a trainee apothecary.

Hoisting my bags to my shoulder, I started toward the door. On the threshold, a dizzying wave of sudden awareness swept through me, and I staggered as my life shifted in plane-change. Fleeting images flashed before my eyes, too fast for recognition. I understood little of that life change from one level to another, never having experienced it before, but recognized it from descriptions I had read. Plane-change, said to be far reaching, meant my decision to leave Olin would affect lives other than my own.

The dizziness passed. I sucked in a breath and descended to the courtyard.

In the early morning's watery sun, my horse, Neh Hah, whinnied a greeting and champed at the bit. Around us, the world came to life as sea-sprite stable lads hurried to their chores. Daniel Scott waited nearby as Mother and Cierva came forward to say good-bye.

"I know you've been restless," Mother said as she hugged me, "and although foreknowledge tells me you are meant to take this journey, it's difficult to let you go." I heard the clink of coins as she pushed a small leather pouch into my hands. She paused, pale eyes coin-bright with tears, yet she smiled. "There may be surprises in store for you, but you are doing the right thing, and I believe all will go well."

"Thank you, Mother," I said huskily, and rather than trying to reach my hidden money belt, tucked the bag into a pocket inside my riding cape. A strange numbness settled over me.

Then Cierva stepped forward to hug me, her usual calm broken as she whispered, "Sim, are you sure you want to do this?"

I could only nod on her shoulder.

"I'll miss you. Please take care of yourself," she said, holding me tightly before stepping away again and pulling her cape around her. Tears streaked her face, but she tried a watery smile, and it tore at my heart.

"You too, Cia," I barely managed to respond. My throat closed, and my eyes burned. How could I leave her? Although she usually seemed content to let things happen as they would, I felt her fear for me. It almost destroyed my resolve to go, and I struggled with second thoughts as I mounted Neh Hah.

Daniel Scott, already mounted, glanced up at Olin's coral walls, damp and glistening in the weak winter sunlight. The black gelding jingled its harness, snorted, and beat a tattoo into the yard's crushed shell.

"Thank you and your people for the hospitality of Olin," he addressed Mother. "Olin is a place of laughter, and Evergreen will be in need of such places." Then he nodded farewell and turned his horse toward the arched opening of the yard.

I too looked up at Olin's towers, ramparts, and curved walls, now shimmering through a blur of tears. I blinked to clear my eyes and saw the two moons, Copper and Silver, gleaming high above the city, only a week and a half from the midwinter full-moon conjunction—a time of feasting and festivity—familiar, safe.

I gripped the reins in renewed panic. Neh Hah snorted and bobbed her head in reaction. Startled, I fought down the fear and steadied my breathing as resolve to reach my father reasserted itself.

With a halfhearted smile and grim determination, I lifted a hand in farewell to Cierva and my mother. Then I turned in the saddle and urged Neh Hah toward the archway.

JOURNEY
Dasimbe Halcon—Winter 1835 AB

We rode west into a raw wind that blew the night's storm further out to sea. A few high clouds remained, ragged horsetails scudding across the brilliantly clear turquoise sky. Raucous gulls, eager scavengers following the storm, wheeled and dove amid the briny air, their piercing cries accompanying the thundering of surf. Both sounds diminished as we traveled inland, leaving only the moaning and whistling wind as our companion. Before long, the warmth of my excitement eased, and bitter cold fingered its way through my thick clothing.

Pulling a muffler high across my face as protection against the wind tracing icy fire on any exposed skin, I peered through a barrier of eyelashes at the road ahead. In the distance on my left, sunlight reflected off the Comber River where it wound its way to the sea. In every other direction, monotonous winter-bare farmlands rolled off into the distance with only the ribbon of road and an occasional farmhouse to break the view.

Ahead, Daniel rode at a brisk trot, lengthening the space between us. I hastened to catch up to one horse length and then settled to stare at his back.

A warlock! The fascination gripped me again. Why had I never seen one before, and what role did warlocks have in the war? Were they aiding North Halcon, or did Daniel act alone, carrying a message to my father as a favor?

The thoughts came in quick succession, but I realized shouting into the wind and being muffled up to my eyes would make questioning him almost impossible. I resigned myself to silence, and my thoughts then turned to my sister and mother.

How would Cia manage without me? I doubted she would share her dreams with her companions in the weaving sheds. As for my mother, I reviewed her parting message and marveled at her gift and show of affection. Her parting hug seemed more important than the gift. I clearly remembered her holding Cia and me close as children, but as we grew older, Mother had grown more matter-of-fact, busy in her life as a diplomat.

A crunching of wheels in the seashell roadbed broke into my reverie. A cart laden with winter fruit and vegetables bound for Olin's market trundled by to my left, the sea-sprite merchant huddled on the driver's seat, bobbing his head in passing. Glancing ahead, I saw that the gap between Daniel and me had widened again, and I urged Neh Hah forward. As the morning wore on, other wagons and riders passed, the road seeming well traveled by heavily clad merchants and a few human farmers.

Midway through the day, Daniel led us off the road to rest the horses and eat. A hillside blocked the worst of the wind, and although it grew too low to the ground to offer additional shelter, an evergreen scrub with blue-black leaves provided fodder for the horses. We hunkered close over the food packet as Daniel divvied up the journey bread and dried fruit provided by Olin's kitchen. He handed me my portion.

I glanced at his blue skin and glittering eyes and swallowed a bite of bread before asking (although I already knew he had a heritage similar to my own), "You're a half breed, aren't you?"

He nodded and finished a mouthful of food before answering. "My mother is an air fairy, my father a human–air fairy half breed, so I'm more air fairy than human."

He bit into his bread again, but I forgot my food and, gaping in fascination, asked, "Air fairies? Who are they? Where do they live?"

He had almost finished his journey bread. "Eat up. We aren't stopping long." He nodded toward the bread and fruit in my hands, and I hastily downed another bite. "The air fairies are a species that live in the high peaks and plateau beyond the Halcon Mountains," he said as he brushed the crumbs from his fingers. I waited for more—but he just grinned. I heard his mental chuckle as he bit into a piece of dried fruit.

I digested his statement along with the rest of my journey bread. Despite the warlock legends, surely nothing existed in the thin, icy air of the peaks rising into the clouds beyond the Halcon Mountains. It was commonly known that the High Tors were inaccessible. His answer made no sense.

Frustrated, I started to ask another question, but just as I opened my mouth, Daniel rose and returned the food pouch to his saddlebag. Then he mounted up. I crammed a last bit of fruit in my mouth and mounted Neh Hah.

The afternoon wore on much like the morning, and long hours of riding left me aching and sore by late afternoon. Although I had often ridden on horseback and slept in wagons at night in my family's frequent trips on this busy road, we had never ridden in midwinter or at the fast pace Daniel kept. Exhausted and chilled to the bone by nightfall, I wanted nothing more than to fall into a warm bed.

Fortunately, we arrived at a small, earthen-floored farmhouse where they took in guests, welcome shelter against the bitter cold. Too tired to notice anything around me, I stumbled inside after Daniel. The warm room and a delicious smell of food enveloped me as a young woman led me to a table and chairs. Daniel, seeming more interested in conversation than food, disappeared into the shadows with our host.

The young woman introduced herself as Tilde and welcomed me to her and her husband's farmhouse with warm bread and a thick, steaming stew. Despite my hunger, I almost fell asleep over the food and barely remembered Tilde guiding me to a raised sleeping pallet behind a partition. After shedding my outer clothes, I fell asleep to the murmur of voices.

When I awoke the next morning, I draped a blanket around my shoulders and peered around the partition's edge. Tilde stood with her back to me as she worked at a table. The rest of the room appeared to be empty.

"Good morning," I said.

Tilde turned from whatever she was doing with a grin that reached lively brown eyes. Dark brown curls glinted in the morning sun. She wore thick trousers and a sweater woven in the rust and greens of the plains' people.

"Good morning. I hope you slept well."

I nodded, grinning, and said, "Very well, thank you," before disappearing back behind the screen. I took down my braids and ran my fingers through the heavy mass of hair before combing it out and braiding it again.

"Where is everyone?" I asked, referring to Daniel and Tilde's husband.

"My husband, Kevin, has already left to his daily chores, and your friend, Daniel, is preparing your mounts for travel. I have hot water, and there is time for you to wash if you like."

"Oh yes, please," I answered as I leaned around the edge of the screen again to smile at her. My eyes must have glowed at the thought of a wash in hot water.

She brought me a robe, and I donned it before she showed me to a small alcove where neatly folded towels lay by a basin ready for water.

"I'm sorry we don't have indoor plumbing yet, except for the toilet. We've only just built this house," she explained as she poured steaming water into the basin. "We have a long way to go before we have the kind of place we want. The toilet is through that door." She pointed to a door off the alcove.

"This is wonderful, thank you," I assured her, and after using the toilet, I proceeded to wash and don fresh underclothing.

After dressing, I left the alcove and approached a window where my breath misted and turned to frost upon the glass. Despite the clear, cold morning, the farmhouse remained snug, and Tilde radiated friendliness.

"How about some breakfast?" she said, indicating a pan of hot oatcakes. "Eat as much as you can. We have plenty, and I hear you have a long day ahead."

At the mention of food, my stomach rumbled loudly. Tilde and I both laughed. "I think that answers your question," I said and then heaped my plate, slathering the oatcakes with honey before attacking them with enthusiasm.

Daniel returned and paid for the night's shelter just as I finished a hot cup of tea. I gathered my few belongings, thanked Tilde for her hospitality, and then asked her to thank Kevin and express my regrets at having fallen asleep before meeting him.

Outside the farmhouse, a fierce wind still howled, scouring the land and sunlit sky. Tilde smiled and waved a hasty good-bye before shutting the door against the chill gale. I pulled at Daniel's sleeve. His eyebrows rose as I offered him coins to cover my portion of the night's lodging, but he took them without comment. Then he rubbed his horse's nose in an absentminded caress before mounting up. I mounted Neh Hah.

"What's his name?" I shouted as we turned into the wind. I nodded toward his horse.

He grinned and shouted, "Bad Boy," and then urged the gelding forward.

I laughed, then pulled my muffler across my face, and followed.

The road turned from shell to cinder as the land rose in a gradual slope toward the west. Aside from that, the second day went much like the first, and before long, I ached with the weariness of constant riding. The brief midday break brought some relief, and again I plied Daniel with questions.

"So you come from somewhere in the mountains and know something of this war in the Halcons. How are you involved, and whom do you work for?" I asked before biting into one of the sweet biscuits filled with dripping jam that Tilde had given us for our journey.

"I work to help keep peace among humans, much as your father does. I'm a diplomat of sorts. But South Halcon doesn't care much for peace at this time." A frown crossed his face and vanished again in an instant.

I found his answer unenlightening. Thinking that perhaps I asked the wrong questions, I moved off the subject of who and what he was. "What can you tell me about the war?"

His amazing eyes searched mine for an instant. "How much do you know?"

"Just that the war is still along the borders and that the rest of North Halcon is safe for now."

After a swig from his water bottle, he stood and dusted off his hands as he answered. "What you haven't been told is the nature of South Halcon's war, how it started, and the potential havoc it could cause if it spreads. It's a particularly ugly story that I haven't the time to tell you now. We have to push on."

Defeated again in an attempt to gain information, I wanted to pull him off his horse and demand that he reveal what he knew. I scrambled to mount Neh Hah instead.

I spent that afternoon's ride plotting my next onslaught of questions.

We stopped that night in a wayside inn, amazingly full in both the tap-room and sleeping areas as every traveler sought shelter from the cold. To avoid undue curiosity over his blue skin and strange eyes, as we entered the inn, Daniel cast a mild confusion ward that affected everyone except me. As we pushed through the noisy crowd to a table, I drew ogling stares, but the men kept their hands to themselves and ignored Daniel. After eating, we took straight to our beds in a small room we shared with two others.

The next day dawned sunny and warmer, the cruel wind having abated. I planned to enjoy this day's travel more than the previous two and left the inn in fair spirits. Daniel also seemed pleased with this day's beginning and slowed our pace from a mixture of canter and trot to a leisurely side-by-side walk—ideal for my next round of questions.

"Daniel, now can you tell me about the war? I mean, how did it start, and why did South Halcon attack the north? What happens when we reach Phoenix? Do we stay long? And how long will it take to reach Halconnida?"

Did he chuckle as he shook his head? With his talent, he had to sense how much I wanted information.

"I have no idea why South Halcon has gone to war, except perhaps to impose their ideas on others." He paused for a moment, looking at the road ahead. "When we reach Phoenix, I have friends to see for news before I decide what happens next. How quickly we travel to Halconnida will depend on what they tell me. If all goes well, we'll see your father soon, and I'll let him explain the details of the war."

I frowned. "Why wait for him to tell me?"

He turned a level gaze in my direction. "Because the news from South Halcon is disturbing. I'll tell you what I know if we're delayed."

"Is that a promise?"

"Yes." His smile sealed the pledge.

Phoenix was a day's ride away, so to help the time pass, I told Daniel of my childhood in Phoenix and somewhat of Olin. In turn, he questioned me about my talent, and I described my sorcerer training. He continued probing the extent of my training at our midday break, and during the afternoon's ride, he asked about my work with an apothecary. A setting sun edged the horizon by the time we topped the last rise above Phoenix.

We reached the city at twilight, and joined the throng of wagons, carts, horsemen, and pedestrians clogging busy streets. Brick buildings glowed ruddy in the lamplight, and sidewalks teemed with evening life despite the chill weather. Shopkeepers had closed their storefronts to go home, or to the quickly filling taverns, for their evening meal. I inhaled the aroma of steamed vegetables, roasted meats, fresh breads, and fruit pies, all more heavily spiced than Olin's fare.

The familiar sights and smells triggered a sudden rush of homesickness, or was it coming-home sickness? I imagined riding up to the administration building to find that nothing had changed, that I could sit down to dinner with my family within its familiar walls, and be back living as we had before receiving news of the war. Instead, I felt like a stranger in the city. Tears prickled my eyes, and as memories of home and family flooded in, my joy at seeing Phoenix again withered.

Daniel had changed his appearance with a confusion ward upon entering the city and seemed intent upon finding his way. Yet he must have sensed my thoughts and feelings, for when we dismounted in front of an inn, he turned his strange eyes in my direction and shook his head. He grasped me by the shoulders.

"Sim, I know you're exhausted and sense that you miss your former life in Phoenix. I understand your frustration and sorrow. War brings nothing but grief." His fingers tightened. "Nevertheless, do what you must and hold to your convictions. Don't deny your destiny." Then he asked, "Can you do that?"

His use of my pet name, not to mention his concern, touch, and glittering stare, unsettled me. And what did he mean by "destiny" and "do what you must"? He talked as if my future held some ordained task. Did he refer to my intention to reach my father in Halconnida?

"What do you mean by 'destiny'?" I managed to ask.

He smiled. "Whatever your future holds."

Then he turned and headed toward the inn door. Tired and hungry, my thinking fuzzy, I gave up trying to understand his cryptic replay for the moment. I entered the inn with a desire for nothing but food and sleep.

That night, in my own tiny bedchamber, I dreamed of my mother in Olin, standing in her room with the barely audible thrum of pounding waves in the background. She sent into my dream, so a storm again raged outside Olin.

"Dasimbe, sweet one."

Mother had not called me "sweet one" since early childhood. I whimpered in my sleep.

"Sim, do not fear your destiny nor draw away from what your future holds. Reach out to it and shift with the changing tides and seasons. Remember, your sister and I will have changed also and no longer be quite as you remember. We all move on."

Then Mother faded from my dream but left a gift behind, a feeling of always-love to calm me in my sleep.

The next morning as I dressed, I puzzled over Mother's message, so much like Daniel's ambiguous statement. They hinted of things to come but gave no information. I shook my head in exasperation and descended the stairs.

Daniel had apparently paid for two nights at the Sheaves and Sickle before going about his business, so I had at least one full day to spend in the city. I pushed aside the sadness of being in Phoenix without my family and, leaving a message for Daniel with the innkeeper, headed for the open-air market near the river and docks. I hoped to hear gossip about the war, and it would be a place less painful to visit than the administration building.

I knew Phoenix's market well, yet today it seemed both familiar and different. The market had not changed, but my circumstances had. I no longer shared the outing with Gloria and my sister but stood alone at the edge of a jostling, hurrying, shoving, and shouting crowd. I savored the air of pageantry presented by preparations for the festival of the winter moons. Brightly colored streamers and decorated lanterns hung from poles, and fireworks stalls spread out beyond normal market parameters. The scene did much to bolster my feelings. Although I had brought little money to spend, I had enough for a pastry or two and felt content for the moment.

I plunged between the outer fireworks stalls and emerged into a crowded aisle between market booths. The din of clamoring venders hawking their wares mingled with laughter and the braying, squawking, clucking, and squealing of livestock. Barge horns blared from the river, adding to the noise. I breathed in the pungent smell of roasting meats, pies both savory and sweet, and the rich scents of ale and cider, along with the smells of incense, leather, and sweat. A rich symphony of colors threaded throughout the stalls: embroidered fabrics and painted leathers from North Halcon, fragrant sea-sprite fabrics from Olin, gaily striped tent awnings, and bright piles of winter fruit and vegetables. Stalls manned by merchants from South Halcon were noticeably absent, along with their finely woven and richly hued spider-silk fabrics, copper jewelry, and gaudy gems.

The morning passed swiftly, and although I heard nothing new about the war and had no tangible goods to show for my excursion, I felt almost lighthearted. For a short time, I had forgotten my need to get answers to my questions.

"Here, here," a nearby merchant shouted and waved me toward his table of hair ornaments. "Something for your pretty red hair."

I wandered over to inspect his wares. Among the multitude of metal and painted wooden filigree combs glinting with gaudy chips of colored stone, the unpainted and unadorned wood combs, carved in delicate swirls and beautiful in their simplicity, caught my eye.

"See anything you like?" asked a voice from over my shoulder.

I started and glanced at the stall owner before I looked over my shoulder.

"You look familiar. Do I know you?" asked the stranger who stood behind me. I had never seen him before. Of medium height and build with sharp brown eyes and brown hair, he wore nondescript clothing, and his appearance gave no indication where he came from. From his accent, I guessed him a Halconian, but north or south? Disliking his attempt to seek me as a bed-buddy, my instincts prickled against him.

"No," I said, and he scowled as I moved away from the table.

He followed me among the stalls. Although uneasy, I felt more anger than fear and decided I had had enough of the market, and the stranger, for one day. I dashed into a narrow gap between two stalls and then wove among several others to lose him before leaving the market.

Carrying nothing but excitement from my excursion to the market, I arrived at the inn to find Daniel outside, packed saddlebags already strapped to his horse, and Neh Hah waiting. So there would be no second night at the Sheaves and Sickle. He had obviously met with his friends while I explored the market.

"Sim, there you are." Daniel sounded relieved. "Get your things and prepare to leave immediately." He returned to tightening the pack straps.

As in the courtyard of Olin, I faced his back as he adjusted the packs on his horse. I wondered if he often chose this activity when avoiding questions.

"Daniel, just a minute. Did you get my message? What's happened, and why the sudden hurry?"

"I'll tell you tonight, I promise. Now please get your things."

Once more, I had to wait for information I might never receive. To know something, anything, I would hold him to his promise. Until then, I knew no more than I ever had, than we ever had, Cia and I.

Cierva! My thoughts flew to her as I dashed up the stairs. I wished I could ask her if she had discovered something new about this wretched war. Mother might have relented and revealed to Cia what had been kept from us.

The urge to talk to Cia grew as I hastily gathered my few belongings. I contemplated attempting a quick long-distance send: a novel idea, as I had never sent far before. Although unsure I had the talent for it, I stilled my thoughts, blanking out the world around me, and put total concentration into a send with Cia as my focus.

"Sim?" I felt Cia's question and suddenly knew that I stood with Cierva in Olin. I heard the distant sound of thundering waves.

"Sim, where are you? Where are you sending from?"

"Cia, I'm in Phoenix at an inn called the Sheaves and Sickle. I still haven't heard anything more about what's happening in the Halcons, and we're getting ready to leave the city. I'm not sure where we're going, hopefully directly to Halconnida. Have you heard anything? Anything at all?"

"No, no more than you. The sprites are silent on the matter. I sense that they're leaving the humans to work this out on their own."

"But we're half sprite and half human." I answered, hoping the war in the Halcons would not alienate us from the sea-sprite world. I felt Cia's mental shake of her head at the idea of anything making a difference to their noninterference before she continued with her own train of thought.

"Sim, Mother hasn't told me what's going on. Perhaps it's better not to know."

"You can't be serious. You must be as anxious as I am."

She hesitated before answering. *"I know Father is safe. We both do, and we'll know if anything happens to him. It doesn't help to question the nature of the war. It won't change anything."*

True enough, we would feel it if anything happened to our father, but knowing that did nothing to help me feel less anxious. Beyond concern for my father and family, the foreboding remained, along with the urgency to do something. I felt more was at risk than we were aware of.

"Sim, this is a long way to send and receive. Will you be all right?"

"I'm fine. The send isn't bothering me, but I do have to go. I'll send again if I can, when and if I have any news. I miss you."

"I miss you too. Please take care of yourself. Good-bye, Sim."

"Good-bye, Cia." Then she was gone. At the break of the send, I felt a painful wrench, not from any physical discomfort or a drain of energy, but from missing Cia.

"Dasimbe."

Daniel stood at the door of my room. No smile lit his cold features, and he looked angry, his glittery eyes swirling more than usual, his jaw clenched, and his lips tight.

"Hurry," he said sharply and turned to go.

Was I being reprimanded? Had I been too slow in getting my things? Tired of waiting for information, of being treated like a child, or worse, not being trusted, I seethed as I grabbed my belongings. I began to wish I had found some other way to join my father and find the information I wanted. If only I had the courage to ride out on my own, I might soon be at my father's side without Daniel's help. That I lacked the courage only fueled my frustration and anger. I stomped from the room.

I still fumed as we left Phoenix, heading south after crossing the dam over the Comber River, not west toward North Halcon. I guessed it was some roundabout route, avoiding a danger in our path. We continued across the plains in the same direction until well after dark.

Instead of finding a farmhouse, Daniel chose to camp in a well-sheltered draw by a creek. In my first night sleeping without at least a wagon or tent over my head, a lace of bare branches hung between a canopy of stars and Evergreen's moons. Almost full, Copper and Silver shed diffused light into a chill darkness that smelled of damp earth.

Small noises emanated from out of the blackness beyond our fire: a rustling in the brush and a splash in the creek. Nothing threatening, yet I cast furtive glances into the night as I ate our evening fare.

Daniel leaned forward after our meal, elbows on knees, to warm his hands over the fire. He glanced up, flame cast shadows dancing across his blue skin. He smiled. "Relax. It's story time."

Remembering his exasperation and savoring my own, I held my grudging silence.

His smile twitched, but he paused only a moment before continuing. "I know you hate being in the dark as to what's going on, and I think you can handle the truth, so I'm going to tell you about the war, where we're going, and what the war has to do with us."

At last! Although after all the waiting I did not expect to be told much. Nevertheless, I leaned forward in expectation, eager to hear what he had to say.

He dropped his eyes to the fire. "The unrest in South Halcon started with a faction in Halcon Rider, a local affair that grew in prominence, until the leaders used force to bring the city's population under control. Eventually, the faction took command of South Halcon's army, and then spread its influence throughout the country. Now it intends to inflict its ideas on the rest of Evergreen."

He paused and seemed far away in his thoughts. I wondered what it was he saw there. Then his glittering eyes met mine, as if weighing and judging what he would say. He made his decision. "Those intentions, and the acts committed within South Halcon, are vile atrocities." His mouth twisted in a frown. "They often torture and then put to death half breeds and those not human. It seems that, except for a chosen few half breeds, they want to purge Evergreen of all but humankind."

He stared across the fire, his eyes reflecting the flickering flames as he sought my reaction.

Stunned and horrified, I said nothing, but my thoughts raced. How could this be? Why would anyone do these things? If what Daniel said was true—my mind screamed in denial.

An instant blanket of mental repression smothered my feelings. "*Quiet, Dasimbe. You're broadcasting your emotions,*" he whispered into my mind. Then a feeling of calm, like a soothing balm, preceded a lifting of the smothering sensation.

"Perhaps that's enough information for tonight," he said aloud.

I gaped at him and then sputtered, "You can pick up my feelings without opening to them?"

He nodded, and his lips tightened. "Yes, and so can others with strong talent, even at some distance. But it's something you can learn to control."

Dread at the thought of my emotions being available for anyone to read joined my horror at his report on South Halcon. I cringed at the thought of revealing anything embarrassing and despaired about what I might have already broadcast.

"How much can you read?"

"Only those fragments of thought accompanied by extreme bursts of emotion. The broadcast is equal to your half breed talent."

I gritted my teeth. "Who can pick up these broadcasts? The sea sprites? My family?" I again pushed down emotions threatening to spiral out of control and tried to remember if I had received such broadcasts from Cia. "Mother should have warned me."

"No human, including your father, can read broadcasts, but the sea sprites can. They wouldn't have interfered unless your broadcast affected them personally. As for your mother—" He shook his head, shrugged, and continued. "Also, it's no longer safe for a long-range mind send. The enemy can pick up a send and use it to find us. You may have already alerted them to your talent in Phoenix. If so, I hope they believe you're still there, out of their reach. Be careful how you use your talent now, Dasimbe."

My eyes widened as the statement and its implications hit me, and then I shuddered as I imagined someone using my send to track us. This explained the flash of anger I had seen in Daniel at the Sheaves and Sickle.

"Daniel, I'm sorry, but you should have warned me earlier about the dangers of sending, and—" I winced "—broadcasting emotions. I had no idea anyone would be interested in me or my talent." A memory intruded. "Still, a stranger did approach me in the market at Phoenix. I thought the man was interested in finding a bed buddy and quickly lost him in the crowd, but now—"

"A stranger?" His eyebrows rose before he frowned and again shook his head. "You're right. I should have warned you of the dangers. The fault is mine, not yours." A rueful grin crossed his face. "You caught me by surprise with the strength of your send. Your mother said you had no training beyond sorcerer talent, and distance sends go well beyond a sorcerer's range." The grin disappeared. "With your lack of warlock training, you had no idea of the extent of your abilities or the dangers of using them."

I nodded, if hesitantly. "True, I never would have guessed that my emotions, or using my talent, brought any kind of danger." Yet I felt I knew the extent of my own abilities. From my sprite heritage, I had some exceptional skill, although not as extensive a range as warlocks were purported to have. And my sorcerer's skills, like those of my father, nowhere near achieved those fabled talents.

I shook my head to clear it. Although disturbed by his news, I had waited long enough to learn about the war and was determined to hear more. "I want to hear the rest of it."

He hesitated, and then nodded. "South Halcon's declaration of war on the north shattered the fragile peace between north and south. All the leaders of North Halcon called to council, like your father, know that peace had been the result of continuous diplomatic intervention and constant vigilance by a group dedicated to keeping it. Nonetheless, the spread of these hostilities surprised all of us.

"Also, South Halcon has more, and better, weapons than we would expect. Mining and foundries have been slow to develop on Evergreen—it's difficult to cajole workers into this hazardous occupation without a great deal of expense, and it takes determination to set up an extensive metalwork operation. That's why the metal, wire, and generators needed for electricity and machines aren't as plentiful as most would like. To have the number and quality of weapons they do, to be as organized and disciplined as they are, speaks of a strong central leader, someone with great charisma and the ability to get things done. We know little about him, except that he's the son of a wealthy merchant of South Halcon. We have a name—Paul Rider of Halcon Rider.

"In addition, in Phoenix I learned that South Halcon is building up a force to the west of Osa Marsh. Unfortunately, my informants don't know why. So we'll be heading into the marsh. We must reach the marsh folk long before Rider's plans, whatever they are, come to fruition, and take whatever information we receive to North Halcon."

I weighed his words. Going into Osa Marsh, so near South Halcon, sounded dangerous.

Daniel loosed his cloak and leaned toward the fire, the silver stars on his left collar catching the firelight as he prodded the embers with a stick before banking them beneath ash for the night. Then he set the night wards.

More questions blossomed like rampant weeds. "Daniel, who are you exactly? I mean, what are you aside from a half-breed warlock?"

Despite the dire news he had just given me, he chuckled, and I recognized the signs of warmth in his eyes. The swirling and sparkling had increased slightly. "Always more questions!" He shook his head. "No more tonight. I'm for sleep. We have a long ride ahead of us. The marsh is still several days away, and you have more to learn than all about Daniel Scott."

I grinned and nodded. "All right, but don't expect me to stop asking questions."

He grinned in return, and then we settled down to sleep.

The wind sighed in the trees as I snuggled into my sleeping bag. After all the information he had given me, I realized that, yes—I should sleep, although I had more questions than before and more to learn than I had dreamed. I imagined I could hear the death cries of those like myself, and disturbing images flashed through my mind. Although well bundled against the night, I shivered, and eventually I slept.

We woke to a sunny morning and several long days of riding. As we traveled, Daniel began teaching me the use of protection wards to screen my emotions and fend off mental intrusion. Although I had used mental guards against receiving dangerous stray thoughts, I had never been taught warding. I learned the similar skill with ease but wondered if I would remember to use it in time to screen bursts of emotion.

On the third day, we approached the town of Leda Springs. In the distance, wind generators indicated where the farming community huddled near access to electricity and water. We passed through the town to the vast farmlands beyond. Denuded of their tall, blue-green stalks of winter maize, they were an endless carpet of bleak, churned earth.

The following days passed quickly as I relaxed into the daily routine of riding and lessons. Each night by the fire, I told a sea-sprite tale and tried to learn more about Daniel and our situation. I learned very little, but my immediate longing for information had been appeased, and I felt my attraction to Daniel grow.

I was beguiled by his awesome talent, his knowledge, strength, and physical appearance, I chided myself. Yet, I also enjoyed his occasional flashes of humor and admired his diligence and patience in training me.

At last, we approached a forest. Near the edge grew the smaller deciduous trees, their branches all winter bare. We rode deeper into the forest, and the smaller trees gave way to towering, evergreen marazuls. Over our heads, the dark, blue-green fronds wove a net against the sun, casting the road into deep shadow.

A week out from Phoenix, thirteen days from Olin, the shadowy forest ended abruptly a few yards before we reached the escarpment above the marshlands. I squinted into the bright sunlight, holding Neh Hah back until my eyes adjusted. Then I edged her forward to view the panoramic scene below. The brilliantly clear day and dizzying height revealed Osa Marsh spread in a vast sea of blue-green reeds that whispered and swayed in rippling waves before every breeze. Between the wavering reeds, sunlit water wove into silver threads and glinting shards of crystal. The sparkling vista undulated into the distance and eventually vanished into a pale blur on the horizon. I sucked in a breath, and although we were far from the sea, I imagined a faint touch of brine.

I heard Bad Boy's hooves click on stone and turned to see Daniel inspecting the ridge's edge to my left. I leaned forward in the saddle, wondering how one got down to the marshes from the top of the escarpment. While I waited for Daniel's direction, I stretched, easing my muscles, and noticed that the aches of riding had diminished over the days. In addition, my clothing fit more loosely than it had at the start of my journey, although I had eaten well enough.

Daniel pointed out a place only a little further east along the ridge top. "There, a well-kept trail that hugs the cliff face in switchbacks all the way to the bottom. It's maintained by marsh folk who trade with the towns beyond the forest. We'd better get started. It's a strenuous descent, and it will take all afternoon to get down."

It did take all afternoon, and we traveled the last two switchbacks after dusk. A well-used campsite awaited us, and exhausted by the long descent, I fell asleep quickly.

We started early the next day and rode swiftly through marsh grass taller than our horses. The level of the land gradually dropped as we crossed sodden patches of ground and numerous rivulets and creeks until we reached the edge of a fair-sized river. There we dismounted, and I looked on in curiosity as Daniel stooped to the water's edge to find and arrange several stones of different sizes in the shallows. When he had finished his arrangement, he began to tap on the stones. I knelt beside him to watch and realized he was creating a repeating rhythm that sent ripples arcing out into the water. Then he stopped and waited.

Before long, the water shivered, and I felt a faint rhythm in the soil beneath us, a rhythm that crept upward into my bones. A type of sending!

At my gasp of amazement, Daniel turned to smile, his glittering eyes laughing at my surprise. "Yes, a type of send, safer and more private than a mind send."

He moved back from the water's edge and sat down.

I settled beside him. "What do we do now?"

"We wait for our escort. They'll take us further into the marsh."

The smell of damp soil and growing things surrounded us despite the winter season, for the temperature in the marsh seldom dropped to freezing. The tall, blue grasses stirred, whispered, and swayed in a fitful breeze and lazy warmth, casting sunlight and shadow back and forth in a rhythm that almost lulled me to sleep.

Despite my daze, I gradually sensed a presence and roused to glance around me. The marsh folk appeared silently, ghosting out from among the tall grasses. A lithe people, as tall as Daniel and lightly furred in swirling blues, teals, and greens, they wore loincloths or skirts in the blue-green shades of the water and reeds of the marsh. Woven strands of shell and twisted bits of reed looped about their wrists and through their hair. As the light shifted, they seemed to disappear, only to reappear as they moved toward us. Their camouflage suited the half light beneath the reeds. If I had not felt their presence, I would never have seen them.

This time my gasp was only in my mind, but Daniel registered my surprise and grinned at my discovery. The furred folk were already busy with the horses, freeing them of their burdens and tackle, shouldering and then transferring the packs to rafts that appeared at the water's edge.

"Daniel!"

"It's all right. They're the ones we've been waiting for. Our horses will follow nearby."

We boarded a raft with several of the marsh folk, who then poled the rafts out between reed clumps lining the shore. Our journey continued by watery channels that twisted through the marsh, winding around countless reed islands. Many of the thickets grew taller than a two-story house. Only my inner sight kept me from becoming totally disoriented. For several hours, we traveled deeper into the marsh until I became weary of the sameness of blue-green mud, water, and reeds and finally slept.

I awoke to a buzz of excited voices and drowsy warmth. The sun had long passed its zenith. Our raft was being poled up to a platform set among reeds as tall as trees. I could see other platforms rising in levels beyond the one we approached. I found it hard to judge how far the platforms spread as they disappeared between the reeds on adjacent islands. The settlement seemed to extend for some distance in all directions with no colors other than those of earth, reed, and water to draw the eye.

On the platform, a group of marsh folk waited for us to disembark. They looked exactly like our polemen although they wore more clothing. We docked alongside the platform and left the raft to approach the waiting group. When we stood before them, Daniel singled out an elderly man who held a deeply engraved staff of blue-black marazul wood.

I watched and listened as Daniel spoke. "Father, again I seek your hospitality. It seems I can't resist the lure of the marsh." He smiled and introduced me to the man he called Father.

"Father, I present Dasimbe Halcon. Dasimbe, I'm pleased to have you meet my foster father, Lam Po Dal of Osa Marsh."

Before I could respond, the old man smiled and reached to clasp my hands. As he looked into my eyes, I sensed a search of some kind taking place although I could not feel it. I also sensed a great strength behind his warm greeting and pleasant demeanor. Then I received his send.

"Bride of the seventh son." Aloud he said, "Welcome, Dasimbe, to our humble marsh. You have much to learn from us."

"Thank you," I said in puzzlement. I did not understand the send or his comment, but he added no explanation to his greeting, only turned and headed toward a ladder leading to a higher platform.

I registered Daniel's broadcast of surprise and knew he had also received the send. Looking to him for enlightenment, I took perverse pleasure in the unexpected break in his emotional screening but received nothing else from him but an intense gaze as he quickly covered his feelings. I shivered as the world seemed to tip slightly in plane-change, although not one generated by any choice of mine.

Before I could question Daniel about Lam Po's comment or the plane-change, he spoke. "Dasimbe, this afternoon we sit in council with Lam Po. Listen to his wisdom. Much that happens now may depend on his knowledge and our choices. Remember how serious the situation is, and save any questions until tomorrow."

As he spoke, a flash of foreknowledge stopped further inquiry on my part. Unlike the usual glints of information I had received in the past, this seemed an imperative. I would stay in Osa Marsh for a time, adding new skills to my talent and strengthening the skills I had.

My thoughts descended into a sprawl of confusion and questions. What new skills? And what about my father and the war?

I had never questioned foreknowledge before, but then, I had never felt an imperative. The idea frightened me, and yet an opportunity to build my talent skills—I felt the temptation, an allure that weighed heavily against previous plans.

"You decide your future tomorrow. It's a frightening thought," Daniel said.

Had he received a glimpse of the foreknowledge or my thoughts? I took a deep breath, reining in my scattered emotions. "Do I have any choice in the matter?"

He nodded. "You decide your fate. Foreknowledge only shows what you will probably choose."

Somewhat reassured, I nodded.

He placed a finger under my chin and looked into my eyes. "To your future then."

When he stepped away again, I smiled. His touch had calmed me, just as on the walls of Olin, it had chased away cold and pain.

We turned to follow Lam Po up several ladders to a higher platform, into a large reed building and the council meeting.

The council met for several hours, and I learned much about the movements of the marsh folk and the enemy. A few days before Daniel and I had arrived in the marsh, a small group of men from South Halcon had passed near the village. They had encountered no marsh folk nor spotted sign of their dwellings, but the marsh folk saw them as they approached the marsh and followed them through to its other boundary bordering on the seacoast fens and beyond to the port town of Fanil. The marsh folk also knew of the troops amassing near their western border on the plains between the marsh and the mountains.

I wondered if South Halcon would attack the marshes. However, this thought was quickly dispelled as Daniel and the Osa elders discussed the possible strategic maneuvers open to the South Halcon army. I had no idea how much foreknowledge went into their assessments, but I trusted their findings and felt a flash of cold fear.

An attack on Phoenix, with troops based below the escarpment to begin with, would move up the switchbacks, their intent well hidden by the difficulty of getting an army up the cliff face and within the forest above. This seemed the plan—a risk, but one well worth taking.

Phoenix, an open back door to the North Halcon region, supported a population unskilled in the arts of war and totally unprepared for any conflict. It also lay close to Olin. Phoenix, a hub of trade and commerce, set to become a hub of war—No! I rebelled at the thought but knew the council presented a true assessment.

That part of the council open to all ended, and I had to leave, but Daniel and the elders met well into the evening. A marsh woman named Omah led me first to a sleeping hut where I deposited my bags and then to a feast the marsh folk held to honor the eve of the midwinter moons. I had lost track of the days despite the closeness of the moons. Tonight, reddish Copper hung almost directly below cool Silver.

I joined the marsh folk at tables already laden with food, hastily filled a plate, and settled to eat. The fish, winter berries, nuts, and small game meats—some wrapped in a paste-like covering made from the crushed stems of a sweet marsh reed—smelled savory and looked familiar but tasted spicier than human or sea-sprite fare. The music of the marsh people also differed from sea-sprite harps and song, but the higher tones of their drums, flutes, and chants had a charm of their own. Although I enjoyed the meal and music, I found it difficult to put aside thoughts of the war to share in the merrymaking. My tired thoughts drifted, and before Daniel and the elders joined the festivities, exhaustion sent me to the sleeping hut and a hammock.

I awoke to winter birdsong. The faint sound of children's laughter mingled with the tinkling of reed wind chimes and the soft slap of water against pilings. A soft haze of light filtered through woven-grass walls. The hammock swayed as I stretched and wiggled my toes beneath a colorful and warm blanket.

A bright wall hanging was swept aside, and Omah appeared. She held a bowl of hot cereal that smelled both familiar and sweet. A towel was draped over her arm.

"Good morning," she said and handed me the bowl as I sat up. She lowered herself cross-legged to the reed matting.

"Thank you," I said as I accepted the bowl. Over its edge, I peered at her.

Numerous pockets fronted Omah's short, green skirt made from a single piece of finely woven fabric. Thin twists of reed adorned with shells circled her furred wrists and ankles. Her blue hair, not much beyond her shoulders, fell in hundreds of tiny braids. Although I had seen the marsh females' short skirts and short hair, I had not noticed any with Omah's braids and found them fascinating.

By the time I had finished eating, I felt truly awake.

Omah smiled and, unfolding her long legs, rose from the matting.

"I'll show you where you can bathe," she said, and towel over her arm, she led me to an opening in the floor where a ladder descended to a shadowy bathing platform that rested just above the water. Reed curtains screening the platform undulated softly in a breeze.

"Thank you, Omah. It's perfect," I said and smiled at the thought of washing away several days of travel.

She handed me the towel. I grabbed my bag for a change of clothing and started down the ladder. Omah grinned and pulled a cover over the opening as I descended.

I saw that other ladders led to similar, screened platforms close to the water, while stilts supported the main platforms in staggered levels high above. A patchwork of sun and shadow filtered down to the reed beds and dark flowing water below.

When I reached the bathing platform, I stripped and, with a sigh of relief, lowered myself into the cool, crystal-clear water. I had my first good wash since Phoenix amid a school of small, brightly scaled fish, only discernible when they met a shaft of sunlight between the swaying underwater grasses. I submerged, and the fish scattered, silver darts flung into darkness. I came up for air and floated on my back, eyes closed.

When was the last time I had felt this relaxed? Surely not since my father had left Phoenix. In this peaceful place, the war and its atrocities seemed far away, and the soldiers massing nearby seemed a sacrilege.

I shook myself out of a daze and clambered back aboard the platform. I toweled dry, savoring the remnants of release I had felt in the water. Then I dressed for the day and ascended the ladder.

Omah hastened me into another reed structure where Daniel and Lam Po sat cross-legged, waiting. They smiled in greeting as I entered, and when I sat, Lam Po served me a hot beverage similar to Phoenix's tea. Small pleasantries over with, Daniel put down his mug and introduced the subject of my immediate future.

"Dasimbe, we're short on time. I'm leaving at once for Halconnida to inform your father of the latest developments. He'll want to start preparing North Halcon's troops to secure Phoenix. Also, Phoenix itself must be warned of what we suspect. I hope you will remain here in Osa Marsh. Lam Po will tell you why."

The old man nodded. "The path to your future starts in the marsh, if you will take it. Here you begin your training, and you will not be idle. You have much to learn, and we have much to teach you."

Although foreknowledge had warned me of this, I wanted more information before making a decision. "What skills can I learn, and why must I stay here to learn them?"

He smiled at my questions. "You can learn to mind-share and shape-change, to deep-heal and to manipulate smoke, air, earth, fire, and water. You will become aware of your true strength and the strength and talent of others. These skills take time to learn, and Daniel will be too busy to teach you. There is much of your heritage you have no knowledge of, and if you do not learn these things, you open a gap in Evergreen's defense. Nevertheless, it must be your own decision to do this. We will not force you to stay."

I stared at him in disbelief. Mind-share! Shape-change! These skills the old man said I must accomplish surely grew out of rumor, legend, and lore, not any true talent.

I turned to Daniel. "Is he serious?"

"Yes." His level look, glittering eyes swirling slowly, told me he meant it.

I struggled with the concepts involved. I had thought I knew the breadth of talent skills, even if my own talent lacked strength. As the daughter of a sorcerer, I knew how to send and open and to receive foreknowledge and not discount it. I also knew the confusion and protection wards Daniel had taught me. True, I had a sea-sprite trick or two that no human sorcerer had, including my father. Cia and I had discovered that we could transport ourselves a short distance. Disappearing from one spot (with a sound like a firecracker) and reappearing at another constituted a favorite sea-sprite game called seek-and-find. We had played this noisy game on the ocean floor, changing the loud reports into tonal waves that sounded something like music. We could also live and breathe underwater as well as our mother if we chose to.

My minor healing skills came from training with a sea-sprite apothecary and only bordered on the awesome skills of a true deep-healer. I admired the sea-sprite deep-healers, highly esteemed members of the Olin community whom I longed to emulate. In the human cities, there were no deep-healers, and doctors took care of healing needs. Could I, part human, learn deep-healing?

Should I believe Lam Po's claim? And what was Evergreen's defense? What had a war in the Halcons to do with Evergreen as a whole?

Daniel leaned forward, as if sensing my doubt and wanting to hurry things along. "Trust us, Dasimbe. You need to learn these things, and Lam Po is an excellent teacher. As my foster father, he taught me much that I can never repay him for. It's your future and your choice, but I hope you choose to learn these skills."

I found it difficult to believe all they said, and yet curiosity and the possibility of learning strange new skills beckoned, and a lifelong belief in foreknowledge was hard to put aside. I thought of my father. He had not asked me to join him. He had been adamant about teaching Cia and me what he knew and would undoubtedly encourage me to develop my talent.

I nodded in acquiescence and sealed my fate, but it felt bittersweet, for Daniel would be traveling on to my father without me.

Daniel and Lam Po smiled at my decision. Then Lam Po nodded and got to his feet. He took his marazul staff from beside the door and left me alone with Daniel.

Momentarily distracted, I asked, "The staff Lam Po carries and the engravings on it—do they mean anything?"

Daniel poured more tea as he answered, "The staff represents a rite of passage of sorts. All marsh folk who travel beyond the marsh acquire them in their first venture outside their homeland. Besides the blue-black marazul wood, blackwhip wood is a favorite of those who reach the foothills of the Halcons. They add the carvings as they go, recording their adventures."

"What a wonderful idea." My eyes lit at the thought of carving a staff, but Daniel brought me back to the moment as he handed me more tea. "I'm sorry, Sim. I know you wanted to be with your father in Halconnida."

"He would encourage me to learn what I can, and I've dreamed of becoming a deep-healer. I have doubts about these skills I'm supposed to acquire but have to admit I'm curious." In truth, I also wondered about Evergreen's defense, whatever that was. Everything combined sounded far-fetched, wonderful, and deadly serious.

"I know you'll tell him everything, and that I love him. Also, please, ask him to tell my friend Gloria Sanchez what's happening. She'll worry when I don't write."

When he nodded, I looked down at my tea and asked, "When do you leave?"

"As soon as I finish this tea."

I nodded in turn, sipping my own tea and suddenly feeling forlorn. I would miss Daniel's company. The days of travel had strengthened the bond I had first felt on the walls of Olin. My attraction to him had grown, and I felt safe in his company.

Then we were outside, climbing down to the lowest level of the reed islands where a raft with Daniel's things aboard was bound to the platform's edge.

Several of the marsh folk, including Lam Po, waited there.

"The horses, what of them?" I wondered aloud as we reached the dock.

"Bad Boy is waiting for me at the edge of the marsh. Your horse will be available when you need her."

I felt a twinge of panic as he started toward the raft. The lifeline to my past, the thread between my home and this strange, watery place, was leaving.

I neglected to screen my emotions. Daniel turned and gently grasped me by the shoulders. "We'll meet again, Sim. That's a promise and foreknowledge. Do you believe me?" His glittering, swirling eyes looked into mine, questing for a response.

"Yes," I replied and managed a weak smile. Then he turned away and stepped onto the raft with the polemen.

They pushed away from the platform and out into the river until the raft caught the main current. While the raft and its polemen seemed to disappear from view, Daniel remained a black shape limned by the marsh, seeming to float above the water until he too disappeared, swallowed by the marsh reeds.

I felt a touch on my arm: Lam Po, catching my attention.

"Come. Today we celebrate the midwinter moons and the start of a new year. Tonight we feast again as Silver and Copper hang in conjunction. Tomorrow we begin your training. You will become a child of Osa Marsh."

OSA MARSH

Dasimbe Halcon—Winter 1835 AB to Summer 1836 AB

Lam Po began my training immediately. As I acquired new talent skills, I absorbed the culture of the marsh. From dawn until dusk, each day became a learning experience. The marsh men and women, even the children, had knowledge to impart. Although a small library (which they called a scribe house) held books containing their history and lore, most of my training took place out of doors. Daily life revolved around the marsh plants and aquatic life. Smaller reeds and grasses were fashioned into craft items: baskets, flutes, and paper, while their homes and the platforms they rested on—and rafts and small boats—were constructed from taller reeds. The largest and strongest of reeds, as big around as tree trunks, were used as stilts to support the housing platforms. The smaller bathing and fishing platforms rested on woven pontoons and rose and fell with the seasonal water levels. The largest pontoons hung under the edges of the main platforms as security against seasonal flooding, and aided in moving the platforms to new locations.

To my delight, I found the interior of the marsh homes held all the brilliant colors the monochromatic blue-green village and its surroundings lacked. I had paid little heed to the bright wall hangings on my first night in Omah's home, but now I noticed the marsh people's obvious love of color. Red and yellow pigments, ground from rocks along the escarpment's edge, appeared in intricately woven baskets, wall hangings, and reed carvings.

I endeavored to weave a basket of my own, threading the beautiful iridescent blue and green grasses of the marsh through reeds dyed with a deep blue pigment highly prized by the weavers in Olin. Taken from the crushed shell of a small snail, the costly blue dye added grace to my first attempt at weaving. Although my basket was small and not as brightly colored or tightly woven as the marsh folks' baskets, the subtle range of colors pleased me.

To help in daily tasks, I learned to fish, and soon came to recognize the different types of aquatic life in the marsh. I also learned to identify other wildlife native to the area and discovered how the seasons affected the abundance around me. And every day, I learned about my own innate talent. In this way, many months passed.

—◆—

"Relax, Dasimbe, and try again. Open, and feel for the bird in a search," Lam Po instructed me in the ways of a talent skill I barely believed in. Yet the lure of learning something new beckoned, so I tried again.

My eyes followed a large predatory nekka in the clear sky, wheeling high above the small island where Lam Po and I sat among the reeds. I reached out in an open to search, imagining the feel of air flowing beneath its scaled wings, and within an instant, I found myself soaring, bound within the bird's body, seeing through its eyes. Startled, I flung up a guard to keep from becoming totally one with the bird. Lam Po had warned me that a person in mind-share with a feral mind did not always return. A thrill of fear mingled with the exhilaration and flashed back to my mind. Adrenaline coursed through my body. Even as I flew with the bird, air buoying my wings, I trembled where I sat with Lam Po.

Through the eyes of the nekka, I looked down from a dizzying height to the marshlands below. I adjusted quickly. The bird focused on small rodents and reptiles that scurried through the reed beds. Although I saw Lam Po and myself sitting in a clearing amid the reeds, the bird had little interest in our presence. I briefly diverted its sight to the marsh grasses wavering in the distance, a view much like the one from the top of the escarpment, but hunger soon drove its attention back to a search for food.

I felt the pang of hunger myself and, with a touch of vertigo, returned to my own body.

Lam Po had kept a close mind's eye on my first venture. "The feeling of dizziness will soon pass," he said. "Now try mind-share with your horse, a little further away. Can you feel her presence?"

I searched for Neh Hah's thoughts. Not finding her immediately, I shook my head. Then remembering what the touch of the bird's mind had felt like, I relaxed and opened to search again.

Somewhere nearby—there! I could feel Neh Hah muzzling content-edly on the tall marsh grasses, her ears pricked forward to catch any way-ward sound. Insects buzzed, and one bit my rump. I flicked my tail. Birds chirped, and in the distance, the small ones' voices called. In surprise, I realized that this was not my thought, but Neh Hah's concept of the marsh folk children. I strengthened my guard, fighting the temptation to delve into what it really felt like to be a horse. The scent of grass was sweet. Life was sweet, other than the incessant insects. I came back to myself and smiled at Lam Po.

His smile went from ear to ear. He let me know by mind touch that he had followed me on my short journey. I felt his pleasure in my accomplishment.

"I am pleased you are eager to learn. Within the next year, you will have to master skills that usually take years of training. Only the fact that you have been taught well by your father in what little he knew, and that you handle sea-sprite talents easily, makes our task possible."

Although I bristled at his assessment of my father's talent, I felt pleased that he thought I could learn what he had to teach.

In the days following, I strengthened my newfound skill, grew more confident in using it, and enjoyed the exhilarating feeling of freedom it gave me. But with this freedom came responsibility. In each search and mind-share, I left my body behind, which, left unguarded, invited attack. Because of the danger, along with the search and mind-share exercises, I learned stronger protective ward-shield skills. I also honed my map skills and learned to recognize exactly what I saw on the ground or in the water, and what to look and listen for in woods or marsh. The creatures of air and earth became my eyes, ears, and nose on these excursions.

Within a few months, I began to feel the marsh as a living entity. Spending most of my time out of doors in mind-share with its wildlife, the marsh saturated my blood and bones as Phoenix had never done. My senses sharpened as I grew more aware of everything around me. There came a day when I felt free to wander the marsh alone in complete safety, despite the danger of natural predators. A large, scaly, feline-like creature called a saor prowled the marsh, and hazards abounded in poisonous fish and plants. I felt and understood the danger, something I had never experienced in Phoenix or Olin.

I began to explore further afield and tested my knowledge. I found small groups of marsh folk in well-hidden villages spread throughout the marsh. All had tales to tell and old lore to share. They continually amazed me with the skills they used in everyday life. Their hands, swift and sure, created everything they needed to enjoy life, and their senses caught every smell and sound. As I absorbed what they had to teach, they welcomed me as one of their own, as a child of the marshlands.

Lam Po next set me to practicing shape-change, a skill the marsh folk used in hunting. I learned the importance of carefully selecting the general size and mass of the creature one intended to emulate. Too large a form became unwieldy and difficult to hold together, although generally it was easier to stretch than to compress to a form. Also, because guidance came from the advanced, computational skills of a large brain mass, the brain's substance was not easily reduced. I learned that to assume the guise of an insect, one had to become an entire swarm, sidestepping the impossibility of shrinking one's mass to the size of a single insect and allowing each entity to contain a piece of the controlling mind.

I found shape-change exhausting. My first attempts held for only a fraction of a second. I gradually improved, and although I enjoyed exploring different shapes, I discovered an affinity for the saor's feline form. This scaled creature inhabited the marshlands and other less inhabited regions of mountain, moor, fen, and forest. Only the smaller, furred felines roamed near Phoenix and Olin. Not only did I enjoy becoming saor in shape-change, but I could also communicate with the creatures in a simple fashion during mind-share. I enjoyed the grace and beauty of the lithe animal. Like the marsh folks' fur, the saors' scales changed colors with the seasons, teal and green in summer, teal and blue in winter—the perfect camouflage.

During this time, a nekka started to follow me, and I learned to distinguish it from others of its kind. As it always seemed available to mind-share, Lam Po said that the nekka had "found" me. I seldom had to search for another bird.

Three and a half months passed swiftly and took us into the sultry summer season. During this time, the marsh folk kept an eye on the massing troops in the west, but the troops had not moved. News drifted in from Fanil. The small group of enemy soldiers stationed there grew restless and rowdy at times but made no other movement. Daniel had arrived safely in Halconnida, but we heard little else from him. Meanwhile, I hunted, fished, and explored—on my own or with the marsh folk—and continued with my training.

I started to learn deep-healing from both male and female marsh-clan elders and delved into their medical books. I had picked up the rudiments of simple healing from my training with an apothecary, but the marsh folk expected more from me. Although fascinated by deep-healing, I had not thought I had the talent for it. Now I discovered differently, but this skill would take years to develop in its entirety.

During my stay in Lam Po's village, I lived alone with Omah, but family members from nearby huts often visited. I grew especially fond of Dixon, a ten-year-old who came on herb-hunting trips with Omah and me deep into the less populated areas of the marsh. Dixon showed me his precious hunting skills and taught me to make a nice reed flute.

—◆—

"Enough play now, Dasimbe," Omah scolded, "Help with these roots. It will soon be too dark to see what we're doing."

Near twilight, the darkening sky seemed to descend into the marsh, casting long shadows between reeds that rustled gently in a dying breeze. The odor of dampness intensified, and midges started to swarm. Although these pests did not bother the marsh people, when I roamed the marsh, I smeared myself with repelling grease to avoid their incessant biting.

Omah had pulled her multitude of tiny braids into a tail for this foraging trip. Like Dixon and me, she stood ankle-deep in water with mud caked up to her thighs.

"Yes, Omah," I said with a false sigh and grinned as I tucked my new flute into a pouch that hung from my belt. I wore a short shift, belted at the waist.

"Here, pull it up by the stem while I slip the bag underneath. Be careful. Don't touch the roots. The poison passes through skin, and it's deadly," Omah instructed.

I prepared to pull on the thick, fibrous stem as Omah opened a bag's mouth near the base of the plant. Then I tugged upward as Dixon looked on in fascination at the emerging lethal roots. As Omah carefully slipped the oiled, watertight bag under the bulbous mass, a noxious smell wafted toward us.

"What a vile smell," I said, wrinkling my nose in disgust as I let go of the plant. Omah secured the bag.

"The poison gives the root its smell," she informed me, "but taken in small doses, it has great healing power." Thus, I learned of buroot.

Omah hefted the bag, and I shouldered others filled with plants we had already harvested. Then I caught the flash of the dying sun's red on scaled wings above us.

"Look, Dixon, the nekka," I pointed out the wheeling bird. My relationship with the nekka fascinated the boy.

My mind flew up to meet my avian friend, yet I felt my body anchored below as I soared in mind-share. Pleasantly surprised at the partial bond in which I could see through the eyes and mind of the bird without fully leaving my body, I reveled in the discovery even as I scanned the marsh.

The area around us appeared clear of any unusual disturbance. After a brief moment immersed in the joyous feel of wings spread on an upward air current, I left the nekka and returned to my own body in full. The nekka greeted me with a shrill birdcall and stayed with Omah, Dixon, and me as we journeyed back through the marsh.

Later, as we crossed a fair-size creek, the nekka again uttered a shrill cry, and I knew this one for an alert call.

"Quiet," I whispered to Omah and Dixon. "Be still for a moment while I check on what the nekka is seeing."

Again I rode the sky and saw through the bird's eyes, this time more fully. The nekka directed my search down the very stream we crossed. A lone man sped eastward. He appeared to be human, not one of the marsh folk. He went swiftly and silently, his goal somewhere further east.

I came back to my own body and reported what I had seen. "To the east of us, a human heads toward the coast, for Fanil I think. Perhaps a soldier from the western troops—maybe a runner. I'll follow him to be sure."

"It's getting dark, Dasimbe, and although you know the marshes well, it may not be safe," Omah cautioned me while Dixon stared in fascination. At the age of ten, all adventure seemed exciting rather than dangerous, until you were face to face with it.

"Yes, that's true," I nodded, but I had already made my decision and formed a simple plan. I broached it with Omah while I mentally ranged ahead with the marsh intruder.

"Then I'll go as a saor to sniff out his intentions, and the nekka will keep watch above. I'll be safe enough as a cat and better able to see in the dark. You can return to the village and tell Lam Po what's happening. I'll report to him as soon as I return."

Omah nodded, her face calm, revealing no fear for me.

"Let me carry your flute for you," Dixon said, his eyes alight, his voice serious. "You might forget you have it and damage it, it's still so new."

I smiled and gave him the flute, then watched as they disappeared into the darkness of the marsh. My way lay downstream.

In the form of a small saor, equal to my own size, I slunk through the reeds, enjoying a cat's night vision. The tall grasses whispered above me, and night insects rose in clouds at my passing, but the midges ignored the scaly cat form.

I continued on, slower now, breathing through quivering nostrils to catch any scent, my ears pricked forward to hear every sound.

There! Man scent, before sound. The nekka screamed above as he caught my mental broadcast of excitement. I actually felt the man stop, tense, and look up. He crouched, peering into the dark, his heart pounding in fear of discovery—or something worse. The contact surprised me so much I almost lost my cat form. Unnerved by feeling his emotions without fully opening to him, I quickly threw up a guard and lost the mental link while still sensing his location. He waited silently nearby. I crouched low and drew nearer, the man smell stronger now, a strange pungent scent. I blanketed any further broadcasts to the nekka to keep him from screaming again. My inadvertent broadcast of thoughts and sudden open revealed my lack of attention to personal wards. I filed a mental note to work on what Lam Po and Daniel had taught me, and then I set my mind to the task at hand.

The man had not sensed me, only I him. He started to move again, still heading east, and I followed, traveling through that night and the next day. He never stopped to rest or eat but ate on the move. Because of his unrelenting pace, I assumed I followed a runner, sent with messages for those men of the South Halcon army who were billeted in Fanil.

By late afternoon, we approached the lower end of the marshlands. The air shook with the sound of water funneling in booming torrents through deep and narrow gaps between horny ridges. Following the human, I climbed a steep trail over shattered rock to a height between rushing rivers. At the top I stopped and watched him descend on the other side as the land dropped sharply in elevation, the turbulent rivers tumbling down in violent falls before branching into the sluggish rivers of the seacoast fens' delta. There, above the fens, I gave up the chase as evening light and thick fog crept up on the wetlands below. While the man traveled into the fens, I would return and report to Lam Po. If a runner had been sent to Fanil, perhaps I should speed up my training.

Remaining as a saor, I sped back through the marsh toward the village. After two days of continuous running, I arrived at dusk the following day, exhausted. Returning to my own shape, I reported briefly to Lam Po before falling into a deep sleep.

When I awoke the next morning, Lam Po had marsh tea ready and waiting.

"Dasimbe, tell me what your journey as a saor was like, and about the man and the nekka," he prompted.

I told him of the adventure in detail, trying to relive it in my imagination. In retrospect, it felt uneventful and took only a short time to tell, yet Lam Po seemed interested. He nodded to himself in thought before he spoke again. "With your skills extending in usage and range, the enemy talents may be able to home in on them."

He pondered, while I wondered if I would have to limit my training. What was the point of having these skills if using them posed a danger?

Lam Po nodded again and finally spoke. "It cannot be helped. You must continue in your training to be ready for future tasks. Work on your warding skills, and never use your talents lightly."

I let out a sigh of relief. The elders would continue my training, and as I had already received this warning from Daniel, I knew enough to take it seriously.

I spent the next two weeks honing my skills and learning to better conceal them. Meanwhile, the Osa Marsh runners continued to report on how the war fared. A stalemate along the border in the Halcon Mountains seemed likely to drag on indefinitely. Although several units of the army training to the west of the marsh had left to join the fray along the border, most remained, and the army grew larger. The marsh elders still believed that when South Halcon attained the volume of well-trained men Paul Rider deemed necessary, they would move on Phoenix.

I still shivered at the thought, and hints of what North Halcon intended did nothing to help.

North Halcon planned to move an army, now under preparation outside Halconnida, to Phoenix when the army to the west began its move toward the escarpment. Already several units had periodically and covertly left North Halcon to descend upon Phoenix. Thus, a small force was gradually building up. It seemed a major engagement of this war would be fought on the plains outside Phoenix, just as the marsh elders had forecast. Yet I continued to hope the assessment was wrong and eagerly awaited news from the runners, hoping to hear something different.

I heard nothing encouraging, but the runners delivered a short missive from my father. Although it held no information the enemy could benefit from if captured, I greatly prized it.

"Dasimbe, things go as well as can be expected. Enough men are being trained to secure our country, but it is an ongoing project. I wish I could see the end of it. I am safe and well. Daniel tells me that you are learning new skills and are well taken care of. I wish you had remained with your mother, but now that you have chosen a different course, I encourage you to develop what skills you can. Daniel assures me you are capable of much more than I taught you.

"I miss you, your sister, and your mother terribly. I think of you often. Take care of yourself, your father, Ciervo Halcon."

Tears filled my eyes as I read the letter. Memories rushed in, and my heart ached. I missed my father, mother, and sister and longed to be reunited soon. Anger again rose against those of South Halcon, but the letter delivered a catharsis of sorts. It strengthened my desire to succeed in my training and aid in the effort against Paul Rider and his army.

One evening not long after my short adventure, Lam Po approached me about the next stage of my training. I had lived in the marshes for four and a half passes of the moon Copper. Half a year had passed, and summer crickets buzzed loud in the background as we sat and talked outside Omah's hut. He told me the training would continue in another village, with a part of the clan that lived east and north of his village. I knew Lam Po must have a good reason for the change, yet I questioned him.

"Why must I go to another village?" While an urge to succeed prompted me forward, dread of leaving my new friends gripped me.

Lam Po smiled. "Several clans split the training, primarily because you must learn to be flexible and see things from a different point of view."

I had long trusted myself to Lam Po's wisdom and would trust him now, but I did not have to like it.

Come midmorning the next day, I said good-bye to Omah and Dixon. Omah handed me a packet of her valuable medicines. I said a heartfelt thank you and added them to my medicine pouch. Dixon gave me a wood carving of a saor. I put it in another pouch along with the flute he had taught me to make and play. Then I hugged Omah and shook hands with Dixon before Lam Po and I left the village.

Fire, Water, Air, and Earth
Dasimbe Halcon—Summer to Autumn 1836 AB

We descended ladders to one of the few platforms edging solid ground and stepped onto a path that funneled into a shadowed world of dim, watery-green light, a reed tunnel that ran between great stands of rush. As the day warmed, the reeds rustled in an overhead breeze, and the rhythmic buzz of insects swelled into a symphony of sound. Unlike my foraging trips with Omah, in which we primarily waded through water, the path remained for the most part dry. Yet the air grew hot and heavy, drenched with humidity. I sought relief from the sweltering heat by dousing myself in the many streams we crossed. Throughout the day, Lam Po questioned me about items along the trail, testing my knowledge. Later, as light dimmed toward dusk, the path ended, opening into a large clearing. We had reached what was to become my new home and training site.

I looked around in curiosity. Most of this village's huts perched on stilts over reasonably dry land, a sharp departure from the marsh norm. Having adjusted to living over water, I found the difference vaguely disquieting. Because we were only a day's walk from Lam Po's village, I hoped he, Omah, and Dixon might visit. I knew nothing of the long hours ahead of me, of how intense my training would be, with little time for visiting.

Lam Po presented me to three village elders: Tostig, Gina, and Tam.

"Welcome, Dasimbe," Tostig greeted me. "I will be your primary instructor. I hear you are eager to learn and learn swiftly." He grinned hugely. "I'm happy to have such a pupil."

"And I hear you are interested in deep-healing," Gina added. "I will continue your instruction in that area."

"While I will teach you the stone-tapping send of the marsh," Tam finished.

All three grinned. I felt honored to be considered such a prize pupil but wondered if I could live up to their expectations.

"We are always delighted to have a new trainee in our midst," Tostig continued. "It's too rare an occurrence. Therefore, the village has prepared a feast in honor of the occasion." He gestured toward marsh folk who scurried about, setting out plates of warm, brown flatbread on tables set in the village center under the twilit sky. Marsh hens turned on spits above nearby fire pits, and water tubers wrapped in steaming fronds lay amid the glowing coals. The scent of roasting meat mingled with wood smoke to tease my nose and awaken hunger.

"Thank you," Lam Po said, and I echoed him.

Then the village elders led us to a table as glow lights appeared overhead, and playing children ran shrieking between huts silhouetted against a darkening sky streaked with red and gold. Even as we settled at the table, villagers wrested food from the spits and embers onto large platters, sending meat juices hissing into the flames. My mouth watered at the wafting aromas, and I eagerly helped myself from the platters they bore to the tables. Then we ate, and before long, a trio of flute players gathered to add lively music to the voices, laughter, and constant thrum of insects. Later, the musicians put down their flutes, and the villagers directed my attention to the central fire.

They began telling their tales, using a form of imaging I had not seen before, either weaving smoke into visible fluid shapes or casting a mental projection into the smoke, some more proficiently than others. It reminded me of evenings spent in the great hall of Olin, and I found myself thinking of Cia, wondering how she fared. I wished she were with me, sharing this experience and all the wonders of the marsh and its people.

Lam Po watched my reactions as I mused and must have felt my thoughts edge toward sadness. I hastened to reassure him.

"This smoke-shaping is fascinating. It reminds me of the sea sprites' imaging in Olin. Why haven't I seen it before?"

"Because smoke-imaging as a mealtime ritual is unique to this village. We all develop different pleasures throughout the marsh. Why don't you try shaping the smoke, Dasimbe? Tell us a tale," he encouraged.

He knew I could manage smoke-imaging because I had told him of experimenting with imaging in Olin.

I looked at the eager faces gathered around the tables as I searched for a tale. Suddenly it came together in my mind. I knew the story I wanted to tell and how I would image it.

"A tale of Olin," I said, in the traditional Olin opening with a brief pause before beginning.

"When sea sprites first came out of the sea, we came only to play a little among the dunes." I projected into the smoke a clear image of sea sprites playing their noisy game of seek-and-find among the dunes and tall dune grasses, adding in the loud popping cracks of several people in transport.

"We liked the whispering sound of the dune grass and loved to mimic the sea gulls' plaintive cry." I took a bit of smoke and fashioned a gull that flew across my image and let out its distinctive cry.

"We were seldom seen. Few humans came to that lonely shore, and we disappeared at any stranger's approach." My image disappeared.

"Back to the sea bed we would go, to play our lovely games of seek-and-find on the sandy ocean floor." I projected the sea sprites playing their game among tall, green, undulating sea plants as brightly colored fish swam by. The loud popping had turned into deep, melodious waves of sound. I received a nice "Ah!" in response to that scene before it too faded.

"But we were seen by a few humans, and eventually legends grew. Sea sprites, they named us, and so we are still called today. In time, a few of our race stayed ashore to sleep in little grass houses among the dunes. We gazed up in wonder at the bright sprinkling of stars in that other ocean above us." I projected this scene of a few huts and bright stars as I spoke and began to sprinkle in more huts as I continued.

"So a colony grew, and we were no longer a legend in the land but a people, and the people decided to build a city. Time was of no importance in this thing we decided to do. A plan was drawn up, a plan for generations to come. Sea sprites build for comfort and beauty, and these things take time and have an order.

"We built the first tower of the sea people as a beacon that would call us home to Olin and the ocean when we traveled the land. Standing taller than any other building in Olin, it rose on an island in the center of a sheltered cove rather than out on the farthest point—a tower of remembrance, not one built for strength against a raging sea." I dissolved the scene of the many huts and began to build a tower out of smoke, tall and ghostly amid sea fog.

"When the tower was finally finished, the people gathered for a far greater task. On a day of ocean calm and lullaby waves, the sky above a brilliant turquoise, we lined the shore, the tower rising tall behind us." I added the smoky people before the now completed tower and continued.

"Linking hands and minds, we made our call as we walked into the ocean, the surf curling around us as we submerged beneath the waves. Every mollusk that could would respond to that call."

In my image, the sea sprites had disappeared beneath the smoke waves while a tingling charge of power filled the air, and I realized I was probably broadcasting a call similar to that given out long ago. I reined in the broadcast and continued.

"So they came—perhaps, in time, from all the oceans of the world—and delivered into our hands the precious nacre to guild our tower. Day and night, month after month, year after year, for many years, so the tale goes, the givers came with their gifts as the city grew around us. None will ever forget that we are forever bound to the sea, and always we have our glistening reminder, our Pearly Tower, to call us home, home to Olin by the sea."

My cheeks glistened with tears as I finished the scene by changing the dim tower shape into a clear projection within the smoke. Shimmering and shining in all its glory, the sentinel eclipsed all other structures in Olin, even the spiraling heights on the cliff. Below the tower, a coral-colored Olin teemed with people, and festive banners snapped in an ocean breeze. I made the image recede to show more of the scene, revealing ships with brightly hued sails rocking on a gentle swell before the city. I pulled out further still, until the scene smudged into a pastel blur, save for that one bright, glowing tower, then I winked the scene out.

In the moment of silence following my tale, homesickness engulfed me. I brushed a hand across cheeks that itched with the trickle of tears and sighed as I remembered how eager I had been to leave Olin.

Excited voices praised me for the tale, and Lam Po inserted gently, "It will not be long, child, before you see Olin again." He had easily read the broadcast of emotion I had not bothered to screen. "Thank you for your tale. It will be remembered by the marsh folk, and some may try to retell it, but none will ever tell it so well as you have done this night."

I nodded, and my tears dried as others told their tales.

Before long, my eyelids drooped, and I stifled a yawn. Lam Po, watching for this, told me I would be staying with Gina. I would miss him when he left. Another leave-taking. I had said good-bye to my father over a year ago in Phoenix, then to my mother and sister in Olin, next Daniel, then Omah and Dixon, and now a farewell to Lam Po. I had experienced too many changes within too few months. The genuine warmth of the villagers around me barely tempered my heaviness of spirit.

Lam Po took me aside. "Dasimbe, you will not be here long. Learn as much as you can, and enjoy your time with these people. I will visit if I can."

I smiled, but it was strained. "Thank you. You've taught me so many wonderful things. And the marsh—I can see why Daniel loves it." I could say this despite my low feelings.

His smile, more genuine than my own, warmed me. "Yes. We are my foster son's second family, as the marsh is his second home, and now we are your second home and family. Learn more about us, and remember, we will always be here for you."

I would have hugged him then if male and female marsh etiquette had allowed it, but I could only thank him again before saying good night. I retired and slept well, for the day's activities and my emotions had exhausted me.

Although I awoke early the next day, I missed my chance to say good-bye to Lam Po. He had gone before first light.

My continuing training started immediately and in some haste, so I had little time to dwell upon my feelings. For my first lesson, Tostig took me to sit by a small fire just outside the village. I wondered why he built a fire in the middle of summer when the marsh shimmered in waves of heat, and a hot breeze rustled the reeds.

"Look into the fire, Dasimbe. Reach into it with your mind. Reach deep, and search for the essence of the flames. Then tell me what you see."

I looked at the fire as if being asked to inspect some strange new creature. I had never reached into an inanimate object, nor heard of it being done, but I reached as he instructed, mentally feeling my way into the flames. They seemed to swirl around me, and I felt a moment of vertigo but continued. Then I felt as if the fire took the air around me and sucked it in, as if I were being eaten by the flames. I started and had difficulty in maintaining my grasp on the essence of the flames. They slipped back and forth, air, reed, and wood being ingested and spat out as heat and light. The constant state of flux confused me.

I came back into myself, thankful to find I still breathed, and reported to Tostig. "It constantly changes, growing and dying at the same time, shifting about as it eats all that is around it."

"Look deeper," he instructed.

I looked again, deeper within the swirling changes but did not understand the bright glittering movements. I grew frightened and withdrew from the flames. "I'm not sure what I saw," I reported.

"Well enough. I have other things to teach you today. Last night you used your talents on smoke. You must learn exactly what it is you did when you moved the air and smoke around to mold and cast your vision, but for now we will see what you can do with water."

He put out the fire and handed me a wide, wooden dish half filled with water. "Look at the surface of the water, as if at a mirror, and cast an image on it."

This I did with ease, as Cierva and I had often created art on a water canvas as children.

"Ah, I see we have found your natural medium. Now quit the image, and mentally move the water upward from the bowl."

I looked up in surprise, wondering why Cia and I had not thought to try this feat.

He watched me expectantly, so I returned my gaze to the water and found I could easily swirl it around the bowl but had difficulty lifting it. I wondered if I must mentally get beneath it to lift it up, but when I attempted this, my effort went right through the water, scattering droplets all over Tostig and myself. He laughed.

"No, no, my child, you must get inside the water to move its essence upward."

As with the fire, he now talked about the essence of the thing. I tried to feel my way into the water, as he said, and found myself reaching into a strange world that, although moving much slower than the fire, did shift about. To my surprise, much of that movement came from living creatures far too small for the eye to see that dwelt within the water. This time, fear did not drive me away as I continued to reach deeper.

Then I moved into a realm of glittering sparks, like tiny suns linked together in a vast shining net that vibrated and seemed to stretch toward infinity. I finally touched an area where the net changed, at first vibrating more quickly as it became tightly woven, then moving less as the bonding became loosely woven. I realized that, where the configuration of moving sparks changed, it became the wood of the bowl and then the surrounding air. I wondered if all things—earth, air, fire, and water—consisted of these tiny moving lights. Did the vast, vibrating net encompass everything? What of myself and all life on Evergreen? Even as I wondered, I played a little with what I had found.

When I felt I had accomplished something like what Tostig asked for, I came back, only to find water misting into the air.

"That is one way to do it. Go ahead and try again," Tostig encouraged me.

All that day I worked with water. Little clouds and splaying fountains soon had us sitting in mud, our wet, stringy hair plastered to our faces, but Tostig seemed pleased enough.

"Tomorrow we will try again with the fire," he said with a smile.

In the next few days, I worked with fire much as I had the water and found it both more complex and simpler at the same time. The water's complexity came from the life-forms it contained, with their own dance of the bright sparks, much more complex than in the water itself. Although the fire contained no life-forms, it consumed them, along with inert organic material and air, and it seemed more complex because of its constant state of flux. The transformation of other substances into heat and light through a constant agitation of the elements was a swift, flickering dance that mesmerized me.

"Tostig, must something always be changed or consumed to create heat and light?"

He nodded and pointed to a twig on the ground a few feet away. "Reach into the twig and see if you can bring together what is necessary to make it change, to make it become fire, heat, and light."

I reached to convert the twig, agitating the elements to form something different from that which existed, to change it from what it was into what it could be. The twig grabbed at the air around it and instantly burst into flame.

"Well done. Now pick a spot in the air nearby, carefully enclose a bit of twig or reed in a ward shield, and then burn what is within the ward."

This meant mentally moving the object, as I had the water, as well as burning it. I did as he instructed, first moving a bit of dried reed to place it within a ward shield that I set as a small cube. Then I worked within the cube to kindle a flame. Applying what I knew, the cube hung glowing in midair for a brief period, extinguishing itself as the air ran out. I let the shield go when the light died, and there was a small "pop" of sound.

"Most light a globe, but you chose a cube. Curious and very well done."

Had this been a feeble attempt at a glow light? All my life I had marveled at the glow lights created by sprites and assumed that I could not light one because of my human blood. Yet, glow lights did not burn out, as my attempt had done. Something else must be involved in their creation. Obviously, I still had a lot to learn.

"How do I make the light last?" I asked.

"That is a different task, and I will instruct you in it soon. Be patient."

During the next few weeks, I practiced with fire and water, mastering the skill of shaping and moving. Before long, I not only lifted water from the bowl in a perfect sphere but also fashioned it into a myriad of other shapes. I could put out or light a small fire with one mental touch. I became aware of exactly what happened when I performed a shape-change, and my clothes and belongings changed with me. I had manipulated their internal structure without knowing what I did.

At the beginning of my second month in Tostig's village, Tam took me to a clearing by the water's edge and knelt to gather stones as I had seen Daniel do. Then he proceeded to tap the stones, adding a small generation of power directly into the stones to form a send through soil and water.

"This type of send is used only in the marsh and is not detected beyond its borders. The enemy, were he here, would not know to look for it," he said and chuckled.

For the rest of that month, I learned the tapping rhythms of the marsh, continued in my work with air, fire, and water, practiced deep-healing, and learned to light a true glow light by speeding up and rearranging the tiny sparks of energy within the ward.

At the beginning of my third month, I asked Tostig, "What of the earth, the rocks, and soil?"

"Now that you have asked that question, you are ready for the answer. Come, and we shall see what you find in a reach." He took me to a clearing just outside the village and knelt on the ground. He told me to do likewise.

"Now place your hands to Evergreen, flat in front of you."

I did as he instructed.

"Close your eyes and reach to feel Evergreen against your palms and fingers. Reach as you have learned to do with water and fire. Then open slowly to the layers of Evergreen and feel it in your mind."

I sent a mental reach down into Evergreen and opened, not to move or change anything, but to understand its composition, to discover how it fit with what I already knew of things. Immediately, I felt pulled into an energy flow I had no control over and went where the flow took me. Just under the surface, life-forms heaved and turned within the soil, while deeper, vast underground lakes lay silent and dark, filled with sightless life-forms of their own. Underground rivers raced through dark caverns and then flashed upward to the surface for a while before disappearing again into the darkness of stone and soil. They burrowed between the roots of growing things, growing things that shot up into the light and spread across the surface of Evergreen.

The soil itself seemed alive, almost breathing. The energy within the soil and throughout all else on Evergreen joined in streams, feeding into larger, tangible currents of energy that pulsed from the surface, down into the depths. The feel of that energy tingled along my skin, on my tongue, and in my nostrils for my body responded to sensation even as my mind traveled within Evergreen.

I went deeper into the energy coursing through Evergreen and saw an agitated matrix of the whirling sparks. The tiny suns within that stream, interweaving and constantly moving, came apart and released energy, much as in a glow light but on a massive scale—bright, hot, and terrifying.

And thought intruded. Although vague and insubstantial at first, it soon solidified into a sense of welcome, acceptance, and belonging. Urgency and demand followed. The urge to grow in knowledge and to protect life on Evergreen flowed through my mind and settled like a seed, before the mental presence dissipated to hover in the background.

Evergreen was aware! Its explosion of life, bursting forth in rivers and trees, up into the mountains, down into the marshlands, out into the oceans and onto the seabed, all of it existed as a sentient entity. Throughout Evergreen, to the very core of the planet, to depths where rock ran molten and fluid, in a bowl of water and a fire's flame, and within my body, the thinking threads of Evergreen felt their way, and the tiny suns whirled.

"Dasimbe. Dasimbe!" Someone called me from afar, and Evergreen gave me back, level upon level, helping me to return to my own body. I jumped in abrupt self-awareness when I returned, my heart pounding as I gulped in air. My fingers dug into the soil, the smell and feel of the marsh helping me regain a sense of self and being.

"Dasimbe, are you all right? Can you tell me what you found?" Tostig asked.

"Yes," I whispered and sat back to put my arms around shaking knees. I took a deep breath before continuing. "It's alive. The whole planet is alive. It thinks and nurtures life. Am I right?"

He nodded. "Yes, and what you have experienced is what we call a joining. You have joined with Evergreen at the deepest level."

"Who knows about this besides the marsh folk? Daniel?"

"All species on Evergreen except humans."

Stunned by this news, I bridled. "And why not humans?"

"I don't know, but it is a sad thing for Evergreen."

How could the sea sprites know about this and I not hear of it? And what about the humans? Did the planet disown them, or—what? Finding no comfortable answers, the human part of me quailed, although I knew through joining that Evergreen had accepted me as one of its own. And what about the tiny sparks of energy? Who knew about them?

"Tostig, who knows about the sparks of energy? Is everyone aware of them also?"

"Daniel spoke of these 'sparks,' as you call them. It is enough for us in the marsh to know that they exist, without naming them. I believe it is the same for the sea sprites and many others on Evergreen. You will have to ask Daniel about the nature of the sparks."

I nodded absentmindedly, elbows resting against knees, chin propped on fingers as my thoughts whirled. I spoke them aloud. "I can't believe I haven't heard of joining or that Evergreen is alive. Is it because of my human blood? And why don't the humans know of this? Many humans believe that some intelligence exists beyond their understanding. They feel, or sense, a force beyond themselves and envision this force as a universal entity. They worship it but aren't connected with it like you are with Evergreen." I shook my head and looked up at him again. "Do others on Evergreen believe a universal entity exists?"

Tostig nodded. "We certainly do, although we don't worship in the manner of humans. For us, everyday life is experienced as worship, and it does not affect our relationship with Evergreen. We feel that Evergreen, and all that lives on it, is only a small part of a universal whole. We feel connected to it and humbled by it. How about you, Dasimbe? How do you worship this entity?"

I shrugged my shoulders. "Not in any formal way. Father warned my sister and I away from human temples and meetinghouses because he felt our half breed status and our talents might be frowned upon. He taught us in private to look for balance and harmony through our connection to the universe. And Mother never spoke of her beliefs or mentioned joining with Evergreen."

He nodded and stood up. "Perhaps your mother had reasons for what she did not tell you, but it seems your father has taught you much as we believe. You will continue to grow in your own understanding of the universe and its power. Meanwhile, we must rush to finish your training within the next month. The energy you use now cannot be hidden from the enemy."

I shivered at his comment, and as I stood, I asked, "Can't the enemy sense the energy used by marsh folk and sea sprites?"

"It seems they are only sensitive to other humans and half breeds, or perhaps they just ignore us at this time."

I shivered again and followed him into the village.

That night, I dreamed of a huge black bird circling above the marsh. Much larger than the nekka, its piercing eyes searched among the villages for something, and I knew that it searched for me, its talons reaching out to find and destroy. Trembling in fear, I struggled to awake from the nightmare. Then the dream changed, and I realized the truth: although manifesting as a dream send, a giant black bird actually wheeled above the marsh. As it hunted, it unintentionally broadcast its intent. With a shrill cry, the bird circled closer to the village I slept in, and as it homed in, I huddled down in terror. The bird cried again and arrowed straight toward the village. My broadcast of fear had alerted it to where I lay sleeping.

I awakened with a sudden start, heart pounding and skin chilled despite the heat. Trembling slightly, I breathed deeply and smothered my feelings, slowed my thudding heart, and cleared my mind. Then I deliberately sought the marsh folks' dreams to project as my own and mentally disappeared. The camouflage worked. The bird faltered in its trajectory and began circling again in wide ranging sweeps, but it did not find me. Giving a last frustrated cry, the bird turned and flew back toward the west. I lay still for a long time, drenched with sweat, muscles tight, before finally drifting into uneasy sleep.

I awoke later than usual the next morning. No one showed any surprise when I arrived late to breakfast.

"You almost had a visitor last night," Tostig said as he approached the table.

"Yes, but I blanketed as much of my fear as I could," I said as I helped myself to a lighter than normal breakfast. My stomach felt queasy.

He seemed to understand and nodded, pointing to the children, who had already forgotten the shared nightmare and ran laughing through the village to their chores or lessons in a normal, happy blend of industry and play. I smiled around a mouthful of food, understanding what Tostig indicated. Like the children, I could relax for a while. I had thwarted the enemy in this first confrontation.

Tostig and I continued with my training throughout that month. Only three months remained until the next midwinter conjunction, and a faint chill had crept back into the marsh.

I honed the skills I had learned to as much practical use as possible, including warding and deep-healing skills, and gradually, I sensed a subtle change in my personality. Beyond a new self-assurance brought on by knowledge of my abilities and skills, I gained a strength of purpose from Evergreen that superseded former interests and desires. I did not join with Evergreen during this time but felt its presence and recognized its influence. The persistent foreboding had vanished, and the need to protect Evergreen's interests—which included ending the humans' war as quickly as possible—became my own.

Foreknowledge hinted at my involvement in the war, and although I still feared the enemy's intention to rid Evergreen of all but a few half breeds, I knew I could—and would—deal with future events as they unfolded. The travel and adventure I had always wanted had become part of my life, even if not in the way I had imagined. The young girl who had left Olin almost a year ago had evolved into a tool, one ripe for Evergreen's use.

On a morning near the beginning of my eighth month in the marsh, Gina appeared at the hut's door before first light, a glow light bobbing over her head.

"Dasimbe, you are needed. A human child is seriously ill. His parents have brought him from their farm to be healed. This will be your first true test of deep-healing, but Tostig and I will be there if you need us."

I arose without question, ready and eager to use my talents in this most personal and rewarding way—to save a life.

Gina led me to a hut already filled with the pungent odor of healing herbs. Soft glow lights hung near the walls. Aside from Tostig, Gina, and me, only the child's parents were in the hut.

"His name is José," his mother whispered, and my eyebrows rose in surprise at a name from the Halcon Mountains.

I knelt by the boy who lay on a raised pallet and ran my hands a few inches above his body from head to foot, mentally scanning as I went. Sensing the problem was within his chest, I placed my hands there as I had once placed them on Evergreen's soil. If I failed in this, Gina and Tostig would take over, but I knew I would not fail.

I closed my eyes to concentrate and then looked within José's body. His lungs labored, filling with a viscous fluid that would drown him before the day ended. I went into the fluid, loosened it from the surrounding tissue, thinned it, and brought it upward through his flesh. Although my eyes remained closed, I knew a mist rose out of the child to dissipate into the air. This first stage of healing done, I turned to the more difficult task ahead.

José's fevered body fought a ravaging infection. Although his lungs harbored the greatest concentration of the invader, I scanned other areas and saw that his body's defenses struggled against an overwhelming force. I added my own energy to the fight for his life, but destroying the enemy took some time.

I sensed when someone gave liquid to the boy, precious help, without which we would have lost the battle. As the invaders became less, José's own defenses rallied. We vanquished the enemy together, although for the boy it was an unconscious battle.

When I lifted my hands from his body and opened my eyes, Gina brought José's parents forward to thank me and to be near their now peacefully sleeping child. Nearly three quarters of the day had passed. I suddenly realized how exhausted and hungry I felt.

Tostig smiled and gave me something to drink. "You did well. Your healing talent is strong. But now you must rest."

"First we feed you," Gina added. "Then you will sleep." She pulled me out of the hut and directed me toward a waiting tray of food.

As she said, I ate and then slept and awoke the next morning to winter's breath nipping the air. By midmorning, the chill would be gone. I remembered the feel of winter in Olin, the howling storms and thundering waves, how I had chafed at my boredom and feared for my father. I missed my family, especially Cia.

I rose and dressed swiftly. Slipping a pair of scissors into a pocket, I left the village. The nekka flew above and called to acknowledge my presence. I touched his mind briefly and then found a sun-warmed spot amid the reeds to settle down and plan my immediate future. I drew in a deep breath of crisp air. I knew my training had ended, and that I would soon leave Osa Marsh. Although I itched to venture forward and longed to see my family, I loved the marsh and its nurturing environment. When among humans, or even the sea sprites, would I feel this close to Evergreen?

With shaking hands, I unwound my long braids and pulled them apart, carefully separating the thick strands. The heavy, red-gold mass fell about me. Like Cierva and my mother, I had always worn my hair long in the sea-sprite fashion. During my journey to and my stay in the marsh, I had cursed the inconvenience of caring for it and envied the marsh women their shorter hair, worn about the shoulders in a length easily put back in a simple tail or short braids. I stood up, my hair spilling almost to my knees, and started to cut.

Tostig was the first to see me when I returned to the village. My hair hung loose to my shoulders.

"Child, is this what you really wanted?"

"I'm no longer a child," I retorted, for my nineteenth birthday drew near. I shook my head, savoring the feel of the short locks. "Besides, long hair is inconvenient, and I'm marsh folk, am I not?"

Tostig nodded, laughing. "We leave tomorrow to meet with Lam Po's village for the official adoption ceremony, although I consider you a daughter to me already, even as Lam Po does."

"I'm to be adopted?" Happiness flooded through me. I already felt I belonged to the marsh and liked the idea of a festive ceremony to make it official.

"It is tradition. We always adopt those we train into the marsh folk."

"How many have there been?" I asked. "Are there others besides Daniel?"

He looked at me a moment before answering. "There are half breeds along the coast who have come in for training although none have required the extensive training you have. Their needs are simple—talents used in hunting, farming, or fishing. Yet they all bond with Evergreen. In the future, if Evergreen decrees, their training may become more extensive."

"Other half breeds like me—sea sprite and human?"

He nodded.

"Wow," I said, bemused, not knowing what to feel or say, but I wondered about these other half breeds as I spent the day helping prepare food to take with us. We worked until well after dark, packing what we had made into baskets. With all the excitement and the holiday mood, I found it difficult to sleep that night. Nevertheless, I awoke early the following morning, and shortly after dawn, I, with Tostig and the whole village, left for Lam Po's village. We arrived near dusk to find people from all over the marsh already gathered for my adoption ceremony.

"Dasimbe, it's good to see you again," Lam Po greeted me and sent, *"Your training is finished and has gone well. You will soon be leaving us, even as Daniel did."*

"It's good to see you too, Lam Po," I replied aloud and asked after Omah and Dixon. I still had the reed pipe Dixon had taught me to make and use and wanted to spend time with my friends. Lam Po granted my wish.

"Eat first, and visit with your friends. They're waiting to see you. Later we will call a council meeting that you must attend."

I grinned my thanks and hurried off to find Omah and Dixon.

I found them waiting near tables laden with food. They plied me with questions as we filled our plates. Gina and Tam joined us while Tostig conversed with Lam Po.

Then I ate, laughed, and after eating, joined the other flute players, adding counterpoint to the background rhythm of drums. I finally paused for a breath.

"What do I do at the ceremony tomorrow?" I asked Omah.

"You will join with us, and we with you, as we all share a joining with Evergreen. Then we eat and eat and eat and be merry," she said and grinned from ear to ear.

"It sounds wonderful," I said and grinned hugely myself. Then we continued with our music and conversation until the council meeting started.

The mellow feeling I carried from the festivities quickly dissolved into the harsh reality of news shared by the marsh runners in council. The South Halcon army had begun its movement from the western plains to the escarpment, and North Halcon's army had responded with its own movement toward Phoenix. My father and Daniel traveled with the troops from Halconnida. At the same time, a small contingent of enemy soldiers headed toward the marsh. In a few days, they would pass to the south of Lam Po's village on their way to Fanil in the east. Fortunately, they had no purpose in the marsh other than to pass through it on their way to join those soldiers already in the coastal town. No one ventured a guess as to the purpose these men had in Fanil, but in a moment of foreknowledge, I knew.

"Please excuse my intrusion," I broke in, "but I speak on this issue with foreknowledge. These troops plan to board ships docked in Fanil. From there, they plan to sail along the coast, terrorizing human farmers into falling back toward Phoenix, effectively cutting them off from any contact with the sea sprites. The soldiers will leave the sprites alone for now. Their main purpose is to sever relations between the humans and all other intelligent groups on Evergreen. The marsh folk they hardly recognize as people," I said with disgust.

Silence greeted this, and saddened at the thought of South Halcon, or any human, following Paul Rider, I wondered at the hardhearted folk of his army.

"Can something be done to stop this?" I asked.

The council buzzed quietly with ideas until Lam Po spoke. "Dasimbe, Evergreen has given you this foreknowledge for a reason. If you warn the sea folk in Fanil, they can put their ships out to sea before the troops arrive. With the council's permission, I will ask you to take this warning to Fanil after the adoption ceremony tomorrow."

All in the council favored the simple strategy and also decided to send a message relating the situation to my father and Daniel.

I agreed, for I felt Evergreen had appointed this mission as my own. I also knew I would soon be back in Olin. Foreknowledge predicted it. I would board a ship in Fanil and sail to Olin. My heart leaped in joy at the thought of seeing Cia and my mother again.

The council ended, and the villagers already slept, so I crept to my bed in Omah's hut, too tired to let my thoughts keep me awake.

The day of my adoption dawned overcast. The marsh folk seemed not to notice, enjoying themselves with feast preparations. Lam Po approached me at breakfast with a broad grin and hot marsh tea.

"Dasimbe, the day of your adoption. How old are you?"

To my surprise, I realized it was my birthday and laughed at myself for having forgotten what I had easily remembered the day before.

"I'm nineteen today. It's my birthday. In all the excitement, I forgot."

Lam Po continued smiling as he settled down with his tea. I suspected that he had known my birth date all along. "Your haircut, it is very fetching," he said before sipping his tea.

"I'm getting used to it," I said and fingered a strand. "I feel freer with the weight and care of it gone."

"It suits you and your new life. You wanted adventure, did you not?"

I nodded as I sipped my own tea. "Yes, but I never expected to get my wish."

We sat in silence for a moment before he continued. "You need nothing special for the ceremony, only yourself. How do you feel today?"

I thought for a moment before answering. "Almost as if today and my adoption were already done and I've moved on, although to exactly what, beyond Fanil and Olin, I don't know. But I feel well and content, and I'm looking forward to the ceremony."

He still smiled, but his eyes held a touch of sadness. "Your foreknowledge prompts you ahead. Indeed, I also feel that you have moved on, save for the ceremony. Yet you will always be one with us, as with Evergreen."

I nodded again, for my ties to Evergreen bound me to these people and the marsh.

Just before noon, everyone assembled in the village center where docking platforms circled an elbow of the river set between islets with some of the tallest clumps of reeds and a few swamp marazuls. The ceremonial gathering spread back from the docks between the huts and reeds onto the platforms, rafts, and small islands that rose in tiers beyond. The morning clouds had disappeared into a brilliant turquoise sky, perfect weather for the ceremony.

I stood with Lam Po at the edge of the largest dock. He introduced me to the people of the marsh and stated my desire for formal adoption. The crowd cheered, and then everyone knelt or sat down. I sat at the edge of the platform, wondering where to place my hands, and then realized water would work as well as soil. I plunged my hands into the river, and the marsh folk began to tap a rhythm on anything handy. The rhythm enfolded me as it built in intensity, and I opened to the message of their drumming. They spoke of the past, of their relationship with each other and Evergreen, and of their hopes for the future, a future of unity among the species. Their story completely absorbed me, and then it stopped as they placed their hands flat on the platforms, into the water, or onto the soil. Then we joined with Evergreen, and with my companions, I again traveled on a journey through the essence of the planet. My sense of belonging, of unity with Evergreen grew stronger by sharing the venture and solidified my desire to serve Evergreen's purpose.

I separated from this joining slowly, rising through levels of awareness to eventually enter my own being, myself, alone. Then, as if waking from a dream, I became aware of everyone around me talking in excitement and bustling about, eager to feast the afternoon away. I took a deep breath and sat back on my heels to take stock and absorb the experience.

From the join, I gathered that the impending battle on Phoenix's plains and the stalemated war in the Halcon Mountains presented only a minor threat to Evergreen as a whole. Evergreen gave the sea sprites, marsh folk, and other species their own natural defenses against what the humans could do. Yet the humans could harm themselves and would try to harm, or use, the half breeds, and half breeds could be a threat to anyone on Evergreen. Why did humans isolate themselves from what Evergreen and the other species had to offer?

"They only hurt themselves," I muttered, but Lam Po caught what I said and knew what I referred to.

"That is so," he said as he passed me a fermented marsh drink I had not tasted before. "You and Daniel will do much for Evergreen, foreknowledge. But we of the marsh are not given to see the fate of humans, only the fate of those connected to Evergreen."

Only those connected to Evergreen. Although I had not long bonded with the planet, the thought of separation from Evergreen made me shiver, and my human heritage became more of a burden with everything I learned. I thought of my father, a good man, if a little stern at times. He took his position as a leader seriously and cared about people. Yet of all the things he had taught Cia and me, nothing compared to what I had learned in the marsh. I had thought he lacked for naught, but he had never connected with Evergreen, and I feared he never would.

Tostig broke into my reverie when he leaned over to give me meat and bread. Dixon joined the flute players, and as the comfortable afternoon wore on, I relaxed and decided to put my concerns behind me for a time. With the nekka watching above, and the eyes of the marsh open to anything of importance or danger, we could indulge in our festivities. Paul Rider must have felt the power of our join. He could only guess at the cause.

Although the feasting continued until late, I retired early, not long after young Dixon. Before sleep would come, I reviewed the day and the revelations gleaned from joining. I thought of the war in the Halcons and of Daniel and my father.

A mist lay over the marsh when I awoke. I arose and gathered my things for the journey.

Omah appeared just as I left the small dwelling. "Lam Po is ready to see you before you leave, Dasimbe." Omah hugged me in farewell. "Be careful, and return to us when you can."

"Omah, I will see you again."

"I know you will, child." We hugged again before parting.

Lam Po and Tostig both waited with a pot of marsh tea. I smiled at that. I had grown fond of that tea.

"I've made my plans, and I'm ready to leave. What will happen to Neh Hah? I run as a saor to Fanil."

"Your horse will be taken care of. When you need her in Phoenix, she will be there."

"Thank you. So I'll be in Phoenix when the armies meet?" I guessed.

They both nodded, and Lam Po spoke. "Yes, although you will probably not be there for long. You will see your family again for a short while. But don't forget, we are your family now also, and we will miss you here in the marsh."

"And I'll miss both of you and all my friends here." I found it hard to express how much these people meant to me. "I will come back," I added.

"Yes, but now you must leave, before those from the enemy's army pass us," Tostig prompted.

I nodded and stood to leave, shouldering my pack. "Again, thank you for all your care and teaching. I'll never forget what you've done for me."

They stood and saw me to the hut door. To my surprise, more than two staffs waited there. Lam Po handed the third staff to me. I grasped the sleek and glistening blue-black marazul wood, its smooth and silky surface warm to the touch.

"You have traveled beyond your home and must carve your staff. I hope your adventures in the marsh warrant some fine work," he said with a grin.

For a moment, I stood speechless, but I beamed in pleasure at their gift.

"Thank you," I finally responded. "I'll treasure it always, and yes—" I grinned. "My first carvings will speak of the marsh."

Then I strapped the staff to my pack and stepped through the doorway. Lam Po and Tostig watched as I disappeared from the village into the morning mist.

As the mist enfolded me, I shape-changed to a saor. Moving swiftly and easily in the silent and lithe form, I savored the exertion, delighting in the freedom of streaking through the marsh like a ghost with fangs, dark and lethal.

Several hours passed before the mist cleared, and the day grew warmer. Still I traveled without stopping and kept on going into the night, reaching the ridge above the lowland fens by dawn of the next day. Before climbing the ridge with its roaring cataracts, I stopped and changed into my own form.

I turned to look back over the marshlands that had been my home for almost a year. Far above the blue rippling of reeds, the nekka flew, morning light glinting off its scales. I smiled. This one friend would follow me from the marsh.

I rested and had a bite to eat. Then I knelt at the water's edge and gathered stones in the shallows. I tapped a rhythm on the stones, repeating it several times before I scattered them. Having sent my good-bye to the marsh, I stood again, shape-changed into a saor, and then ran into the noisy heights above the fens.

Fanil and the *Ra Shavel*
Dasimbe Halcon—Autumn 1836 AB

The Ra Shavel *skipped the waves lightly, sun dancing in
the salt-spray flung skyward by her bow. Appropriately,
"sun dance" is the human translation of* Ra Shavel.

— *Entry in Dasimbe Halcon's journal*

Remaining as a saor, I crept down through the waterfall's mist and the tumbled rocks of the ridge to the edge of the fens. The lowland growth had already changed into its winter colors, more blue than green, a dark teal mimicking the ocean. I headed north and east around the wetlands, frightening birds into white, whirling clouds of agitation. Scales and feathers glinted in the sun. Large predators slithered through sucking mud and slick grasses, their gaping jaws eager to snare whatever passed. My nostrils quivered at the rich, heavy odor of verdant growth mingled with decay. The water, free moving in the marsh, had become sluggish in the fens. Beyond the wetlands, Fanil stood on a rise above a sheltered river estuary.

I smelled brine before I heard the sound of distant surf. Both scent and sound grew in intensity as I neared the coast, and by the time I reached Fanil, the constant thrum of the sea, the cries of seabirds, and the salt-laden air had inundated my senses.

While the nekka remained above the fens to hunt, I shape-changed into the guise of a sea sprite and approached the town on a path between

92

submerged fields of cultivated winter rice, a pale version of the wild, dark-green rice in the fens. Late afternoon sunlight streaked the sky with gold as I entered the small seaport.

A crushed-shell road ran straight through the town. To my right, stores, taverns, and docks lined a river where sea-sprite vendors along the waterfront did brisk business with sailors who had just finished unloading their catch or cargo. On my left, hillside roads wound uphill between gaily decorated wooden buildings perched on tall stilts. The setting sun caught brilliant splashes of color on carved and painted eaves.

I maintained the thinner, paler version of myself to hide my presence from any enemy soldiers and followed Lam Po's directions to the town's council house. I saw nothing of the soldiers already in the town, and the sea sprites ignored me as I passed. The sprites sensed me as a stranger and would know something of why I came to Fanil but went about their business with their usual aloof gaiety.

I found the council house set on wooden piles near the town center and mounted the wide, sweet-smelling wooden steps. Crossing the porch, I passed through open double doors into an airy room with tall windows and a high ceiling. Bars of hazy sunlight gilded interior walls paneled in the same aromatic wood as the entry steps. Brightly colored cushions lay in a horseshoe shape on the polished wooden floor. Other doors gave entry to the room, and a sea-sprite male emerged from one of them.

"Can I help you?" he asked as he approached. The question addressed a human, not a sea sprite. Stranger or not, no sea sprite would have been asked if she needed help. Their communal link took care of such things. While in the building and out of sight of humans, I had no need for disguise, so I changed back to my own, more human form and answered his formal question.

"I bear a message from the council of Osa Marsh to the council of Fanil. Can we meet quickly?" I queried in just as formal a manner.

Not asking why, he only nodded and then led me to a cushion before leaving the room.

One by one, the council members entered and found places on the other cushions. They smiled, nodding a greeting as they arrived, and then talked quietly among themselves as we waited for the room to fill. When the head elder rapped knuckles on wood for attention, the room fell silent. Then he nodded in my direction. It was time for me to give the marsh council's message.

"My name is Dasimbe, and I come from Osa Marsh, where I sat in council with Lam Po Dal and the other elders four nights ago. I bring the following message from that meeting." I paused for a moment before plunging into the body of the message. "Soldiers from South Halcon have been massing on the plains west of the marsh for some time now and have started their move toward Phoenix. A small contingent has separated from their army and heads toward Fanil to join the humans already here. They plan to board however many ships they need, leaving only a few soldiers to watch the town. From the ships, they plan to foray into the country-side along the coast, driving human settlers toward Phoenix. If they find humans that cohabit with sprites, or find those of mixed sprite-human blood, they may slaughter them outright. Their purpose is to totally sepa-rate the species and, perhaps in the future, instigate war between humans and the other people of Evergreen." I hastily lowered my eyes to hands that twisted together in my lap. My cheeks burned. For the first time in my life, I expected censure for my human blood. Yet I raised my head again and continued.

"I intend to thwart their plans, with your help. The marsh council's request is that you put all your ships to sea, for whatever time it takes to discourage these men from their task. We believe the soldiers here will grow restless and possibly attempt to pillage the town. The liberal use of protection and confusion wards should take care of that problem. When the soldiers grow frustrated with their situation, perhaps they will return to their army. This will surely anger Paul Rider, their leader, but we feel it best to let him know that not all will go as he wishes. This is what the marsh council sees. Can we count on your aid in this?"

I expected some discussion and questions, but the head elder surprised me with an immediate answer. "We have been awaiting your arrival in Fanil. We knew South Halcon planned some movement based from here, but not the details nor the motivation. Thank you for supplying this information, child of the marsh. We will do as the marsh council suggests." A huge smile lit his face as he added, "It is a good plan, and we hope Paul Rider thinks so too."

I had forgotten the sea sprites' refreshing and lighthearted disregard for things that seemed serious to a human. This, along with the tangy sea air and the aromatic wood scent, helped lighten my mood and ease my embarrassment.

"Thank you for listening and for your help," I said in genuine gratitude.

"We do what we can. Meanwhile, one of our families will be glad to house you, and we all have children who will vie to show you Fanil."

"Wait a minute," one of the council members interrupted, laughing. "What chance do I have here?"

I glanced at the speaker. Up to now, I had paid little attention to the council members individually, except for their leader. I was surprised to see that not all were truly elders. A younger sea sprite had just spoken, elder in title only. Red highlights glinted in his fair hair, and his eyes, unlike the light gray of most sea sprites in Olin, were a mischievous blue threaded with silver. A broad smile lit his fine-boned face.

"I would be glad to show you around tomorrow, and you may spend the night at my place if you like." I blushed at his frankness as everyone hooted in laughter at his remark.

"Thank you. I'll pass on spending the night, but you may show me around Fanil," I managed to respond.

He let out an exaggerated sigh as he got to his feet. "Ah well, tomorrow then."

I stood up with the rest amid good-natured teasing and realized how tired I felt. The head elder noticed this.

"Dasimbe Halcon, my name is Santil. You are welcome to stay with my family tonight. My wife and children will be thrilled to meet you."

I paused at his use of my full name. Even though I had not introduced myself as a Halcon, he knew who I was. I wondered if he knew my parents and realized that I represented my family as well as the marsh council.

"Do you know my family?"

He smiled broadly. "I know who they are. I frequently visited Olin in my youth when your mother was a young woman courted by many. She left several broken hearts when news came of her marriage to your father in Phoenix. But then, Ciervo Halcon had swept all Olin off its feet in the previous months, so what did they expect? Yes, your parents inspired many a tale in sea-sprite lands, and they are still talked of today. When you and your sister, Cierva, were born, we all knew of it."

I chuckled at his reply. "My family is noteworthy," I agreed. The sprites loved a good story or debate, and my parents provided material for both.

He led me through Fanil's early evening bustle to a sweet-smelling wooden house on stilts. His wife and children greeted us at the top of the stairs and welcomed me into their home. He introduced his wife as Betan, named after the brightly colored but poisonous fish of the reefs, and then introduced his children: Clea, a girl of sixteen, and Otan and Datan, boys of fourteen and twelve. They dressed much alike in the lightly woven tunic and trousers worn by sprites for everyday wear. The boys favored their mother with fair hair and pale gray-green eyes. Clea had her father's curly black hair, and her gray eyes were only a little darker than my mother's. All had the sprites' thin, angled bone structure and iridescent skin.

Betan led me to a cushion by a low, round table already set for an evening meal. Glow lights bobbed overhead. The children followed with their happy chatter and deposited themselves on other cushions while Santil went to help Betan bring in the food. My mouth watered at the delicious aroma of seafood wafting through the house.

"Do you always eat in your own homes rather than communally?" I asked Santil when he returned with a platter of vegetables and a huge bowl of green rice.

"Once a week and on feast days, we eat a communal meal. In summer, we tend to eat outside with a group of neighbors. How about you? How does your family eat?"

He sat down, and Betan set a great plate of steaming shellfish on the table and joined us. Then we all helped ourselves to what we wanted.

I answered as I filled my plate. "In Phoenix, I ate with my family in the human fashion in our own dwelling, except for feast days. In Olin, almost everyone dined communally, although I could take a light meal in my room if I wished. I had to fetch my food, of course. In Osa Marsh, meals are communal and very similar to the communal gatherings in Olin, with storytelling and music along with the food."

"You're so lucky to have traveled," Clea said before biting into a juicy tidbit. I only smiled as I bit into my own succulent bit of meat.

After the meal, the children clamored for a story from their father. Although tired, I offered my services for a very brief tale.

"Would you mind a short story from a stranger tonight? I would love to tell you a tale of Olin. Have you been there?"

The children cried, Yes!" as their parents smiled.

"But I've never been there," Otan said.

"Me either," Datan added before they all settled down to listen.

"Have you heard of the Man Pearl?" I asked and received another no. I sat down on a large cushion in front of the fire, and Santil and Betan joined their children.

"A tale of Olin," I began, as was the custom. "Among the treasures and many strange wonders displayed in the Pearl Tower of Olin, there is a giant man-shaped pearl. Different explanations exist about how the Man Pearl came to be, but no one truly knows how it was formed. Some say a long-ago artisan shaped a light framework of wood and glazed it with clay and then pearl, and so it may be, but there is another story that I prefer to believe.

"Yiddlaw and Yallow, two very mischievous young brothers, were playing seek-and-find far out in the ocean, approaching the deeps where larger sea life grow. It was Yiddlaw's turn to hide, and Yallow barely had time to blink an eye before Yiddlaw vanished, as is customary. Yet Yiddlaw departed from custom when he chose to hide in a place only he knew of and smothered his communal link. Yallow searched for a long time, but he could have sought forever and never found his brother. What is the fun in that? Believing his brother played a joke on him by returning home to eat the special treats their mother set out for them, Yallow left the ocean.

"Meanwhile, Yiddlaw lay curled up inside a very large oyster, where he quickly grew bored and fell asleep. The oyster, being irritated, started to work on covering this larger than usual object. Something in the secretions worked as a sedative, and Yiddlaw slept for a very long time. He awoke hungry and promptly vanished back to shore, only to find that Olin had grown larger, and Yallow had changed into an old man. Although Yiddlaw had not changed much, no one recognized him, not even his brother, and no one believed his tale, even when he took them to find the man-shaped pearl hidden within the giant oyster.

"The people of Olin transported the Man Pearl to Olin and hold it as one of their greatest treasures, but no one remembers what became of Yiddlaw, the foolish boy."

The children laughed, and I yawned as they begged their father for a tale.

Betan took pity on me and led me to a loft room under the eaves. The low murmur of voices amid night breezes, and the sound of surf lulled me to sleep.

The next morning after bathing, I rummaged through my pack for my sea-sprite day dress, not worn in over a year. I shook out and donned the pale-green, iridescent midcalf tunic and matching pants. Folding my short marsh tunic carefully, I packed it away and joined Santil's noisy brood for a light breakfast.

Before long, the young council member arrived to show me around Fanil. He introduced himself as Rask O'Meral. Clea remained quiet in the background, but the boys clamored to come with us.

"I'll go as a sea sprite. The human soldiers must not see me," I explained, and Rask nodded.

As we walked downhill toward the town center, Rask pointed out the intricate carvings on the raised buildings, some painted, many not. All the buildings faced the crushed-shell roadway that wound down to the docks on the river below. Under almost every home, a small winter garden flourished in raised beds surrounding a central flagged area. The homes perched high enough for the sun to reach the gardens for some of each day.

"In the summer, the sun is more directly overhead, and the gardens remain cool," Rask explained as we neared the lower level of the town and the main road paralleling the docks. "We seldom eat indoors then. Everyone heads for the garden to eat or to visit with friends."

To our left, almost due east, the main road led to the ocean. To our right, it retraced my route into the town from the rice fields and fens.

Otan and Datan, already bored with following us, hurried off to their own pursuits as Rask angled to the left. Ahead, the sea breathed a rumbling welcome home. I felt my pulse quicken in response.

Rask's low laughter intruded. "At last, our escorts are gone. Now tell me about yourself, Dasimbe. You originally come from Olin, correct?"

I tore my mind from the distant sea to respond. "Yes, from Olin and Phoenix. My mother's kin name is O'Meral, like yours. My father is Ciervo Halcon, a human sorcerer from North Halcon. They were married in Phoenix, where we live for most of the year, but we spent a great deal of time in Olin."

"We are distant cousins then," he said with a grin, "despite your mixed blood. A fascinating heritage. Do you know many like yourself?"

I shook my head. "The only half breeds I know are my sister, Cierva, and Daniel, the man who took me to the marsh. He is an air fairy–human half breed. I know other half breeds exist, but I've not met any, and I don't know how many there are. How about you? Are you from Fanil?"

"Ha, no. I'm an undersea brat. The city of Meral is my home although I've spent time in Oscat and in the Babal Trench. Now I represent Meral in Fanil. Have you been to Meral?" he asked, turning inquisitive blue eyes in my direction.

"Several times as a child. Is it truly as beautiful as I remember?" I pictured the glowing underwater city set amid seaweed that rippled in flowing curtains towering far higher than the tall coral buildings.

"Yes, it's the most beautiful place on Evergreen—but I'm prejudiced of course," he said with a huge grin. "I love my home yet feel a need to see more of the world, and I envy you your travels. Have you been to the mountains?"

I noticed a touch of awe in his voice, and because he could never visit the mountains, I said nothing to inspire him. "Several times as a child, to visit my grandfather in Halconnida, but I hardly remember the visits. Halconnida is nowhere near as impressive as Meral." Although Halconnida had its own charm, I told the truth.

We had passed through the town as we talked and continued along the road until it started to curve to the north following the coast. In the distance, the road climbed into the bramble that grew beneath the headlands. Eventually, it breached the headlands to cross forest and farmland.

We stopped at the edge of the dunes overlooking the ocean.

"Welcome home," Rask said with a grin.

I drank in the view. The winter sun warmed my face and glinted off water that ran high after the last storm. A hazy horizon blended ocean and sky, and restless waves rolled in to crash and churn on the shore, a sight and sound wonderfully familiar. I breathed in the salty air, and my eyes stung. *Not quite home yet*, I thought. Olin and Cia waited further up the coast.

"Thank you, Rask." I remembered my host. He understood the lure of the sea and had remained silent as I gazed at the ocean. He only nodded and smiled.

We shared the quiet solitude awhile longer and then walked back to Fanil, the sun already high as we headed to the wharves. The sprites prepared to put their ships out to sea—loading food, water, and trading goods as last-minute repairs were completed and inspected.

"When will the ships be ready?" I asked.

"Another day perhaps. Our scouts from the marsh continue to arrive with news of the enemy's movements. We have just enough time to do what is necessary. Fortunately, Lam Po Dal has always been in close contact with the council here. We were well forewarned. The marsh folk must trust you greatly to have chosen you as their messenger."

His statement made me feel proud that my adoptive marsh clan thought so well of me and dulled the sting of missing my true family.

"I have been adopted by the marsh folk, and we joined together with Evergreen. My purpose and theirs is the same—peace among the species.

Do you understand what Evergreen intends?" I still had questions about who knew what about Evergreen and its purpose.

His brows furrowed in thought. "Evergreen's intention? Some of it. I've not been in a joining recently." He shrugged. "It's a serious thing with us. We enjoy it too much and have difficulty pulling out of it. This you have done in the marsh?"

"Yes."

He only nodded in reply, and we walked in silence for a while. He occasionally pointed out some sight in the town or on the water and then indicated a roadside vendor.

"It's past midday. How about something to eat?"

At the aroma of seafood and savory rice wrapped in flatbread, I grinned and nodded. "Great idea. I'm hungry."

We purchased our food and ate as we ambled up the hill toward Santil's house.

"I really do wish I could show you Meral, but you're returning to Olin, aren't you?" Rask asked, as he brushed crumbs from his fingers.

"Yes, if a ship will take me." That he knew I planned on going to Olin didn't surprise me. I had not shielded my thoughts and feelings at viewing the ocean.

"My family owns a ship that will leave for Olin when the others put to sea. I believe the *Ra Shavel* has room for passengers."

"*Ra Shavel*. Sun dance. I like the name," I said, translating the sprite words.

"I still think you should accompany me to Meral," he said, grinning again, and I knew that he teased. "But I doubt you'll change your mind."

"You're right. I'll not change my mind, but I'd like to see Meral again someday."

"Perhaps I could arrange for your visit," Rask continued the banter as we approached Santil's house. "But today I'll see about your passage on the *Ra Shavel*."

I smiled at his offer. "Thank you, Rask. I appreciate your help." Then I changed the subject. "Where are the enemy soldiers?" I had seen nothing of them during our walk.

"We seldom see them. They've found that Fanil has nothing they're interested in. They barely keep an eye on us and eagerly await the arrival of their friends." He chuckled and sent me a brief view of a ward set to confuse the soldiers.

At the false image of quiet dockyards, I knew that the soldiers saw little that they were not meant to see and much of what did not exist.

When we arrived at Santil's house, it was already midafternoon. I thanked Rask for showing me Fanil, and he left to book my passage on the *Ra Shavel*.

Later that day, Santil took time from his position as harbormaster to ask me what my plans were. I told him I planned to travel to Olin and mentioned the *Ra Shavel*.

"I am happy to hear Rask is of help to you," he said with a smile and then ambled off back to the docks.

Rask had left Santil's house with a promise to return that evening. He arrived with three companions: his younger brother Dom, Dom's friend Pacel, and Pacel's sister Jacin. Dom resembled Rask with light-red hair and silvery-blue eyes, while Pacel and Jacin both had white-blond hair and pale, hazel-gray eyes. All younger than Rask, they appeared nearer my age and filled the house with laughter.

Santil and Betan suggested we take an evening walk through the town, now lit by glow lights. Considering the exuberance of the company, it seemed a good idea. Again, I went as a sea sprite, one of two girls in a group of five young people. A chill hung in the air, and few people took advantage of the calm reigning before the next storm.

Rask pointed out the ships. "Thankfully, they're ready to put out to sea tomorrow. Two runners from the South Halcon army arrived late this afternoon, and the soldiers aren't far behind. The men quartered here must be in better spirits tonight."

His assessment appeared accurate. A group of four soldiers appeared a few moments later, drunk and staggering further along the docks. My heart sank at the sight, and my joy of only a moment before wavered.

"Perhaps we should return to the house," I said, and the others agreed. They must have felt my unease and intense dislike. Although comfortable living among the hard-working and boisterous people of Phoenix and the plains, I had avoided their drunken revels. Now, faced with a group of the enemy's army, I felt loathing. I doubted every soldier in South Halcon agreed with Paul Rider's ideology, yet they fought for him and planned to wreak havoc along the coast—good reason for my animosity.

Although the soldiers posed no threat, we returned to Santil's house and settled before a fire that chased off the mild winter chill. My gloom diminished as we talked of the impending departure of the ships to sea.

"I'm going with you on the *Ra Shavel* to Olin," Rask suddenly stated.

"And I as well," said Jacin.

"We're all going with you to Olin," said Rask, indicating the others. "Yesterday we decided that we can travel with you as far as Phoenix if need be. You need traveling companions, Dasimbe."

They all nodded in agreement.

Surprised by their suggestion, for a moment I said nothing, but sudden tears stung my eyes at their offer of companionship. Tackling new adventures on my own, and the continuous farewells, had affected me more than I realized. The offer of friendship from those I barely knew deeply moved me.

"You're right. I need companions, and I'll be glad of your company."

Dom laughed. "Great, it's all set then. We leave tomorrow. I'm ready for an adventure," he said, and the others echoed agreement.

"What time do the ships put to sea?" he asked Rask.

"By midmorning, well before the enemy soldiers arrive. The town plans to set new confusion wards shortly before the ships set out."

Santil approached, bearing hot, spiced drinks. "Yes, we will enjoy setting the wards and seeing the results," he said as he set the tray with its cups on a low table beside us. His twinkling eyes promised mischief. "And it will do you good to have traveling companions, Dasimbe. Besides, these young people are restless and bored in Fanil."

"So true, but no offense to Fanil," offered Rask, and we all laughed.

"None taken," Santil said with a smile.

After finishing our drinks, we all parted company, and despite my excitement, I drifted into an easy sleep.

In the morning, after gathering my few belongings, I relaxed by playing the marsh flute while Clea read nearby. Otan and Datan were at the docks watching the ships make their final preparations to leave. Clea seemed downcast and dropped the book into her lap.

"What's wrong, Clea? Are you worried about the safety of Fanil?"

She shook her head and brooded for a moment before she spoke. "No, I'm not afraid, but you're taking everyone with you."

By everyone, I realized she meant those young adults in the town who were a little older than herself, those whom she considered exciting and aspired to be like.

"They'll be back," I said, without foreknowledge this time but wanting to reassure her.

"Can I come with you? I have an aunt in Olin who is fond of me. I would love to visit her."

I wondered how long had she been thinking this up. "I don't know, Clea. What would your parents think? Have you asked them?"

She brooded again and did not answer but returned to her book, so I continued playing my flute.

"That's pretty, Dasimbe. Is it a marsh tune?" asked Betan, who appeared in the doorway holding a bundle of clothing to her chest. "No, don't stop playing to answer."

I nodded and continued playing, changing the tune to fit the rhythm of the nearby surf.

She entered the room, giving her daughter a touch on the shoulder before sitting down next to her. Clea, still brooding over her book, did not respond to her mother's touch.

"Dasimbe, I have a favor to ask of you," Betan said at a pause in my playing.

I put down my flute and smiled. "Yes?"

She continued with the usual sea-sprite aplomb. "Clea is sixteen and has seen very little outside Fanil. She has never been to Meral undersea and only once been to Olin as a child. It is time she visited Olin again. I would like to send her on the *Ra Shavel,* if you would companion her."

Clea dropped her book in surprise.

Surprised also and not entirely pleased, I did not answer immediately. Was I to be responsible for the child?

"Mother, thank you," Clea said before turning to me. "Dasimbe, I'm only a few years younger than you, and I'll not be any trouble. Please say yes."

I had a feeling she would be aboard the *Ra Shavel* no matter what I said, and she would be better off in our group with everyone keeping an eye on her.

"All right. Betan, I go in the company of Rask, his brother, and his friends. Is this suitable company for your daughter?"

She nodded. "Yes, it is."

"Good. They will help me accompany Clea. She'll have plenty of people to keep an eye on her."

Betan smiled. "Thank you. She has been restless for some time. Clea, come with me. I have some things to give you before you leave." Then she turned to me with the bundle of clothing. "Here is something for your trip to Olin—a gift for helping us against the enemy."

"Thank you," I answered, taking the bundle. She nodded, and she and Clea left the room together.

I put away my flute and laid the soft tunic and trousers across a chair. Admiring the honey-colored fabric, I fingered the fine, iridescent weave of shimmering sea grass and thought about the people going with me on the *Ra Shavel*. I barely knew them and hoped no complications would arise from their company. Yet the sprites' ability to avoid personal or group peril would counter any danger they faced. I decided to let it go at that and folded the clothing away.

The next morning, as Santil, Betan, Otan, and Datan saw us aboard the *Ra Shavel*, I made brief contact with the nekka, directing its attention to the docks and our ship. All along the waterfront, the people of Fanil gathered in small groups to see the ships off. Confusion wards, already in force, covered nearly half the town. I wondered what the human soldiers were allowed to see.

"Good-bye. Fair winds to Olin," shouted the crowd as the *Ra Shavel* slipped away from the dock. Clea waved energetically to her parents, and they to her.

We passed five smaller ships, and their sailors waved, grinning as if our leaving Fanil were nothing more than a merry jaunt. Then the dark, blue-green river water changed to a lighter teal as the *Ra Shavel* entered the ocean. The captain ordered more sails set upon leaving the sheltered estuary, and we picked up speed. Barring problems from winter storms further up the coast, it would be a four-day voyage to Olin.

Aboard the *Ra Shavel*, passengers and crew alike faced astern to watch the other ships head out to sea. Colored sails caught the wind, and the ships scattered, bright butterflies skimming the waves. The ships would use the necessary leave-taking as an opportunity to visit and trade with Meral or Oscat, and one would follow the *Ra Shavel* to Olin. The fishing fleet had gone out as normal and would return under the cover of night and wards to unload their catch.

The *Ra Shavel* lived up to her name and danced the waves, the ship's prow flinging great clouds of sparkling sea spray high into the air. Wood groaned as the ship lifted and plunged. Her sails thrummed and rigging hummed in a salty wind that swirled across the deck and tugged at my bound hair. Exhilaration surged through me, and for a moment, I felt freed from thoughts of the war and my part in it. I hugged myself in joy. I was going home.

That night I slept well, in a cabin I shared with Jacin and Clea. The next morning I arose to the feel of the *Ra Shavel* moving in a wind that had abated very little. I hurried to dress and found Rask and Dom at the ship's rail. Small, silvery flying fish, for which the seaport of Fanil had been named, flashed alongside the ship, their scales reflecting sunlight. Eyes wide at the sparkling sight, I reached to grip the rail and sucked in a deep breath, savoring the taste of salt on my tongue and the feel of the sun and a brisk breeze.

"Let's get something to eat," Dom shouted against the wind. Spirits high, we went to find breakfast. Pacel, Jacin, and Clea joined us as we ate.

The carefree feeling did not last. Just after midday, as I played my reed pipe on deck, a mental touch sent a chill down my spine. I turned to those nearest me.

"Rask, Dom, did either of you feel a stranger's mental touch just now?"

Both shook their heads. "What exactly did you feel, Dasimbe?" Rask asked.

"I'm not sure, but it sent a shiver down my spine."

I felt it again, like a cloud covering the sun, an intrusion I did not like. I shivered again and warded my thoughts against whatever it might be. A sharp bird's cry rent the air, and we all looked up. A bird, much larger than the nekka that flew along the coast parallel to the *Ra Shavel*, flew directly above, perhaps the same one that had circled over the marsh while I slept. I shivered, remembering its intent to find and destroy me, and hastily shape-changed to my sea-sprite form.

Rask turned concerned eyes in my direction. "Dasimbe, is it looking for you? Maybe we can help by setting a confusion ward over the ship," he suggested.

"No," I said, shaking my head. "Do nothing to attract its attention. The enemy is looking for a half breed and any unusual use of mental energy. Perhaps if it seems we have nothing to hide—well, you get the idea." At Rask's nod of understanding, I continued. "I hope it looks in vain. My minor shape-change is using little talent. I doubt it will find anything."

Pacel, Jacin, and Clea joined us, concern showing in their faces.

"What does the bird want?" Jacin asked.

"It's looking for Dasimbe," Dom told her.

"We should play a game of seek-and-find to rattle its brains a little," she said with a wicked grin.

We all looked at her in surprise. I would never have considered this unusual ploy. Yet this frivolous game's exorbitant talent expenditure would cover any one individual's talent and surely confuse the bird—the perfect cover.

"Yes." I tucked the flute away and rose to my feet. "Shall we have a game?" My face lit with a smile as wicked in intent as Jacin's.

With the loud cracking sound of a minor fireworks display, we disappeared one by one into the waves and hopscotched across the ocean floor in a vanishing-and-reappearing chase after the ship above. Each of us choosing a different tone for our sound waves, we filled the sea with music.

We played the game for several hours, getting lost in the joy of it and losing track of time. When we finished our game, the bird was gone.

After this incident, I kept a mental watch open and became aware of more than one mental talent inland along the coast. Prowling the deck, I touched the edges of thoughts. Impressions came and went, broadcasts of feelings mingled with ideas. None seemed threatening. Puzzled and concerned, I approached Rask.

"What is it?" he asked, seeing my frown.

"I feel the presence of mental talent, nothing threatening, but is it Paul Rider's half breeds, or the half breeds who live along the coast?"

He smiled. "It isn't Paul Rider's half breeds you feel. I doubt he has many to spare, and he doesn't trust them out of his sight." He turned and grasped the rail, gazing at the distant shoreline. "Those you sense are sea sprite–human half breeds, the offspring of farmers and fishermen. No threat to us or Evergreen."

"Yes, Tostig of the marsh mentioned them. But why isn't Evergreen recruiting them? I thought all half breeds were needed in this war."

He turned to me with a frown. "I suspect your involvement has to do with your upbringing. You've been trained by a sorcerer and know more of the human community than those that dwell along the coast. Your training with the marsh folk went as smoothly as it did because of what you already knew." He nodded toward the shore. "They're more sea sprite than human and use their talent in simple ways."

I stared at him, silent for a moment, and then nodded. Just as Tostig had said—simple folk. Although curious and filled with longing to meet others of my kind, I realized that with little talent training, they remained vulnerable to mental attack. For their own protection, they were best left alone. I continued to feel their presence as we traveled northward.

In the following two days, our group became more closely knit. We spent hours in conversation and played rounds of seek-and-find. Sometimes I played my flute, and the others made up songs with ridiculous lyrics that had us rolling with laughter, effectively putting a halt to my playing. I had never felt this close to sea sprites before and enjoyed the rapport with my fellow travelers. Always with those in Olin, even my mother, I had felt a reserve, an awareness of my different heritage. I had learned to live with the feeling, not noticing it much, but now the closeness of my new friends made it obvious. Perhaps my joining with Evergreen had changed things. It had certainly changed me. Whatever the reason, I hoped the results would hold true with the sea sprites of Olin.

The air grew perceptively cooler as the *Ra Shavel* danced her way north. On the last day out from Olin, we ran before the next storm, the smell of rain and lightning growing stronger as clouds built into a dark wall behind us. The captain of the *Ra Shavel* had timed our arrival to take advantage of the winds while coming into port between the worst of the blows.

That afternoon, I dressed in the clothing Betan had given me and stood at the rail of the ship with my friends. Although the sky darkened behind us, the curved and spiked walls of Olin appeared in silhouette against a rose-gold sunset. The Pearly Tower speared the horizon, shimmering in orange, pink, purple, and gold, beckoning us toward Olin.

"It's beautiful," Clea whispered in awe.

"Yes," I whispered. The sight of Olin at sunset gripped me as never before, and joy bubbled as I sensed my mother waiting on the docks with Daniel by her side. I felt for Cierva and did not find her. Although tempted to whisk myself instantly from the ship to Olin, I waited with my friends but unintentionally broadcast my eagerness to be ashore. I tried to dampen my impatience to little avail.

Rask turned from the sight of Olin to grin in my direction.

I shrugged and took a deep breath. Although the enemy posed no threat this near Olin, I still fought to screen my emotions in an effort to master the screening wards.

Still taking advantage of the prevailing winds, we seemed to fly at the gap between the breakwaters protecting Olin's cove. The captain wanted the *Ra Shavel* put in safely before the storm hit. Then we flashed through the gap into comparatively quiet waters and maintained our speed almost to the wharves. However, before we reached that point, deck hands furled the sails and set out oars, so that we reached the dock at a more sedate pace. Then they threw out ropes, tied the ship to the dock, and hastily shoved a gangplank across the water just as another ship appeared on the horizon. Our sister ship from Fanil sped toward safety, just as we had done.

My companions and I disembarked into the already gathering twilight as huge winches swung cargo pallets to the docks and sailors scurried to ready the ship for the storm. I saw Daniel first. He was a full head taller than anyone else on the busy dock. Mother stood beside him. I hastened to reach them, urging my friends along with me, and clamped broadcast wards firmly in place to screen my heightened emotions.

"Dasimbe," Mother said, her voice husky as she stepped forward to hug me.

"Mother," I whispered in her ear and blinked, my eyes filling with tears. After a moment, I stepped back to really look at her and Daniel.

Mother beamed, obviously pleased to see me, and although Daniel wore his usual black from head to foot, he smiled and the slow swirling glints in his eyes indicated his pleasure at my arrival. My attraction to him surfaced like a punch to the stomach. Then I surprised myself by giving him a hug and felt his astonishment—and satisfaction. Did he feel the same as I did? Although giddy with questions, I reluctantly stepped back to introduce my openly curious friends from Fanil.

"Mother, Daniel. These are my companions from Fanil. This is Rask O'Meral, his brother Dom, Dom's friend Pacel, Pacel's sister Jacin, and Clea, the daughter of the Fanil harbormaster. Everyone, this is my mother, Dalia O'Meral, and this is our friend and a fellow traveler of mine, Daniel Scott."

All of those from Fanil seemed intrigued and curious at Daniel's strange appearance, and Clea openly stared. Sea-sprite etiquette prevailed, however, for they could feel he was a friend to the sprites and greeted him enthusiastically.

My mother suggested that we retire to the warmth of Olin before the storm hit. As the jolly crowd headed from the docks toward Olin's main spiral, I turned for a last look at the *Ra Shavel*, now riding higher in the night-dark and increasingly choppy water. Within moments, she would be towed out into the bay to weather the storm. Glow lamps lit the busy scene as the other ship docked to unload its passengers and goods.

"Thank you, *Ra Shavel*, for bringing me home. You lived up to your name," I said before turning again toward Olin.

Daniel stood there waiting and turned to walk with me. Overcome with questions, excitement, and stories, I hardly knew where to begin.

He spoke before I uttered a word. "Welcome home, Sim. It seems you've acquired a retinue during your travels."

Responding to the laughter dancing in his beautiful, glittering eyes, I grinned as I said, "Daniel, I've met so many people, it's hard to keep track of them." Then I grew serious. "I came to love the marsh folk and found it hard to leave them despite the fact that I missed my family. The marsh folk have such faith in us." I shook my head in wonder.

His look turned as serious as my own. "I believe it's Evergreen the marsh folk have faith in, not us." Then he asked a question. "How did you like your joining? I felt the group join not long after I left Halconnida with the army."

I sensed the importance of this question to him and hardly knew what to say. How could I explain the awe and joy I felt at joining with Evergreen and the subsequent sense of belonging and purpose? He must have known what it meant to me.

Finding it difficult to describe the experience, I sent my feelings as I spoke aloud. "You know what it meant to me. I enjoyed it. What else would a half breed feel?"

He nodded. "And how about your training? Did the marsh elders convince you to expand your talents into the realms of legend and lore?" He was grinning again.

I looked at him in surprise and then laughed as I realized how easily he would have picked up those thoughts and feelings at the time I held them.

"My training went well, thank you, and I learned marvelous things. However, for all my experiences, I'm glad to be home. I missed my family, and by the way," I added, "Cia's not in Olin. Do you know where she is?"

"That's your mother's story to tell, but I believe Cierva is safe and well."

Disappointed and curious at the same time and eager to question my mother, I quickened my pace.

"What were you saying to the ship?" Daniel asked as we neared the entrance to Olin's main coil.

"The *Ra Shavel* is her name. I wanted to thank her for a good journey and for bringing me home to Olin. I feel I'm saying good-bye to a very important part of my life, a part of growing up I'll never forget."

He nodded and laughed. "I expect you never will. And how do you feel about the future?"

"I'm excited about it and nervous at the same time, but I feel confident, thanks to Evergreen and the training of the marsh folk. Yet, I wonder— why are we so important to Evergreen? Why us?"

"That question is not easily answered, not tonight anyway. Come inside with everyone else. Evergreen, and your questions, can wait awhile."

Eager to hear news of my sister, I nodded, and we entered Olin with the others.

Cierva in the Northern Forest
Cierva Halcon—Winter 1835 AB to Winter 1836 AB

A few days after Dasimbe left Olin with Daniel Scott, and a day after her surprising send from Phoenix, I attended a morning council meeting and later sat weaving at my loom, believing these daily activities and my habitual calm masked the growing concern I felt for Dasimbe and her future. An irritating restlessness, something I had felt little of in the past, accompanied my shuttle as I shoved it through the warp with more force than usual. Over and over, I reviewed what little I knew of events beyond Olin.

I felt little fear for my father. I knew he trained North Halcon's troops far from the actual battle, and he understood any future dangers he faced, but Dasimbe—she could walk into hazardous situations completely unaware. The send from Phoenix only increased my worry and stirred thoughts of trying to follow her, but how could I travel and with whom? These, and my fear of leaving Olin on my own, kept my vague plans frustratingly impractical. I thought her send part of a possibly dangerous and yet exciting adventure. Would she try the extravagant use of talent again? I would never have dreamed of attempting such a feat myself, but neither would I have left Olin with a virtual stranger. Dasimbe's adventurous streak had finally born fruit, and despite my fear for her, for the first time in my life, I envied my sister.

After afternoon council, I accompanied Harrin and Jalin, my mentors in council, to our favorite walled courtyard near the meeting chamber. Settling onto a coral bench set on crushed shell amid evergreen sea ivy, I glanced up at the turquoise sky, clear after the last storm apart from a few stray wisps of cloud. The air within the courtyard held a hint of the chill wind gusting outside Olin. I closed my eyes, savoring the scent of the sea and the touch of winter sun on my face.

"Tell me what's bothering you," Harrin prompted, breaking into my silence.

So he had noticed my distraction in council.

I looked into serious, silver-gray eyes, void of their usual merry glint, and then glanced away as I struggled for words to explain the cause of unfamiliar emotions. "It's the war in the Halcons and what it has done to my family." I looked up again. "Our lives have been disrupted. Dasimbe left Olin a few days ago with a stranger from the Halcons, and we haven't seen Father since last summer. I'm having difficulty concentrating in council and on my weaving."

"Your family is caught up in an ugly situation that has nothing to do with your life in Olin," Jalin said, summarizing my dilemma. "It must be very difficult for you."

Loath to share my frustration, I gritted my teeth and muttered, "I can understand why Dasimbe left."

"Are you thinking of leaving also?" Harrin asked.

"I've thought about it, but where would I go, and how would I get there?" I glanced at him again, not expecting an answer. "My father doesn't need me underfoot, and I don't know where Dasimbe is. There's nowhere to go." I shook my head and stood. "I appreciate your concern, but there's nothing anyone can do."

They remained seated as I excused myself and headed for my room.

Three days later, fate intervened in a letter that changed my life and set me on my future path. Mother approached with the folded note as I sat at the large loom in her room, struggling to give my weaving the attention it deserved.

"Cia, I want you to read a message that has arrived for Daniel Scott. It's nothing private or secret."

I put the shuttle aside and took the note from her outstretched fingers. Curiosity aroused by her request, I hastily scanned its message. It read,

"Daniel. We in the forest receive only rumors of the war in the Halcons and have disturbing dreams. If you are still in Olin, please send news or better yet, bring yourself to visit me. Your loving sister, Celeste."

I looked up at my mother, eyebrows raised in inquiry, wondering why she had wanted me to read the note, but I only asked, "Where does this letter come from? Who is this 'we'?"

"It came from the Northern Forest, not the mountains, and was delivered by a messenger who waits in the great hall. I don't know who the 'we' is, except for Celeste." My mother settled beside me at the loom, saying nothing further about the mysterious Celeste or Daniel Scott as she continued. "We should inform her of what little we know, and I can think of no better representative than you, Cia. Perhaps it's time for you to leave Olin as Dasimbe did. You can deliver the news to Daniel's sister and then travel onto Phoenix."

A touch of fear mingled with my thrill at this unexpected opportunity to leave Olin, but I doubted I would make a suitable messenger. "What can I tell her? I know little about the war," I reminded her.

"I know." She nodded. "Therefore, I'll give you all the information we have at this time." She paused for a moment before adding, "And it will not be easy to hear."

Then she stood with her usual grace and gestured me toward her seating area. I left the loom to settle on a scarlet cushion while she went to a shelf and took down two delicate shell cups. She filled each with water and a sprinkling of tea leaves and brewed the tea by heating the cups in her hands. Then she mentally whisked the spent leaves to a garden bed and joined me on the cushions, handing me a teacup before telling me of the uprising in South Halcon, an uprising that had grown into something more serious. She told me of Paul Rider, of the hatred he felt toward other species and those of mixed blood, and of what he did because of that hatred.

"And that's even though he is of mixed blood himself and uses his talent despite his beliefs. He's filled with self-loathing," she added.

I shivered despite the hot tea. The disturbing atrocities she described sickened me and made it difficult to imagine people committing them.

How could anyone do these things? Why would someone want to? What would he gain?

Mother had paused, looking for a response. Stilling my thoughts, I asked (not entirely sure I wanted to know more), "Why does he hate other species? And what species are they?" My short list of known species held no candidates. "I thought only humans lived in South Halcon."

Although she did not display it, I could feel her relief at my reaction. What had she expected—hysterics, tears, anger?

"I have no idea what motivates a man like Paul Rider, perhaps fear. As for which species live with humans in South Halcon, a few sea sprites from the Babel Straight trade in Halcon Rider, our inland limit in that region. But another species has settled there, one from the west, from an area beyond my knowledge, although I have sensed them in a joining."

I flinched at the idea of sea sprites facing the evil she had described. As for this other species—what did they look like? I had only recently met one of the legendary warlocks. Now Mother talked of another species, and she knew of them by using something I had never heard of.

"What is a joining?" I asked as I set my empty cup on the low table.

Mother sighed. In regret or resignation, I wondered. "I'm sorry, Cia. There is no time to teach you about joining now, and I regret the necessity of keeping Evergreen's sentience from you and your sister. I tried to assure you the least discomfort among humans."

"Evergreen's sentience?"

"Evergreen is aware, and it communicates. It speaks to us in joining."

At first disbelief warred with what I knew of my mother—if she said it, then it must be true—but how could Evergreen speak? I gritted my teeth in dismay and a touch of anger. How could she have kept from Dasimbe and me something this important, this monumental? Bad enough to only just learn the nature of South Halcon's war, but now I had to confront my ignorance of another species, joining, and Evergreen's sentience! What else did I not know about my world? More than ever, I wanted to leave Olin, to run away from my ignorance reflected in every familiar turn of the coral halls. I had already decided to take Mother's offer, and she knew it, as she knew the betrayal and hurt I felt.

I pushed aside these inconvenient feelings and asked about something concrete, the place I would run to. "Tell me about the Northern Forest. I've heard rumors that the forest people live in trees and have multiple partners in marriage. Are the rumors true?"

My question seemed to lighten the tension between us.

"Yes," Mother said. "They're true. However, you must visit the forest elementals to understand their ways, and they can teach you about Evergreen and joining." Then she smiled and stood. "But beware of their men. They enjoy a healthy flirtation and may try to beguile you into a tryst or group marriage. I trust you are strong enough to avoid that temptation."

Frustration and anger subsided at the thought of learning more of Evergreen and its people, and I chuckled at her humorous warning.

I waylaid Harrin and Jalin at the end of that afternoon's council meeting. Seated in our habitual courtyard, I relayed all that Mother had told me.

"All true," Harrin said of the war, "although I had not heard of the western species before. Interesting." With eyes unfocused, he seemed to wander off into his own mental arena.

"Your mother wanted to tell you more about Evergreen, its sentience and joining, but it seemed unwise with you living among humans," Jalin added.

"What can you tell me?" I asked.

She paused before answering and smiled. "I think your instruction is best left to those in the forest, and you will enjoy joining among them. Foreknowledge."

The next morning, eight days after Dasimbe had left Olin, I hugged Mother good-bye while Harrin and Jalin looked on, and the forest messenger waited. We stood just inside an archway to the stable yard. Outside, a howling storm again spewed sea spray and sleet in all directions. Only seven days remained before the midwinter moon conjunction, but I had no desire to remain until after the seasonal festivities. Our farewells said, Mother gave me another brief hug and then lowered the archway's force shield. Huddled within my thick riding cape, I followed the messenger out into the gale.

Our saddled horses stood just outside, shielded from the weather by the stable master who dropped the shields as we mounted up. Then the storm engulfed me, along with a wave of plane-change. Startled, I gulped a breath of stinging, sleet-filled air. Although I had never felt plane-change before, I recognized it and knew what it meant.

The forest messenger had already started for the courtyard's gateway, and despite the foul weather and disorientation of plane-change, I hurried to follow. One packhorse carried everything we needed for six long and bitterly cold days of riding across the winter-bleak farmlands between Olin and the Northern Forest.

Our road arrowed north, traversing the wild scrublands bordering Olin. Dark evergreen foliage, close to the ground and coated with ice, formed a glazed mat to either side of the roadway. When we reached an old quarry, the road bore northwest, skirting the pit of tumbled blocks with their sharp, ice-rimed edges. Long ago masons had cut granite here, supplying blocks for administrative buildings in Phoenix, but now, the deserted quarry boomed, and the misty, sleet-filled air shivered as the sea crashed into nearby cliffs. The roar gradually faded as we headed inland. By early evening, we had traveled far enough to reach farmland and leave the worst of the storm behind us.

We spent that bitterly cold night, and the ones that followed, in farmhouse inns along the way. The sky cleared, but the air kept its brittle chill. Although the human messenger I traveled with—a dark-eyed, black-skinned farmer named Sam West—did not take kindly to questions, he was otherwise fair company and talked easily enough if given free rein on subjects he chose. He boasted that farms bordering the forest had the best soil on Phoenix's plains, and I believed him, for the turned earth of the fields became darker, and began to clump into great black clods as we drew nearer the forest's edge. I knew that much of the produce sold in Phoenix came from this area, part of the broad and fertile region bordering the more arid plains surrounding Phoenix. Without the Comber River's narrow greenbelt and these rich farmlands, Phoenix would not exist.

Drawing closer to the forest, we passed through several towns, all bustling with activity. Like Phoenix, the inhabitants of the area had a varied human heritage, and all looked healthy and prosperous, the cold weather having no effect on their exuberance.

At the end of the fifth day, a dark, indistinct wall rose in a hazy smear to fill the horizon from east to west. It disappeared beyond sight in either direction.

"Sam, is that the forest?" I puffed into the chilly air.

"Yes, that's the Northern Forest all right."

Our next day's travel brought the forest closer, its dark bulk dominating everything in the vicinity. I had seldom seen anything larger than a copse before and gawked at the seemingly endless brown tangle of trunks and branches confronting us.

We entered the forest itself late that afternoon, passing from blustery plains into the softly rustling realm of trees. The road looked well kept, and smaller byways branched off to meander away beneath trees that were, for the most part, bare. A few hardy birds—green-and-golden-scaled mites and green-feathered wrens—twittered about, while small animals scurried through the ground cover, but I saw no humans.

"Where are the people and their homes?"

"The elementals don't live in houses like we do. They live in their trees, and some live in the creeks."

"But what about the humans?"

He gave me a strange look and then burst into laughter. "You don't know anything about the forest, do you?" He shook his head. "No humans build or farm in here because we'd have to cut down trees, see? And we can't cut down these trees. They belong to the tree people. Some of the trees further into the forest are their homes. They live in them."

I looked around me and up into the trees but saw nothing out of the ordinary, only bare branches laced against winter sunlight.

Sam saw me looking at the trees and grinned. "You won't see the forest people until they want you to, until they come out. Even the humans among them are hard to find, unless you know where to look. They live deeper in the forest, in woven houses high up in the largest trees."

I nodded and, with nothing yet to gawk at, reined in my curiosity.

The forest changed, the smaller bare-branched trees giving way to taller, darker evergreens, primarily marazuls. Not long thereafter, we left the main road for a smaller byway, and a thick, blue-green canopy of feathery fronds closed in high above us. A few blackwhips grew beneath the towering marazuls, although the whips thrived best at a higher altitude.

The air grew warmer. I took off my gloves and cape and unwound my neck scarf, placing them all in my saddle pack. Further into the forest, I noticed several species of trees I had never seen before. One species grew as high as the marazuls. A dark bark clothed their vast trunks, and thick, wide-spreading branches sprouted gray-blue fringed leaves. Another, smaller, species had trunks covered with a gold-green bark patterned in swirls and spirals. Its tiny red-gold leaves hung from slender, rope-like branches. Interspersed between these trees, the more familiar shrubbery and nut-bearing trees grew profusely, and all bore leaves despite the winter season. Indeed, the temperature held only a touch of chill.

The strange forest quivered with life and sound, and movement flickered between occasional shafts of sunlight. Sam ignored the twittering, rustlings, and unnerving shifting shadows, shifting shadows that became shadowy forms flowing from tree to tree. Whispers and soft laughter joined the forest sounds. A half-seen escort accompanied us through the forest, and winter had turned into spring.

Deep twilight had fallen by the time the trail emerged in a small hillside meadow where the air seemed almost balmy, and a light breeze spread the spicy scent of windflowers. The sound of water splashing over stones promised a stream nearby.

"This is it. We're here," Sam said. He smiled, his teeth a brief flash of white in the gloom.

A woman appeared, a tall wraith ghosting from among the nearby trees as we dismounted. Long, midnight-black hair flowed loose over a short, pale shift, its color indistinct in the waning light.

"Hello, Sam. I see you've brought a visitor."

Her voice held a touch of laughter. Other folk stepped quietly out from among the trees and formed a small gathering around us. Even in the dim light I could see that the woman who had spoken had large, dark irises shot with shards of light, and the same blue skin and high cheekbones as Daniel. I knew she must be Celeste.

"Yes, ma'am. Cierva Halcon of Olin and Phoenix brings news of your brother."

"A friend of my brother's." She greeted me with a warm smile while her glittering eyes looked me over.

I hastened to correct the assumption. "Actually, we met only briefly, but I know the news he carried. You are Celeste?"

"Yes," she said, nodding, and then gestured us toward the trees. "Both of you, please come and share your news while refreshing yourselves."

Then she clasped my hand and pulled me from the glen into the darkness between the trees. Within a moment, we came to a smaller clearing beneath one of the towering trees with gray-blue fringed leaves.

"This is a guardian tree, and that is our house." She gestured upward. "There you can rest, take refreshment, and tell us your story."

I looked up. Barely discernible against a sky still touched with twilight, a circular shape nested high amid the thick branches and feathery leaves of one of the largest trees I had ever seen.

Celeste's elemental companions scampered up spiraling stairs toward the distant tree house. Sam and Celeste stayed with me as I, in my heavier clothing, made a more sedate ascent. I ran my hand along the bark as we climbed, amazed at the girth of the tree, and breathed a sigh of relief when we finally reached the large platform. A snug shelter waited, inviting me with its woven hangings, glow lights, and a small aromatic fire set on a large circular plate. Although the temperature had dropped as we climbed, the fire added a touch of warmth along with its pleasing scent. As we settled on amber-colored cushions, I noticed that Sam accepted everything as ordinary and guessed that he had been up in a tree house before.

Celeste served refreshments and then introduced me to the others who had climbed the tree. "Cierva Halcon, these are my sister-wives, Sarah and Shea. These are my brother-husbands—Brice, Peter, and Shawn. Our group belongs to the diamond clan."

Two males, Brice and Shawn, and one female, Shea, looked much alike with almond-shaped hazel eyes, sandy hair, and tawny skin etched with dark whorls. Peter and Sarah both had dark brown skin and short dark-red curly hair. Aside from Sam and me, who wore riding leathers, they all wore short, sleeveless tunics in soft shades of green and gold. Gold filigree armbands, twisted into a diamond shape, encircled their upper arms.

They all greeted me at once in a babble of voices. Then Shawn clapped his hands to catch their attention, and that brought some semblance of order to the gathering.

"Brothers and sisters, quiet for a moment. Let Cierva tell us her news. I know Celeste is eager to hear of her brother, and we all want to know what's happening in the Halcons." He turned serious hazel eyes in my direction and leaned forward to hear the news.

The others followed suit, so I told them my story from its beginning in Phoenix, when our family had first heard of the escalating war. I told them of my father's leaving for Halconnida as my sister, mother, and I left for Olin. I mentioned Dasimbe leaving Olin with Daniel and then recounted my mother's revelation about the nature of South Halcon's threat and its leader's intent.

"This man, Paul Rider, he must be demented," Shawn muttered.

"A twisted man," added Celeste. Her eyes, catching the firelight, flashed with tiny, whirling flames.

"He has everything wrong," Sam said, shaking his head.

Silence reigned for a moment.

"I'm glad you came to tell us," Celeste broke the silence and leaned forward to take my hands in hers. "I miss Daniel and welcome any news of him and what goes on in the world. Please feel free to stay here as long as you like. We would love to show you the forest."

The whole group chorused an agreement, men and women alike. Perhaps my mother's warning about the males had been a little strong.

"You also, Sam. You are always welcome," Celeste added.

"Thank you, but I'd best be heading home. I can't leave my responsibilities on the farm for much longer. Besides, tomorrow we feast the midwinter moons. When you need me again, send someone," he said as he rose to his feet.

Brice, Peter, and Shawn accompanied him as he descended the stairs, discussing the war in the Halcons as they departed.

"Our brother-husbands will see that your horse is taken care of," Celeste said as I watched them disappear below the platform's edge.

"Thank you," I said and turned back toward the three women.

"Tell me about Olin. What's it like?" asked Sarah.

"And about Phoenix," added Shea.

Celeste and Sarah said they had been to Phoenix, but neither knew it well, and none of them had been to Olin. I told them something about each.

Later, their immediate curiosity sated, I asked, "How about you? Do you all live in this house, or do you have more than one?"

They all laughed, and Shea, sputtering to a stop, answered my question. "No and yes. We all gather here, but only Celeste, Sarah, and Peter sleep here. We elementals sleep in our trees. Would you like to see mine? Come with me, and I'll show you." She stood, pulling me up with her.

Celeste smiled, and Sarah grinned as Shea led me to the staircase. I hesitated at the top of stairs now lit with glow lights and eyed the darkness beyond the tree.

"Perhaps tomorrow after you've rested would be better," Celeste offered.

"No, I'm all right," I said, more concerned about the darkness than fatigue.

I followed Shea down the stairs, but when she stepped away from the light and disappeared into the inky blackness of the forest, I paused before inching forward, feeling my way into the night.

"Shea, I can't see a thing. I'm going to trip over something. How do you do this? Can you see in the dark like a cat?"

A soft laugh came out of the night. "No. I adjust my eyes to the aura of things around me. Don't you do that?"

I found myself shaking my head as if she could see me. "No, I've never heard of an aura. What is it?"

"Wow! How do you get around in the dark? Never mind, maybe I can explain. An aura is an object's color or, as Celeste defines it, radiating particles of energy. The energy's strength registers as color, and the colors reveal what an object is. Normal eyesight can't pick it up, but an open can, so I open to what's around me in a search for the colors, the auras. I've done it for so long, I hardly think about it. Why don't you try it? It's easy."

I hesitated, remembering my father's explanation of how all creation emitted energy in some form, even a clump of soil or a rock. Could it be as easy as she said? Curiosity won over doubt, and I reached out, opening in search for the energy radiating around us, and easily felt the faint, vibrating waves of energy flowing through the forest. But where was the color? I felt Shea's mental presence, a gentle nudge toward understanding.

Suddenly, the nearby landscape leaped into dazzling color, surreal and gaudy in its display. Against the stark blackness of night, tall columns of blue brightened inward to green and yellow. A hazy mass of light green shifted and stirred overhead. I recognized these as trees, and Shea herself glowed in much the same way, only her limbs radiated red while threads of orange wove through a bright, white center.

"I can see you and the trees," I said, pleased at my accomplishment.

Then she led me through this display to a nearby tree. Much smaller than a guardian tree, it could never have supported a platform, but a vibrant, orange core radiated at its center.

"This is my home. Now watch," she instructed.

Her shimmering form went up to the tree and stepped inside, filling the core with a glowing white that sent threads up within the thin, gold-green branches. Although she disappeared from view, I could discern her mental presence.

"See what I mean?" she sent. 'This is my home, an elemental tree. I am elemental Shea. As an elemental, I'm part of this tree and the forest. My tree and I are truly bonded. As the sea sprites cannot go far from the ocean, we cannot go far from our trees." She stepped out again into the night.

"But that is not the case with all of our group," she continued as she started back through the trees and pulled me with her. "Sarah and Peter are true, blood-born brother and sister and fully human. Therefore, unlike elementals, they can travel wherever they wish, but they cannot mate with each other, only with the rest of us. Celeste is of human and air-fairy blood, so she can go anywhere on Evergreen, and she could have mated with whomever she chose. Nevertheless, she chose us, and our group is highly honored. Otherwise, we are a normal forest marriage group," she informed me. I could hear the pride she felt in her mates.

Normal? What she counted as normal amazed me. I still marveled at her bonding with her tree as I struggled to maintain night vision and organize crowding thoughts and questions.

"Your family sounds pretty unique to me. And what is an air fairy? I've never heard of them before," I admitted as I realized that Daniel and Celeste must have gained their unusual looks from somewhere.

"Celeste says that they're a species that lives in the highest mountain peaks. Like sea sprites, they remain very attached to where they live."

Another species! How many were there? I grinned in the dark, almost chuckling. I had wanted to shed my ignorance and learn more of the world. Now, even as I faced the challenge of developing a new skill, I digested information that sparked more questions.

Shea continued. "I never heard of air fairies until Celeste came to the forest as a foster child. She often tells us of her home in the mountains. Perhaps she'll tell you more if you ask her."

I remained silent, concentrating on the trail and absorbing the wonder of night vision while imagining the lives of the forest people. I had questions aplenty.

"Switch to regular sight," Shea said, as the surrounding area brightened, and the trees became hazy, losing their distinct form. I did as she said, and the forest instantly returned to semidarkness, faint light filtering between the trees. The light increased as we approached the well-lit guardian tree.

Ahead of us, Brice, Shawn, and Peter had returned and waited at the tree's base.

"What have you been showing her?" Shawn asked as we approached.

"How we live in a tree," Shea answered with a grin and started up the staircase.

Before I could follow, Shawn stepped close, a smile teasing the corners of his mouth. A dimple appeared. "I'll have to show you my tree."

His hazel eyes danced as he brushed fingers across my cheek and laughed softly as my flesh heated at the sensual interest in his touch. I pulled away.

To a lesser degree, I felt interest from Brice and Peter and wondered if what my mother had said about the forest males might be true. Their laughter chased me as I climbed up the tree behind Shea.

That evening, visitors bustled up and down the tree's staircase, the air throbbing with excitement as plans for celebrating the midwinter moons flowed through the conversations around me. I relaxed and enjoyed the bustle, thankful no one suggested I move up and down the long flight of stairs as the forest folk did. They went lightly clad and like sea sprites, seemed oblivious to the chill. I still wore my heavier clothing, glad of it now the day's warmth had vanished, although Celeste's tree house remained snug, and the forest resisted the worst of winter's grip.

Eventually the guests started to filter back down the tree, along with Celeste's marriage group. The last to leave, Shawn, cast a provocative smile in my direction from the top of the stairs, his eyes crinkling in merriment as I blushed in response. Then he disappeared down the stairs, and Celeste started laughing.

"Is he flirting with you?" she asked and stopped laughing when I protested. "I meant no offense," she explained, "and it wasn't an accusation. The forest people have a looser protocol about matters between a man and a woman than humans do. For the most part, we bed whom we choose, all of us, male and female, although primarily within our group. I see Shawn's interest in you as natural and beautiful."

I sorted through my feelings before replying. I found I enjoyed Shawn's interest and the physical sensation it aroused. Unsure of how to handle this, I hid my unease by asking more questions.

"Isn't there a problem with jealousy? And isn't it confusing when a woman becomes pregnant and children are involved? How do you know who a child's father is?"

"In answer to the second question, two people match their periods of fertility when they decide to have a child. No male delivers sperm nor female nurtures an egg unless they desire to, so a woman always knows who has fathered her child. Even the humans have that choice in the Northern Forest."

I believed her explanation because I knew sea sprites had a similar choice. The sprites chose a lifetime mate with whom to have children but partnered freely with others before that. Only humans had little control over their fertility.

"As for jealousy, it isn't unheard of, but it's rare," Celeste continued. "Before people join a group, they must know and care for all the members. I love my sister-wives, and we support each other emotionally. I love my brother-husbands and would never stop their contact with any of my sister-wives. Although a pair usually bonds closely to have a child, they still encourage physical and emotional contact from the others. We try to balance each others' needs because we truly care for each other."

I tried to reconcile that concept with what I knew of humans and found it difficult to imagine the arrangement succeeding. The question of paternal parenthood remained, and in trying to attract a mate, humans often found themselves lacking something they wanted more of—looks, skills, or goods. Their competitiveness generally went against sharing mates, and jealousy ran rampant.

Maybe because I was part sea sprite, I found the group concept intriguing. Sea sprites rarely felt as if they personally lacked in anything. Mate attraction and choice became a matter of shared interests and ideas, attachment devices that would work well in a group.

In a moment of insight, I realized that, unlike humans, all sea sprites and elementals appeared attractive, never lacking in appeal, never disfigured, ugly, or even plain. Why? Everything I learned raised more questions.

I looked at Celeste. Although not an elemental or sea sprite, she too held the allure, the attraction and beauty, and seemed perfectly at ease in her surroundings.

"I envy you. You seem content here, and the forest suits you. You even dress like the forest folk, while I—"

I plucked at my heavy clothing and shook my head. "Are you like the sea sprites, unaffected by changes in weather?"

Celeste laughed, shaking her head briefly as she answered. "No, I'm not unaffected by weather. I adapt to it by changing my metabolism and the air around me, something you can learn to do. I can teach you how if you like."

I did not understand what she meant but leaped at the offer. "Yes, I'd like that. Please teach me anything you can. My father taught my sister and me what he could, the talents of a mountain sorcerer, but nothing else. Most humans know less than I do."

"I know. I've been among humans. But what did your mother teach you?"

Her query triggered emotional confusion as my questions about Mother's motive for secrecy resurfaced. Was it truly because we lived among humans that she had neglected to teach Dasimbe and me more of Evergreen and our talent? How much difference would it have made in our lives if she had taught us what she knew? How much had we missed?

"She didn't teach my sister or me anything about our talents, but neither did she discourage us from picking up skills naturally in play," I added. "We learned to transport from one place to another and to breathe under water when we played seek-and-find with the sea sprites. Is that the sort of thing you mean?"

She nodded and started to pull out bedding. "Yes, and there's so much more you could have learned. I'll teach you what I can, in whatever time we have, but for tonight, it's late, and I'm tired. We'll see what you can do tomorrow."

Tired from the journey and from absorbing new information and experiences, I agreed. I thanked her for the bedding and, bundled in blankets, quickly fell asleep.

I awoke to a low buzz of voices and opened my eyes to winter sunlight filtering through the gray-blue fringed leaves. Shifting further from under the covers into slightly chill air, I saw Sarah, Shea, Peter, and Celeste talking quietly over steaming drinks and warm morning cakes, the smell of which woke me completely.

"That smells good. What is it?" I asked, letting them know I was awake.

"Spiced cake. We saved some for you," Sarah said. She smiled and pointed to the plate in front of them. I hastily pulled on my warm outer clothing and joined them in their circle around a large pot of steaming tea and the plate of cakes.

"What kind of tea is that?" I asked. It had a strange, pungent odor.

"Mixed-bark tea," Celeste said, pouring me a cup.

Sarah, Shea, and Peter started to plan my day as I sipped the tangy tea, definitely a morning brew.

"Now hold on a minute," Celeste cautioned the others just as Brice and Shawn appeared at the top of the stairs. "First, we have to get her dressed properly."

They all looked at me thoughtfully.

"Do you always dress like that?" Shawn asked as he joined us around the tea and cakes.

"Only when I'm cold," I answered.

"How do you get cold?" Shea asked.

As I wondered how to explain, Celeste answered for me. "She doesn't change with Evergreen's seasons. She's never joined with Evergreen."

All except Peter and Sarah seemed stunned by this, and because I obviously had no explanation, Peter offered his example. "I never joined with Evergreen until I came here to the forest, and I was cold every winter," he admitted. I flashed him a grateful smile.

A moment of silence greeted his confession, and then Shawn said, "She needs a joining with Evergreen, and we always have a group joining for the moon conjunction. Yes?" His eyes and voice danced with excitement.

Everyone agreed, and Shawn jumped to his feet, excusing himself to help prepare for the group celebration. He stopped at the top of the stairs and turned to Celeste. "Will she have time for both an individual and group joining?"

Celeste only had time to nod before Shawn and all the others disappeared down the tree. I remained with Celeste, the tea, and one last spice cake.

"Are we rushing you?" Celeste asked through her laughter.

"I have no idea. Are you?" I felt both excited and nervous about the haste to do something I knew nothing about.

"We may be. As soon as you finish eating, we'll see. You must join with Evergreen before you join with the forest people."

After I finished the last cake and my tea, we went down from the platform and back through the nearby trees to the windflower-covered hillside.

"This place is beautiful," I said, blinking in the sudden profusion of light.

Sunbeams caressed the tree-framed meadow in bright folds of warmth. Hidden in foliage, birds and animals rustled, chirped, and cast brief shadows. At the meadow's edge to our right, my mare contentedly nibbled grass by the creek I had previously heard but not seen.

Celeste smiled and knelt in a swath of clipped grass that ran along the edge of the meadow near the trees. "Kneel down across from me, and then I'll explain what to do."

I knelt facing her.

"Now place your palms on the grass and earth in front of you."

Again, I did as she instructed, placing my hands in the short grass.

"Have you opened before?" she asked.

"Yes," I said quietly and nodded, wavering between excitement and fear of the unknown.

"All right. Close your eyes, and open to Evergreen, just as in any other open, but do it slowly and then reach a little. The results may surprise you. Go ahead and try it. I'll keep watch."

I nodded again, too nervous to respond with anything more. Then I closed my eyes and took a deep breath as I pressed my fingers into the soil and opened to Evergreen.

At first, I felt only the top layer of soil, crawling with burrowing insects and plentiful grass and tree roots. The trees drew me, and instead of going down into the earth, I felt myself rising into roots, a trunk, branches, and leaves. I felt another entity, the inhabitant of the tree, and although a stranger, he welcomed me, but I felt like an intruder and pulled away from this exploration. I went back through the roots and into the soil. Not sure of what would happen next, I reached down and then let myself go wherever Evergreen took me. Evergreen pulled me downward.

Carried along in the cold flow of a deep underground river, I went out from under the forest and into the sea. Although familiar to me, the ocean felt different than before, for I no longer existed as a separate entity relishing its cool depths but became part of its very substance. I felt its life force, its being, as if it were my own and exulted in the feeling. Then I reached outward to Evergreen again. Time ceased to exist, as I flowed and ebbed with the tides, flowed in molten streams through the earth, and blew with the wind to high mountain peaks and back again to the sea.

Eventually, I grew tired and felt myself drawn back through Evergreen, away from the planet's intimate contact. Returning to my own body, I gripped the grass and soil beneath my fingers where I knelt by the hillside, eyes still closed.

I sighed, savoring the scented breeze and the sun's soft warmth before I opened my eyes to an early afternoon sky. Then I sat back on my heels to look around. Celeste sat on the grass in front of me.

"How do you feel?" she asked.

I smiled as I recognized the pleasant presence of Evergreen in my body and mind.

"I feel wonderful but tired. Did you stay with me?"

"Yes." She nodded. "And now you should rest for a while. Not everyone has the strength for two joinings in one day, but you have the strength of a half breed to aid you. Let's go back to the tree house."

The last of my energy sapped by the spiraling climb to the platform, I easily fell asleep and awoke to late-afternoon sunlight filtering through overhead leaves. The air, warm and still, held the mixed scents of something savory and something sweet. Mouth watering, I sat up to see hot herbed rolls and a baked spiced apple awaiting me.

"How do you feel?" Celeste asked again, putting aside a small notepad and pen.

"I feel fine, but I'm famished," I said, eyeing the food.

"Ha, I think that's a good sign. Here, eat up. That was quite an experience you had today, and you'll experience something similar tonight."

"Is joining always so tiring?" I asked as I reached for a hot speckled roll and almost purred in pleasure as I bit into its warm, richly seasoned flavor.

She picked up the pen and notebook again as she answered. "No. Once you get used to it, it's exhilarating. But initially it can be overwhelming and perhaps frightening."

She continued her writing as I ate the spiced apple and thought about what she had said. I had felt tired, yes, but not frightened, only curious and excited.

The sunlight gradually failed, and shadows deepened. Then the sky darkened into night, and stars began to glitter through the treetops. When Copper and Silver rose in their full shining splendor, those stars would pale. A cool breeze stirred the leaves, and then night's chill descended. I shivered slightly and drew nearer the small fire that blossomed like magic in its wide dish.

"Celeste," I said, interrupting her writing, "when will you teach me to adjust to the weather?"

"Actually, you have the capability now." She looked up from her notepad. "Think about what you did when you opened to Evergreen. When you walk the sea floor and transport yourself, it's the same principle. You've always been able to manipulate the elements and should be able to keep yourself warm. Perhaps you were never taught the skill because humans lack this ability. But the sea sprites do it naturally, do they not? Use your talent. Go ahead and try it."

I had thought the sea sprites were unaffected by cold. Now I learned that they manipulated the elements to warm themselves. As she said, I had always known how to manipulate the elements but had not thought to use the skill beyond what I had learned in play. Why had I never been shown this simple feat or thought to try it?

Incredulous at my easy acceptance of an uncomplicated life, I squelched any doubts and thought of ways I might warm myself.

I could change the air against my skin or adjust my body's warmth or a little of both. I tried a little of both, speeding the atoms against my skin and increasing my output of body heat. As my skin and body began to warm, my heavy clothing became uncomfortable. I stopped monitoring the air and concentrated on the easier task of increasing body heat.

"I did it," I whispered, hardly believing how easily I had performed the task.

Celeste grinned. "I believe you are beginning to see what you've missed learning and what you are capable of. Joining with Evergreen has enhanced your abilities. Can you feel Evergreen's presence?"

"Yes," I answered. I felt Evergreen in my body and mind as a background of warmth and a whisper of support and encouragement. "Do only the forest folk feel Evergreen like this?"

"No." She shook her head and spread her hands in an open gesture. "All the species I know of, except humans, have joined with Evergreen and feel it in their blood." She returned her hands to her lap. "Humans can join with Evergreen but don't do it naturally because they aren't aware the possibility exists. While sea sprites and elementals are born with the knowledge, humans have to learn about it, and the lack of understanding can make joining difficult to achieve."

I thought of my father, who, as far as I knew, had never joined with Evergreen. Had Mother shared this experience with him? Would he have found it difficult, as Celeste suggested? Regardless, Sim and I should have known about this, and I longed to share with her the sense of belonging I received from Evergreen. I vowed to learn all that I could and share the information with her when we next met.

"What about the joining tonight? How is it different from what I did today?"

"You'll find out soon. In fact, it's nearly time to meet with the others." She put aside her writing and rose to her feet. "Shawn asked to lead your introduction to the forest people. I'll sit next to you and guide you in what to do." She looked up at the now rising moons, her eyes dancing with speckled reflections of light. Then she glanced down again with a smile. "Your joining with us will coincide with the midwinter-moon celebration."

"An auspicious omen, surely," I answered, as I shed an outer layer of clothing.

Then we left the tree house and descended into a forest already immersed in darkness. I followed Celeste using auras, happily practicing the skill until we approached the meadow where the rising full moons bathed the clearing in a frosty light too bright for night vision. A crowd greeted me, one much larger than I expected, and long tables laden with food rested on a level area edging the natural hillside amphitheater. Celeste's group waited near the top of the rise, and as she and I passed through the diamond clan, they handed us a fermented drink to toast the moons' conjunction.

When we reached the top of the hillside, Shawn clapped his hands above his head for attention. The glen grew quiet, except for the babbling brook and night sounds emanating from the surrounding forest. The air, smelling of damp and a hint of windflowers, caressed my skin.

"It's time," Shawn said, and the people sat down, putting mugs and cups aside. I sat beside Celeste.

Shawn spoke again. "I present Cierva of Olin and Phoenix to join with the forest people, if it pleases you. Is this your wish?"

Everyone cheered a resounding "Yes!"

"Do as we do," Celeste whispered.

Some of the people sat with their hands to the earth as I had earlier. Others, nearer the trees, placed their hands against bark. I put my hands to the grass and Evergreen's surface.

"Now we'll sing to you," Celeste whispered again. "Close your eyes and listen."

The singing had already started as a low hum that grew in volume and changed into a harmonious interweaving of voices and the rustling of leaves. Soon, the songs became stories and formed pictures in my mind—a type of send. The pictures changed, reflecting the history of the Northern

Forest and its blend of tree and folk. Flowing through the telling was joy and a feeling of their love of Evergreen. Evergreen wove itself in and out of these stories, which grew into a tapestry of life. I barely noticed when the singing stopped and the joining began. I entered their lives, their trees, and their bodies. I felt their closeness to each other and to Evergreen. I felt part of the oneness, as they accepted me into their join. Thus, we went into the soil and life of Evergreen—it was within us, and we within it. Our experience together felt much as the join on my own had, only now, as I shared the experience, I became truly aware of the unity of all Evergreen.

In time, I felt drawn back to the meadow and again entered my own body. After orienting myself, I felt a flood of exhilaration.

"And what did you think of this joining?" Celeste asked.

No words could easily describe the experience or how I felt, but I made an effort. "I can never repay what you have shared with me. It was wonderful, and I thank you."

Shawn had been listening, and as Celeste nodded understanding, he grinned and pointed to the food-burdened tables lit by Copper and Silver. "You must be hungry. Let's join the others."

The rest of the gathering had already flowed downhill toward food and drink. We followed, joining the crowd by the tables. After another drink and a sampling of what the tables had to offer, I returned to the tree house. No longer needing help to find the way, I went by myself while the others continued celebrating.

Within a few days, I wore a sleeveless tunic like the others, as everyone within Celeste's group had some piece of apparel to share until I could purchase my own. Very few of the forest folk wove their own fabrics but instead bartered with roving vendors for clothing made by the sea sprites.

Then members of the group took turns in showing me the forest, its waterfalls, meadows, wildlife, and their trees—the small golden-green barked trees covered with spirals matching their skin makings. I also learned of the forest community as a whole and as individuals and watched them at work and in play. The diamond clan consisted of several marriage groups and their children, but only Celeste's group had humans and their tree house.

After an afternoon of gathering winterberries with Sarah, we stopped to relax in her favorite place, a sun-warmed ledge of rock near a short waterfall. The rush of water tumbled into a deep, clear pool cupped by weathered rock and overhung with lush ferns, even in winter. An oasis of tranquility, the pool lay upstream on the same creek that ran through the glen.

We lay on our backs, staring at the sky as Sarah twirled a piece of winter grass in her fingers and told me her story.

"When I was a child, I used to skip out of work or school and into the forest every chance I could get. I joined for the first time when I was eight, and soon after that, my parents gave up on me." She shook her head and laughed. Then she sobered.

"But Peter was older and didn't have the freedom to roam that I had. He did more work on the farm when not in class and had little time or energy left for play. My parents were hard on him, especially my father. I guess if I'd been older, I would have been just as overworked. Anyhow, Dad slowed down somewhat as the farm became more prosperous. Then he hired seasonal help and gave Peter some slack, but it was too late. Dad had pushed him too hard and for too long. Peter's response was to spend more and more of his free time in the forest with me, and eventually we stayed here."

She paused a moment and then continued. "When Peter decided to join me in the forest for good, Dad took it pretty hard, but now he has another child to dote on. My younger brother's name is David. He'll have an easier time on the farm than Peter did and will probably stay there," she finished.

"How well do the farmers get along with those in the forest?" I asked, remembering Sam.

"Well, newcomers like my folks find association with those of the forest strange at first. It took my dad a while to realize that the Northern Forest helps to keep the farm free from disease and pests. His farm is especially bountiful. Thankfully, David will grow up accepting the association as normal because there is an abundance of trade back and forth between farmers and the forest folk."

She turned to me with a grin. "You've visited us at a time of festival, so it may look as though we have little work to do. But that would be a misconception." She turned back to peering up at the sky as she explained.

"Although we have no farms, our vast orchards and nut groves yield a magnificent harvest. When the nuts and fruits are in season, we work in shifts day and night. Then we trade our surplus with the homesteads and towns. We collect berries year-round. They grow continuously here and only seasonally outside the forest. In spring, we harvest the special barks and moss we use for tea, much of which is sold in nearby towns. The sea sprites living on the coast nearby also trade for our berries, fruits, nuts, and tea.

"In addition, we teach local farmers to better care for the earth, although many have lived around here for generations and pass the information down to their children. Of course, some families lose a child to the forest life, but the elementals don't encourage it. Just think how crowded the forest would be if everyone decided to live here." She laughed and rolled onto her stomach.

"Enough about my family," she said and jumped to her feet. "Come on. Let's get wet while the sun shines." Then she stripped, with little regard for the cold, and leaped into the pool. She came up sputtering, water glistening on her brown skin and red curls. Her eyes danced in mischief. "Come on in," she shouted.

I hesitated, wondering if my new skill at regulating my body heat could handle the task. The water would be winter-cold, but I took a deep breath and disrobed, went around the pool's edge to a shallow incline, and gingerly eased my way into the icy water, adjusting my body temperature as I went.

"Don't adjust too much. A little cold is good for you," Sarah said and laughed as she splashed me.

She was right. The frigid water tingled and invigorated.

I grinned and splashed her in return, enjoying the novel experience of playing in the nude, something I had never done in all my adult years of living among sea sprites and humans. Perhaps the sea sprites would have swum in the nude, but any clothes they wore playing seek-and-find dried immediately on exiting the water, leaving them free from continuously robing and disrobing.

Our laughter and splashing mingled with the rush of the falls. Soon tendrils from my braids hung dripping around my face, and I submerged completely, swimming through the frigid crystal-clear water to near the base of the falls. I emerged from the water sputtering as Sarah had done.

"Hi, Shawn," she shouted to someone behind me on the rocks.

Startled, I turned to see Shawn already half undressed. He quickly discarded the rest of his clothes and came to stand at the edge of the pool. He flashed us a grin before diving in.

I swam to where I touched bottom without going into the shallows. Shawn came up into the middle of the pool and shook back his hair. Then he laughed and flashed another grin in my direction. I blushed and dropped my gaze, embarrassed at the heat I felt. Why did this flirtation bother me as no sea-sprite encounter had?

He laughed again, and Sarah shouted, "Catch me." She dove into the water, and Shawn followed.

I thought seriously of disappearing out of the pool, but in the same instant, I felt like a coward and envied the others their spontaneity and lack of restraint.

Sarah burst out of the water first and swam toward me, laughing and splashing. I retaliated, splashing back and trying to appear at ease, but I looked at her, not at Shawn emerging from the water behind her. Then Shawn had come closer than I expected, and Sarah leaped out of the water like a fanil fish.

"Wait," said Shawn, taking my wrist before I could follow her. "Don't be frightened. I'll not hurt you."

Transfixed by his voice, I paused, pulse racing, and stared into hazel eyes filled with warm laughter. Water sparkled like jewels on his lashes and in his water-darkened, shoulder-length hair. Glistening rivulets ran down his tawny skin. Fear mingled with my excitement. Although I had experienced all this before in frivolous sea-sprite sexual encounters, new emotions entwined with the heat of desire. I longed to belong, to bond both physically and emotionally with Shawn and the forest group. This was no game.

From the corner of my eye, I could see a clothed Sarah disappearing into the trees.

"My mother warned me about this," I muttered, but she had not told me that females aided in a seduction. I cursed Sarah silently.

"What did your mother tell you?" Shawn asked. He had drawn closer, his voice lower and huskier than usual. He still held my wrist, and my pulse pounded beneath his fingers.

"To beware of seduction," I answered but did not pull away from his grip as he leaned forward, his warm breath caressing my lips before his lips touched mine.

His kiss deepened as he reached his other hand into my hair, his thumb brushing my jaw in a touch that tingled. Then he released my wrist to slide his arm around my waist, pulling me against his body. Where his skin touched mine, my body flamed, igniting an agony of pleasure and need, a need that melted any remaining hesitation. I became a willing and eager participant in the seduction.

We exited the pool, touching and exploring each other's bodies, sating sexual desire that went far beyond anything I had experienced in youthful sea-sprite tangles. When exhaustion forced us to rest, Shawn suggested we stay the night by the pool. As we curled up together, using our clothing as a bed and mutually adjusted body heat for warmth, he told me of his plans.

"Tomorrow I'm heading for the nut groves bordering the forest to the north. We of the forest check on the groves periodically, rotating the responsibility among the clans, and usually gather berries and nuts on our return. I chose the assignment hoping you might like to see the groves." He faced me, looking for my reaction.

"I'd love to," I said sleepily as I curled closer.

We left early the next morning and spent another night together in the forest before we reached our goal the following day. Nut-bearing trees became more plentiful as we neared the groves, and they bore nuts well into the winter season, just as they did deeper in the forest.

"The trees in the groves bear fruit only in season," Shawn explained as we passed from the wild tangle of the forest into neat rows of bare-branched trees, each hung with a strip of colored cloth. I saw several rows with white strips and then further in, red.

"How far do the groves go?" I asked, for I could see no end to them, "and what are the colored strips there for?"

"The groves extend the length of the forest, from east to west, and reach to the North Range foothills where the orchards begin. Our fruit trees grow best at cooler heights. The colored strips identify an individual's area of responsibility. Yellow is my color."

"The grove must be hundreds of square miles. How do your people take care of it all?"

"The forest nurtures itself, including the groves and orchards," he answered as we continued into the grove, "but we help." He stopped to examine a tree where the red-tagged rows gave way to yellow-tagged trees. "If there are any problems in the land, it will show in the fruit and nut trees first. We check the branches, trunks, and roots for any sign of disease. The forest has a healing effect on these trees, but we check them anyway. In return for our husbandry, the forest provides sustenance for all life within its borders and then some." Still fingering the tree, he shrugged and added, "It's all part of our bond with the forest."

The sky clouded over, and a cold drizzle began to fall as he moved from tree to tree, replacing the old yellow strip with a new one as he finished each inspection. By the time he had examined several rows, bare branches dripped dismally in a gray mist, and I dripped like one of the trees.

Shawn, finished with the yellow tagged trees, finally stood and turned to notice my bedraggled state. Then he shook his head. "Cierva, I'm as wet as you are, but you look worse."

"I guess you're used to this, but I'm not," I retorted, frowning at the weather. Out from under the forest's cover, no amount of heat-regulating skill could counter winter's gloom, and I missed the protection of my rain cape and its hood.

He laughed at my frown and, grabbing my hand, pulled me back toward the forest at a quick trot. I felt instant relief when the thick evergreen canopy closed overhead. The forest's warmth crept back into my bones as we left the gray sky and black, dripping grove behind.

We collected nuts and berries as we went, eating a few when we grew hungry. Again, we prepared to sleep under the forest eaves, using mental talent to dry a patch of ground and shield ourselves from rain filtering down through the forest canopy.

Shawn propped himself up on an elbow next to me and leaned in to brush his fingers against my cheek as he spoke just above a whisper. "Cierva, what will you to do in the future? What do you want to do? Will you return to Olin or stay in the forest? We'd love for you to stay. Maybe join our marriage group." He smiled and confessed, "We've talked about it, about you joining us. What do you think?"

I stiffened in confusion as joy mixed with a touch of dismay. Any thoughts of leaving the forest had left me cold and I had avoided thoughts of the future and returning to Olin. I needed more time here, to hide away from an unknown tomorrow, yet had not considered staying to join the forest marriage group. My ordered and structured life previous to this adventure left me unprepared to make such a choice. I missed my former life with my family; a father, a mother and Dasimbe, and still hoped for a reunion, but that possibility seemed so vague. Tears prickled my eyes. That life would never return to what it had been. *What should I do?* I went cold again and shivered at the thought of leaving the sheltering forest. *This place and its people! So warm, so loving.* My heart swelled at the thought of them. Then a wave of peace flooded over me, and I felt the presence of Evergreen envelope me in the feeling of home and belonging. Confusion ebbed somewhat, and Shawn awaited my response.

I took a breath and steadied myself. "I'm sorry I'm taking so long to answer, but all the changes in my life – I'm overwhelmed. I would like to stay in the forest, but haven't thought about it before because all of this; the forest, joining with Evergreen and now you, is new to me." I knew my eyes pleaded for understanding, and returning his touch I reached to caress his face.

"I think I understand," he said, and a small frown crossed his face, "although I've not experienced what you have. Yet, I want you to consider what I've said, the proposal of joining our group."

I nodded, and then added, "I'm considering it."

The remainder of our hike back to the diamond clan's trees passed in a blur of berry picking, lovemaking, and exploration of each other's lives. I told him of my family, of how isolated a half breed's life could be, and of how I worried about Dasimbe.

"Have you met Celeste's brother, Daniel?" I asked. "That's who Dasimbe left Olin with."

He shook his head as he reached for berries along the trail. "He last visited Celeste just before I joined the marriage group, but as she tells it, he is someone to be trusted. Your sister is safe enough in his company."

Then he described his life in his parent's family group near the sea sprite town of Osak. "Osak is on the eastern edge of the forest near a river mouth and the ocean, ideal for trade with tree and river elementals, sea sprites, and humans from nearby farms. It's an interesting town, and I've always been fascinated by sea sprites. I've several good friends among that lot in Osak." He chuckled and reached to daub berry juice across my lips. "Maybe that explains my attraction to you."

We approached the diamond clan's trees hand in hand near midnight, using night vision to navigate. I heard faint chatter from the tree house, but no one seemed to notice our return.

"Can I see your tree?" I whispered.

"You certainly will," he whispered back, and I felt his smile as we approached his tree. Then he released my hand and deposited his food sacks at the tree's base. Stepping forward, he disappeared into the tree's orange-and-white center.

"*Put your hands upon my bark,*" he sent. "*Then close your eyes and join with me as you did with Evergreen. Think yourself into the tree.*"

Although nervous, I placed my hands on the tree and opened to join with him within the tree, at least in mind.

"*Come closer,*" Shawn sent, and I reached to feel the tree's form and bonded, melding to entwine with both the tree and Shawn at the same time. Warmth, love, and a feeling of comfort and home engulfed me. With the elemental bonding complete, I slept.

Celeste approached me not long after breakfast the next morning. "Cierva, can you come up this afternoon for tea and cakes? We need to talk over what your plans are."

I assured her that I would and spent the rest of the morning with Sarah and Shea, shredding and bundling the pungent tea bark for trade. Without a doubt, I had completely forgiven Sarah for her part in my seduction.

After a morning of work, they took me to a creek that led to a river, where they hoped to introduce me to a river elemental. None showed up, so we turned toward home.

"They're slivery slick creatures and fickle lovers," Sarah said. "I'm sorry we didn't meet one."

Shea hooted with laughter and said, "Their loss is our gain." Then she explained what she meant. "Before joining our group, Sarah had several affairs with the river folk. They are fascinating, gorgeous creatures but loyal only to their own kind. They seldom mate with other species."

As we continued through the forest, they told me about the town of Osak, repeating much of what Shawn had said. Sarah and Shea made it clear that a visit to the seaside town, with its mixed species and cultures, was quite a treat for them. By the time they finished telling me about Osak, we had returned to their group of trees.

Later, over the promised tea and cakes, Celeste asked, "What are your plans, Cierva? Have you thought about staying with us in the forest?" Then she sipped her tea, peering over the cup's edge for my answer.

I lowered my cup and nodded. My bond with Shawn had changed everything. "Yes, I've thought about it, and I would love to stay. Although I had thought to follow Dasimbe, I've not heard from her since she left Phocnix with Daniel. And now—" I hesitated briefly. I recalled earlier dreams of bonding with someone in Olin, near my family. A comfortable dream, I thought ruefully. Now I cringed at the thought of leaving the forest. My fondness for Shawn and this marriage group, their acceptance and warmth, and our mutual bond with Evergreen bound me to them. Without a doubt, I wanted to stay.

I continued. "My plans have changed. I know she's all right, and I don't want to leave the forest."

Celeste smiled, and setting her own cup aside, she leaned forward to grasp my hands. "And we don't want you to go. Shawn told me you talked it over, and we all agree. We would like you to become our sister-wife."

I said nothing immediately but grinned like a fool. "I'd like that," I managed at last, "but my mother must be informed, and at some time in the future, I must meet again with my family, foreknowledge."

Celeste nodded. "You and I will join Daniel and your family in Phoenix in the near future. Foreknowledge also. However, the time between is our own. That's all I'm given to see, but I feel the Northern Forest is your home now."

I leaned forward and hugged her.

"All right," she said as we sat back again. "I'll tell the others, and we'll make it formal.

After we finished our tea and cakes, she rose to inform the others of my decision. Shortly thereafter, we all met for an impromptu bonding ceremony in the meadow. Late-afternoon light flooded the glen, and despite the short notice, food-laden tables stood waiting. Although excited, I faced the group calmly as they gathered in a circle around me.

Celeste then gave instructions. "We will approach you for individual opens first. After that, we'll open as a group. Are you ready?"

I nodded, and Celeste reached forward to run the back of her fingers across my cheek. I opened to her thoughts and emotions: a joyous welcoming of love and acceptance in a sensual caress from the inside out.

One at a time they met me in open, and each bonding, each expression of love, felt different, unique to the individual. Then, we opened in a group. I had never imagined such passion in an open with several people, but this open accomplished that. Moving about me in mental touch, they begged for my attention, very bewildering, unnerving, and yet enjoyable! I came out of the open excited, hungry, and thankful for the food waiting nearby.

As we headed for the tables, Shawn presented me with a diamond-clan armband, placing it around my upper arm.

"I'm married," I realized, "and this is my group. Seven of us."

Already attuned to the others, I found sharing love within the group interesting. Within a few days I began to recognize when one of them needed affection. We all took the responsibility of caring for each other, male and female alike. Although I enjoyed intimacy with each of the group, my bond with Shawn would remain strongest.

"I'd like to be a father," he said only a week after my joining the group, and he actually blushed. "I've never asked anyone before, but would you like to be a mother?"

My eyes widened and eyebrows went up as I barely kept my mouth from dropping open.

Just one surprise after another, I thought, and then my imagination took flight, but I found imaging being a mother almost impossible. Yet, I opened myself to the possibility.

"I never thought about it before," I answered, "so I'm not sure. Let me think about it." But I felt myself warm to the idea as I looked into his hazel eyes.

I thought about having his child for another two days before deciding, and that night as we lay together I told him I wanted his child, and he pulled me to him for a kiss that deepened with passion. We broke apart for a breath and instantly felt the disorienting sensation of plane-change as a shifting of probabilities occurred, and we knew the decision made to conceive a child would have consequences beyond what we knew.

"What is the cause of the plane-change?" he said in a whisper.

I shook my head. "I don't know, but I feel our child will be special to Evergreen and some purpose is already set."

His eyebrows rose, but he made no comment. Then he smiled and pulled me close again.

The next day, Celeste approached me with a grin. "I see the change in your aura, and all of us could see this coming. You'll be the first in our group to have a child. How do you feel about that?"

Again, I grinned foolishly. "Excited, happy, and maybe a little nervous."

Celeste chuckled. "I think I'd feel the same."

That spring, I finally met both male and female water elementals, devastatingly attractive creatures with long, lustrous, glistening manes of hair—all outrageous flirts, as Shea and Sarah had warned. Flaunting their nude, silvery sleek and yet muscular bodies, they seemed disappointed that only Shea and Brice responded with a brief liaison.

In late spring, our group traveled to the sea-sprite town of Osak. As we neared the coast, the road widened, and the trees thinned. Then I smelled the sea. Breathing deeply, I inhaled salty air, and it stirred fond memories of family and Olin. Then we left the forest to enter the town, and I stared in curiosity at its wooden buildings raised on stilts, so different from coral Olin. I also gawked at the bustling mix of humans, sea sprites, and elementals, so unlike the predominately unmixed populations of Olin and Phoenix. Celeste drew stares, but no one stopped to obviously gape. After an afternoon exploring the market, we visited Shawn's parents and their group in the forest near the edge of Osak. We spent the night with them but hardly slept, as almost everyone used the excuse of my pregnancy to celebrate until dawn.

By midsummer I had grown huge, much to the delight of our group, and Shawn often "talked to the baby," as he put it, while rubbing my stomach. I missed several foraging trips during this time, but at least one of the group remained with me until the others returned. Before long, Shea was expecting a child by Peter, and Celeste talked of having a baby but did not mention who the father would be. Sarah had her eye on a young human male, and I wondered if we would make him an offer. We had all come to care for Chris and wanted him to join us. The pairings in our group up to that point had mated an elemental with either a human or half breed. If Chris bonded with us, and he and Sarah mated, it would be the only full human mating. Musing on the other combinations possible within our group, I realized we could easily populate a small village with an interesting assortment of people.

I had sent word to Mother of my group marriage and of my pregnancy. We kept in touch by messenger, and in late summer, only a few days before the birth of my daughter, Mother arrived with Sam.

She grinned as she dismounted from her horse. "I see you paid no attention to my warning."

I knew what warning she referred to. "Oh, I paid attention, but it did no good." I laughed and then glanced at Shawn. "The charm of the forest males overcame any hesitation on my part."

"I'm glad to see you well and happy," she said as she hugged me, and my feelings of past betrayal dissolved. Then she turned to meet my forest family and soon had them unloading large loom parts and weaving supplies from the back of a packhorse.

I clapped my hands in delight at the unexpected gift. "Thank you, Mother. Now I can weave my own cloth, and I'll teach the others. I'll have more skeins shipped from Olin to Osak when I need them." Ideas bloomed even as I thanked her.

The day of our daughter's birth arrived near the start of the harvest season, with most of the clan already having left for the groves and orchards. Only our group remained behind. Shawn stayed by my side to help Celeste and my mother deliver the baby, as the others waited beyond a partition in the tree house. As our baby was born, emerging healthy and hollering into the world, Evergreen's presence surrounded us like a warm blanket. Although Evergreen had some future purpose for this child, for now she was ours. Shawn beamed from ear to ear as he handed me my daughter.

"She is named Serena, for the ambiance of the forest," Shawn announced at her small naming feast and joining a few days later.

When we joined with Evergreen, Mother stayed aloof, not sharing the experience. I asked her why, and at the same time, I finally asked her why she had never taught Dasimbe and me to join or adjust to the weather.

"Sea sprites have difficulty withdrawing from a join, and most only link with Evergreen a few times in their lives," she answered. "As for teaching you, I didn't want you to feel any more alienated from humans than you already did. I've had to hide much of what I know to live among humans, and it hasn't been easy."

I nodded understanding. With the connection I felt to Evergreen and the forest, I would find it difficult to live among humans again for any length of time.

I deeply regretted Dasimbe's and my father's absence from Serena's birth and naming. I had wanted them to share my joy. Mother told me what she knew of Dasimbe's whereabouts, news sent by wire from Daniel in Halconnida, and not long after Serena's name day, Mother received foreknowledge that Dasimbe would soon arrive in Olin.

She calmly packed up her belongings and left the forest to return to Olin. It would not be long before they both left Olin for Phoenix, and I knew I would meet them there.

Meanwhile, the harvest beckoned, and our group left to join the other forest folk in the orchards. Shawn and I shared carrying a sleeping Serena in a sea-grass sling I had hastily woven on the new loom.

The orchards, breathtaking in their expanse, stretched for hundreds of miles along the Northern Forest border between the nut groves and the mountains. They carpeted the foothills and crept into the lower mountain passes. Forest folk, both elemental and human, worked feverishly to glean a vast variety of apples, pears, and persimmons. The clear fall bright sky and the fruits' fantastic range of colors, textures, and wine-like aromas saturated the environment and our senses.

Time flew, and Serena blossomed, growing heavier in the sling, which soon became a back carrier. I often stopped harvesting to feed her, and in the evenings, I set her out on a blanket. She soon raised her head to look around and before long, rolled over with chortles of glee.

Then the day came when Celeste approached me about leaving the forest. Before she spoke, I felt her purpose as a knife to the heart and clutched a sleeping Serena closer. She whimpered but did not wake. I loved Evergreen, yet foreknowledge loomed as a specter, and I rebelled against what it asked me to do.

"Cierva, we should leave for Phoenix. Is it too soon for you to part from Serena? Foreknowledge told me you would go, but perhaps I saw wrongly."

"No," I said and touched fingertips to Serena's cap of downy black hair. I swiped at tears threatening to spill onto her face. A touch of bitterness edged my voice as I continued, "You didn't see wrongly, but I have no desire to take this journey, despite foreknowledge. I'm only thankful that Serena will have our sister-wives and brother-husbands to care for her."

Celeste said nothing as she sat beside me, her head next to mine, both of us gazing at Serena. I knew she had no more desire to leave our family than I did.

Our clan left the orchards with fruit-laden wagons. When we reached our trees, Shawn took me aside as the others unloaded fruit and supplies to put into storage.

"You're leaving soon," he said simply as he pulled me close.

I nodded against his chest, my throat too tight to speak. He stroked my hair and then lifted my chin and looked into my eyes.

"You will return," he said, his voice rough. His eyes glistened. Then he smiled wanly. "It's good that Celeste will be your companion. But with two of you gone, it will be lonely."

"I don't want to leave," I said.

He nodded. "I know, but you must. Evergreen calls you." Then he drew me close again.

Celeste and I left the clan a few weeks later, and although Serena hardly noticed our departure with all the care and affection she received from the group, Shawn displayed obvious distress, his face reflecting his feelings. He held Serena in his arms as we said good-bye, and I could see the pain in his eyes. I glanced at Sarah and Shea, glad that they would comfort him, but I knew he would miss me. As Celeste and I rode away from the group, concern and sorrow etched all their faces. My tears rolled unchecked.

The tears gradually dried as we traveled back along the route I had taken with Sam nearly a year ago, but my heart remained heavy. The air cooled as the marazuls and guardians thinned, and bare-branched trees took the place of evergreens. By the time we neared the edge of the forest, the climate had changed, and winter ruled. We reached the last of the trees and faced a bitterly cold wind scouring the plains.

It took all my control to keep my body temperature adjusted. Celeste and I hastily donned heavier clothing. Then she reached across to grasp my hand.

"Be strong, Cierva. We will return to the forest," she said, and I knew she spoke for herself as much as for me. I tried a weak smile and nodded.

Then we rode out from among the trees and headed toward Phoenix.

Return to Phoenix
Daniel Scott—Winter 1836 AB

As Dasimbe and Cierva discovered more about Evergreen and their talents, I rode as a messenger, scout, or trainer, as need demanded, along with my brother Stephen, who had recently arrived from the war along the border between North and South Halcon. We worked with Ciervo Halcon to prepare for the confrontation with Paul Rider and his army while another brother, Benjamin, worked in Halconnida with the governing council. Ciervo had met several of the Guide Scouts who traveled Evergreen in their true form and seen the results of our talent. Recognizing us as the legendry warlocks, he accepted that our talent exceeded his. I had met him in council sessions during his visits from Phoenix before the war, and he knew me as someone with uncanny knowledge of what transpired across Evergreen, one who helped keep the human settlements at peace, even as he did. He had come to value my judgment and advice.

Shortly before the army left Halconnida for Phoenix, I approached Ciervo after a grueling day of training and another meeting of commanders had ended.

"Daniel, what news?" he said as he sat back in his chair, pouring wine from flagon into mug. He sighed and looked me in the eye. "Something good I hope."

Weariness etched his drawn face, and I cringed at adding additional worry to his concerns.

I shook my head. "Not bad news exactly, but foreknowledge, and a plan you may not be comfortable with."

He nodded. "Fairly warned. Go ahead."

"After we reach Phoenix, I will continue on to Olin. Dasimbe will be arriving there shortly, having finished her training in the marsh. She, Dalia, and I will then return to meet you in Phoenix. I believe Cierva and my sister, Celeste, will also join us there."

Briefly digesting the statement, he said, "What are you suggesting? That I put my family in danger?" Through tight lips, he added, "Foreknowledge or not, it's my wife and daughters you're talking about. I want them as far from the battlefield as possible."

I stood my ground, explaining the reason for their presence in Phoenix while I ignored the fact that I had no idea how Evergreen intended to use our talents.

"Dasimbe's mental talent now far exceeds your own, and Cierva has developed her skills in the Northern Forest. Your wife has always had the strength to defend herself," I reminded him. "In unison, they make a formidable enemy, and their combined talent is needed in the battle against Paul Rider."

His eyes blazed with anger by the time I finished, and I felt his struggle with the concept of using his family's skills in battle. He had no idea of the strength of his daughters' talent, and using his wife's skills for warfare would never have occurred to him. Yet, he knew warlocks, and he trusted my judgment, especially in matters of talent, and I had previously assured him of Dasimbe's training and growth in the marsh. Despite his obvious distaste for the situation, he knew talent skills could be a powerful weapon.

"Then bring them to Phoenix safely and see that they remain safe. I'll hold you responsible." His eyes flashed green fire as he spat out his response.

By the time we received word of South Halcon's move toward Phoenix, a well-prepared army waited to move out from Halconnida. I left with the troops on a bitterly cold winter's morning but pushed on ahead of Stephan and the army, covering five days travel in three by going short on sleep. I stopped in Phoenix only long enough to report the pending arrival of Halconnida's army to the city administrators. They knew of Paul Rider's intent and were prepared to receive North Halcon's troops. However, now that South Halcon's army moved toward them, they grew uneasy, not entirely trusting North Halcon to protect them. I did not stay to reassure them but left again immediately. I could feel Dasimbe nearing Olin and wanted to be there for her homecoming.

I arrived in Olin under a lowering sky, but thundering waves, blustery winds, swirling rain and sleet were noticeably absent. As I dismounted, I remembered that in winter, ships reached Olin by sailing between storms and often ran before a storm, using prevailing winds for speed.

After seeing Bad Boy to the stables, I reported briefly to Dalia Halcon with a private message from Ciervo and news of the army's expected arrival in Phoenix. Then, shown to a bedroom, I fell into a well-deserved sleep.

I awoke by midmorning, bathed, dressed, and went in search of food. Although I could eat in the main hall between gatherings, I had to fetch my food from the kitchen. After eating, I sought out Dalia, who remained working at her enormous loom as she gestured me to a seat nearby. Outside a window, weak sunlight challenged the clouds.

"What do you know of your family's part in the upcoming battle?" I asked as I took a seat.

"You know as much as I do, Daniel. We'll all be there. That's all I know for sure," she said as she threaded a shuttle across the warp. I sensed Dasimbe's impending homecoming occupied her attention, distracting her from all but the repetition of her weaving. Although she hid her impatience well, she waited for the day to pass and had no inclination to discuss the upcoming battle. I left her to her weaving.

Later that day, she found me in the library, a dry, tunnel-like system of rooms especially designed to preserve books. She asked me to join her on the docks to greet Dasimbe, a formality, as she knew I would be there.

Near sunset, we waited on the crowded dock for Dasimbe's ship to appear. I shielded my eagerness to hear of her time in the marsh. I had felt her join with the marsh folk, sensed her growth in talent and knowledge, and felt her deep connection to Evergreen. However, in this moment of joyful reunion with her mother, I would refrain from immediately asking for details of her training.

A ship's sails appeared on the horizon, and I felt Dasimbe's broadcast of emotion and her attempt to dampen it. I also knew she had friends aboard and wondered how they would influence future events but knew they had a part in our mission. I felt Evergreen's direction, stronger than ever before. The planet manipulated us like the pieces of a puzzle being sorted and set in place.

The wind picked up, blowing an errant strand of hair across my eyes. I brushed it aside and glanced at the sky. In the west, only a few thin streaks of pink-stained cloud moved toward the setting sun, but in the east, a wall of dark clouds cloaked the division between sea and sky.

The ship came in fast before the storm. Plunging ahead, she shot through the entrance to the bay, then hastily took in sails and slacked off enough speed to arrive gracefully at the docks.

I could feel Sim's presence through the bustle of disembarkation. Then I saw her and her new friends in the crowd streaming along the dock. She caught sight of Dalia and me and smiled, her face glowing with joy and the vibrancy of youth. Her natural beauty I remembered, yet she had changed in some manner difficult to discern from a distance in the quickly fading light.

When she and her friends reached us, she stepped forward, tears filling her eyes as she hugged her mother, and they whispered greetings. Then she turned to me.

"Hello, Daniel," she said and then hugged me also. Despite her shielding wards, I felt her joy at seeing and touching me. A sudden warmth and satisfaction engulfed me before she released me to introduce Dalia and me to her traveling companions.

Her friends stared at me in unabashed curiosity. I gathered none of them had seen an air-fairy half breed before, but like all sea sprites, they felt my connection to Evergreen and greeted me warmly. I sensed that the eldest, a redhead called Rask, was near my own age of twenty-seven. His brother Dom, Dom's friend Pacel and his sister Jacin seemed much younger. Clea, with her dark curls, seemed still a child.

Introductions finished, we joined the crowd filtering away from the darkened docks toward the city. Behind us, Olin's sprites gathered the traveler's baggage and took it to their appointed rooms. I managed a few words alone with Dasimbe before entering the main coil of Olin, and although full of questions as always, she agreed to wait until the morrow to discuss everything except for Cierva's whereabouts.

We headed straight to the main hall for the evening gathering, where the sprites from Fanil, appreciatively agog, admired the gleaming nacre-covered walls. No sooner had we sat down than storm winds sent a first, faint whistling vibration through Olin.

"Mother, where's Cia?" Dasimbe immediately asked. "I know she's well, but Daniel wouldn't say where she is. He said it's your story to tell."

Dalia nodded and thanked a server who deposited a large platter of rice and seafood before us. Then she turned to her daughter. "I believe there is enough time before festivities start for a brief version of Cierva's adventure."

As I had not heard Cierva's exploits, I listened attentively from across the table as Dalia recounted Cieva's story.

Dasimbe's mouth gaped briefly, and her eyes widened at the tale.

"She is happy in the forest with her group," Dalia continued. "Even so, we will see her in Phoenix, foreknowledge. I believe Celeste will accompany her. That is as much as I can tell you tonight."

After a moment of silence, Sim said, "Thank you, Mother." Then she shook her head and chuckled. "Cia sure has been busy," she added. "I can't believe she's married and has a child. We'll have a lot to talk about in Phoenix." The laughter left Sim's eyes. "We'll see Father in Phoenix also, but I'm afraid our reunion will be short. Nevertheless, foreknowledge tells me we'll make good use of our time together."

Dalia nodded, her face masking the feelings I sensed roiled beneath its calm exterior. "True, we will make the best of it," she said. "Now eat, and drink your wine, Dasimbe, and after imaging, you can tell us of your travels."

By this time, the winds gusting outside had increased to their traditional howl. Although mental shields muffled the worst of the sound and kept the city snug, the sprites from Fanil expressed amazement as Olin vibrated with the thunder of waves crashing against coral and stone. They had heard tales of how raging storms battered Olin, but apparently, only Rask had experienced the city's winter season.

As we ate, harpists began to play, and one by one, as the sprites finished eating, they started to hum. I glanced at Sim, absorbing the changes I had barely seen on the dimly lit docks and felt the bonding pull, the attraction. Her face had slimmed to reflect more of her sea-sprite heritage, and she had cut her red-gold hair. Out of its braid, it would probably fall only a little past her shoulders. I imagined it unbound and thought it would suit her. It would definitely be more practical for travel. When she turned to me, her eyes danced with inquisitiveness.

"Daniel, tell me of your travels. I heard you left Halconnida with the army, yet here you are. How did you arrive so quickly? And how is my father?"

I had nearly finished my rice and shellfish. Now I paused to answer her questions. "Your father is in good health. I left with the troops from Halconnida but went on ahead to pass word to Phoenix of the army's impending arrival. Then I immediately left for Olin because you and your mother are needed in Phoenix."

I instantly regretted the last phrase as her eyes lit with more questions. I tried to stem the tide of inquisition. "Sim," I said, with a pretence at sternness, "Let's not talk of future plans tonight. I'll discuss plans with you and your mother later and would prefer not to repeat myself."

To my surprise, she laughed and, eyes twinkling, said, "All right, Daniel. I'll contain my curiosity, but I expect a full accounting when the time comes."

I grinned at her easy acceptance.

When the traditional singing and imaging started, the sprites from Fanil added their own embellishment of fanil fish skimming the top of gossamer waves beside the *Ra Shavel*. After the singing reached its crescendo and faded away, the sprites asked Dasimbe to recite her adventures.

"Listen carefully," she said. "I expect someone will want to image this story in the future." She spoke with excitement of her life and friends in Osa

Marsh and Fanil, describing the reed houses, the saor, and the nekka. She told them about the training she had received, of her joining with Evergreen and her adoption into the marsh folk. The gathering broke into applause. Even her friends from Fanil seemed impressed with all she had done, while she seemed to feel most profoundly her training in deep-healing.

Rask and Jacin helped finish the story with comments about their voyage aboard the *Ra Shavel,* making special mention of the large, black bird that hovered above the ship. While the hovering bird had been both frightening and exciting to them, I sensed that Sim had thought it dangerous, and she had the right of it. The bird had undoubtedly been spying for the enemy who, while hating those who had the ability to shape-change, used their talent. I silently applauded Jacin's idea of seek-and-find as a means of confusing the bird.

The sprites thoroughly enjoyed the recounting of Sim's adventures, and Dalia seemed equally pleased with what she heard of her daughter's accomplishments.

"Are you satisfied with what you hear?" I asked her.

Dalia nodded and smiled only slightly before replying. "She must learn all that you know, Daniel. Her training in the marsh has been toward that end, has it not?"

I nodded also, wondering how much Dalia sensed or knew of Dasimbe's future.

"Sim will continue to learn as much as she is able to, and yes, I'll see to it."

She nodded again and, seeming content with this answer, asked nothing more.

Not long after, Dasimbe's friends excused themselves from the feast, claiming tiredness from their journey and the excitement of arriving in Olin. They thanked Dalia and asked to be shown to their rooms. Sim decided to follow their cue.

"Mother, I'm going to retire for the night." She smiled. "I'll be better company tomorrow."

"Go ahead, Sim," her mother responded, and Sim rose from the low table.

I stood also. "I'll walk you to your room," I offered, thinking to escape the remaining festivities. Sim glanced in my direction and smiled with a brief nod.

"Good night," I said to Dalia.

"Good night, Daniel," she replied. A glint lit her eyes, and I caught the impression of a mental laugh. Having no desire to explore the thoughts of this complicated woman, I did not ask what she thought humorous.

Sim chattered about her exploits in the marsh as we walked through the coiled halls to her room. My mind wandered, but I grinned at the mention of a black marazul staff. My own staff remained in High Tor. What would the adventure ahead give me to carve at my next homecoming?

As we approached her door, Sim started laughing.

"What's the joke?" I asked, smiling.

"While you're daydreaming, my mother is pondering our leaving the feast together. She'll draw her own conclusions from what she reads from you. Do you mind? And what is your intention?" she teased, green eyes glinting in mischief.

She flirted with me, expecting some response. I felt instant heat as the bonding attraction flared. Caught by surprise, for a moment I said nothing. I wondered if she knew her own intentions but found the situation humorous and decided to play along.

"My intention is to walk you to your room. Is there something more you want from me?" I confronted her with a straight face, trying not to laugh.

"Daniel, don't be obtuse," she retorted. She seemed in a wickedly playful humor and continued the banter as we stopped in front of her door. "Perhaps you're too wrapped up in Evergreen's business to see what's in front of you." She brushed her hand against my face in a touch that felt like fire and leaned forward. "I'm attracted to you and would like to be more than friends."

Caught up in a game I should never have joined in, I accepted her challenge and pulled her toward me.

I knew the kiss was a mistake the minute my lips touched hers. As open as any woman I had been with, she returned my kiss with a passion that surprised me. The kiss deepened, and I responded, the bonding fires building into an inferno. The temptation to bond completely in union and joining jolted me out of any complacency I had concerning her. With no screening in Olin for the energies created in a half-breed union, this was neither the time nor the place for such a release of emotion.

I pulled away from her, although I could see in her eyes that she expected more from me. I had to deny us both that pleasure.

"No, Sim. Not now, not yet," I said and touched her hair with fingertips that already sparked flashes of energy between us.

I watched as the dazed look in her eyes turned to hurt and anger. "All right, Daniel, but the time may not come again."

She entered her room without another word and closed the door. I blamed myself for causing her distress, a careless mistake I would not repeat.

The following day, she avoided me, not asking questions as she intended. I left her alone and spent time with the sprites from Fanil. Within a few days, I had a reasonable grasp of their character and capabilities. Then Dasimbe again monopolized their time, and I proceeded to obtain supplies for our journey. I made no move to meet immediately with Dasimbe and Dalia about our plans to confront the enemy. However, Dalia soon noticed that Sim avoided my company and approached me.

"Is there something wrong between you and Sim?"

Although I had no desire to discuss the issue, I needed to give Dalia an answer. "I unintentionally offended Dasimbe by starting something I can't continue at this time."

"That's cryptic, Daniel, although I can guess at what you mean."

Because I shielded my thoughts and emotions well, she could only conjecture about the cause of the rift by reading Sim's emotions, a possibility that made me uncomfortable. She could easily assume that I played with her daughter's affections.

"Perhaps you can, but things aren't as simple as they seem. No matter what my intention might be, any sexual contact between two half breeds like Dasimbe and me won't go unnoticed. We can't join or bond without half of Evergreen knowing, and this is no time to reveal ourselves. Paul Rider can't even suspect we exist. Sim doesn't know this and believes I'm rejecting her. Is that clear enough?"

"Perfectly, but why not explain it to her?"

I found the Halcon women exasperating in their belief that all questions could be answered easily and all issues dealt with effortlessly. Nonetheless, I gritted my teeth and managed a smile as I answered. "You think this can be discussed rationally? We aren't talking about a casual sexual union but about strong emotions and having to guard against bonding for an unknown length of time. Do you have any idea how difficult that will be? And what of the things I can't tell her about myself? That causes constant tension. Although I intend to reveal everything to her eventually, dealing with Rider is my first priority."

"*Men!*" I caught Dalia's exasperated thought before she answered. "Not entirely clear, but I understand her curiosity regarding you and know that's a problem. I'll have a talk with her. She'll understand more than you think."

I accepted her offer without comment but wondered how she meant to explain the situation.

In the next two days, I exercised Bad Boy and my talent outside the city, obtained the rest of our supplies, divided them into manageable packs, and otherwise prepared to leave Olin. I met with Sim, her mother, and her friends each night at the sea-sprite gathering and frequently heard the sound of a marsh pipe wafting through the courtyards when the weather remained free of storms. I envied Sim her skill with the flute and missed the marsh whenever I heard her play.

A few days before our departure, she finally approached me as I gazed at a sunlit sea from the same parapet where we had first met in a winter storm. The sun picked up the red-gold of her loosened hair as she walked toward me. Lifting a hand to brush back a stray strand caught by the fitful breeze, her green eyes remained guarded and serious, but she smiled.

Her grace and beauty took my breath away. Yet, like all sea sprites, she totally disregarded her physical attributes, unlike the elementals and air fairies, who flaunted their beauty, using it to affect humans.

"Hello, Daniel," she said and paused briefly before continuing. "I'm sorry for misunderstanding you and to have been offended over nothing."

She held her head high as she offered that quiet, subdued statement, so unlike the cheerful and questioning Dasimbe I knew. I wondered what her mother had said to her.

I smiled, searching for words to heal the rift between us. "Sim, I'm sorry I hurt you. That wasn't my intention, but any involvement at this time could be dangerous. The outflow of energy in a half-breed union and joining can't be screened in Olin. Paul Rider is probably not aware of us at this time, and it's best he not know we exist."

Dasimbe said nothing for a moment. Cocking her head to one side, a slight, inquisitive smile lit her green eyes. "Then you are interested in a union and joining at some point in time. That's not what my mother led me to expect." She laughed. "She told me to forget what happened, that it was only a kiss, and that anything sexual could be dangerous." Her eyes flashed in challenge.

So Dalia's attempt to defuse the situation had not relayed my intentions, only the warning.

"For now, that's true. It's best to forget what happened. But in the future, we can hope for more." It was a plea on my part for patience.

Sim smiled. "Of course. There are more important things to think about now. Perhaps we will feel the same in the future."

I realized then that for all her growth in talent, she little understood the feelings emerging between us. I wanted to shake her, to wake her from her misunderstanding. Yet revealing the nature of my feelings—and even a casual touch—could spark something more dangerous, so I let it go with a nod. "You, your mother, and I will meet tomorrow to go over the final details of our journey to Phoenix."

"Yes, tomorrow," she said and turned toward the ocean. Gazing out, she took in a deep breath before closing her eyes briefly. "I love the smell of the sea," she said and then turned and left the parapet.

I stood alone, gazing out to sea until sunset turned to dusk.

The next afternoon I met with Sim and her mother to discuss our leave-taking of Olin in two days' time. The supplies and pack animals had already been purchased, and only the minor detail of arranging for the mounts remained to be taken care of. Both Dalia and Sim knew that Evergreen had planned to reunite their family in Phoenix. Sim officially informed me that her friends from Fanil would join us, but I had already included them in our number, purchasing the extra supplies and horses. However, that sixteen-year-old Clea intended to accompany us surprised me, and I balked at the thought. Yet the other sea sprites supported her decision, and she would not be dissuaded. So we would ride out of Olin as a party of eight. When Celeste and Cierva arrived in Phoenix, our number would be ten.

Two days later, we left Olin as another storm bore in from the east, its dark maw devouring the ocean and sky. Rain threatened with large, lazy drops, but we traveled quickly, pushing our horses at a fast pace for as long as we dared, and left the storm behind us. The day remained overcast and chill but luckily lacked a cutting wind.

After a short stop to eat, we slowed our pace, and Rask rode up beside me.

"Daniel, you're our leader, aren't you? What happens in Phoenix? Is there really going to be a battle?"

I smiled, wondering if like Sim, he always asked a multitude of questions at once. I nodded and replied, "I lead this group, but only because I know the situation, and hopefully the armies will confront each other far outside Phoenix, not in its streets. Unlike the people of North Halcon, those in Phoenix are ill equipped to defend themselves. Halconnida's troops should be there already, making sure the city has a good stock of food and that the dam and river are secured. What do you know about fighting, Rask?"

"Nothing," he said with a laugh. "We sprites have only good-natured spats. War is a human concept, and it sounds revoltingly serious."

"War means killing," I informed him flatly.

"Human hell," he muttered.

I nodded, and after a moment's consideration, I presented him with a challenge. "You and your friends have volunteered to accompany Dasimbe into a dangerous situation and are caught up in Evergreen's plan. Nevertheless, you can still return to Olin if you wish. Until now, the sprites have kept out of the war, even though it involves species other than human."

His smile faded and posture stiffened as he turned sharp blue eyes in my direction. "Our little sea-sprite group isn't entirely ignorant of Evergreen's purpose, even if humans confuse us. We have no intention of avoiding what Evergreen has planned. Besides, Dasimbe needs our companionship."

Then his shoulders relaxed again, and his smile returned. "Now, what does Evergreen have planned for us?"

I grinned at his response. I liked this affable and yet spirited sea sprite. His good humor covered a quick and agile mind.

"There has already been more killing than Evergreen will tolerate. The anticipated battle would be a disaster. It must be stopped," I told him.

"Yes, but how do we stop it? I've heard that humans in the mountains fight with each other continuously."

"I haven't an answer to that, but Evergreen will guide us."

He paused, thinking, then continued. "Will we be joining with Evergreen?"

I nodded. "When we've all gathered in Phoenix. But Paul Rider's spies must not suspect anything but the North Halcon army."

"Who is all?"

"Myself and my sister, Celeste. Dasimbe and her sister, Cierva. Their mother, Dalia. And your group from Fanil. Ten in all."

"Will that be enough to do whatever is needed?"

I shrugged my shoulders slightly as I answered. "It's not us, but Evergreen that Paul Rider should be worried about. We are only its pawns."

I pushed aside the discomfort that acknowledgment gave me. Before this war, I had seldom depended on Evergreen for guidance. I had joined with the planet for the joy of it and represented High Tor as a Guide Scout. The war had changed everything. Now I received frequent foreknowledge and strong direction from Evergreen, and I had no idea how far Evergreen could, or would, extend its influence.

Before Rask could ask more questions, the rest of the sprites from Fanil rode up beside us, full of their own questions, and Rask tried to answer them all at once. I hastily fell back, escaping the babble of voices to ride beside Dasimbe and her mother.

Dalia smiled and nodded, but Dasimbe seemed absent. I looked up to see a nekka arcing in a large circle over the plains ahead of us. We rode on silence until Sim returned to her own body.

"Did you see anything interesting?" I asked her.

"No, but the nekka enjoys my company from time to time. What did Rask want?"

"Rask was full of questions, as you usually are. I couldn't tell him much, but he seemed satisfied. I left him to answer the questions of the others. Sea sprites are always asking questions," I said, teasing.

"And other people are always secretive," she retorted. Then she smiled. "But it's true that sea sprites are curious and eager to learn in their youth. Some mellow with age though and become more reserved," she added matter-of-factly.

I grinned, enjoying her reply, and then noticed the nekka had circled to fly directly overhead.

"Are you holding the bird in some kind of bond?" I asked, genuinely curious. I had never heard of such a thing yet had no explanation for what I saw.

Dasimbe chuckled. "What a strange idea. No, the nekka just enjoys my company in mind-share. Lam Po said it had 'found me.' It's been nearby since I made contact with it in the marsh. I spent time in mind-share with it even in Olin. Surely others have done this."

"Not that I've heard of," I answered and wondered if Evergreen had prompted this bond.

"Then I feel privileged," she said.

We rode on in silence, and again I studied the changes in Dasimbe. She wore her shorter hair pulled back in a braid for riding and rode easily, with a grace she had not displayed a year ago. No longer the child-woman who, although pleasant to look at and amusing at times, had been exasperating with her questions and naïveté, she now radiated the self-assurance of an experienced and talented woman. I had grown fond of her then, but my feelings toward her now were on an entirely different level.

I also noticed her marazul staff, a well-executed saor already carved crouching at the top. Beneath that, a winged shape flew as a work in progress—the nekka, I guessed.

"What are you staring at, Daniel?" she asked, evidently noticing my inspection.

"I was admiring your staff. You have a good start on the carving."

She smiled. "Thank you. And where's your staff?"

"At home. I knew I wouldn't have much time to carve anything during this trip."

"I'd like to see your staff," Dalia interjected. "It would probably tell a lot about you."

She laughed, and Dasimbe joined her. I smiled at Dalia's attempt to make light of my continuing secrecy.

That night we stopped at the farm where Dasimbe and I had spent the first night of our previous journey to Phoenix. Having sensed our approach, Tilde and Kevin watched for us. Sim, Dalia, and I dismounted outside a newly extended farmhouse while the rest of our group dismounted near a small barn and began caring for the horses.

"Dasimbe, you remember Tilde, and this is Kevin." I started introductions. "Tilde, Kevin, this is Dasimbe and her mother, Dalia Halcon of Olin. The rest of our group will remain outside to care for the horses and packs." I explained. "They'll make camp, and you can meet them later."

"Of course," Kevin said as he turned to greet Dalia and Dasimbe. "I'm glad to meet you."

"And I you," Dalia said.

Sim nodded and smiled, her attention riveted on Kevin, who made no effort to hide the fact that his skin color and eyes matched mine. Although she gave no overt sign of surprise, her eyes widened slightly.

I noticed Tilde giving Dasimbe a brief hug as Kevin ushered us into the house.

"I'm only sorry we can't fit everyone in the house. There's only one bedroom and a loft, but now we have a real floor." He grinned as he stomped his heel on the wood, its fresh scent mixing with the smell of hot stew and freshly baked bread. He led us to a large wooden table, where he gestured for us to sit.

"We'll spend the night outside with the rest," I said as I sat down. "Any news from Phoenix?"

Kevin nodded as he and Tilde joined us at the table. "Halconnida's troops reached the city two days ago, and the South Halcon army has almost finished its move up the escarpment. The bulk of Rider's troops are in the forest preparing to move onto the plains. By now, Paul Rider is aware that his plans and movements are known. He'll be furious, in a hurry, and rethinking his strategy somewhat. That large an army takes time to move. You have maybe a week and a half at the most to do whatever you can to stop this madness."

No one said a word but waited for my response to his statement.

Elbows on the table, I rubbed my chin thoughtfully, letting them know I did not ignore Kevin's comment, only pondered it before answering. "That's not much time. But perhaps we can create some kind of diversion for the enemy until the others arrive in Phoenix."

"What others?" Kevin inquired.

"Celeste and Dasimbe's sister, Cierva. From Celeste's send, I know they'll not reach Phoenix for almost a week."

Kevin nodded, and for a moment, no one said a word. I guessed he had discussed the war with Tilde, as she seemed to understand what we talked about.

"Not to change the subject," Kevin said, breaking the silence, "but how is your family, Daniel? I haven't heard much from either Celeste or High Tor lately."

Dalia and Dasimbe turned inquisitive eyes in my direction. I silently cursed Kevin for mentioning High Tor.

"I believe they're all well, but we can't communicate often over such a distance without Paul Rider picking it up. You probably know as much as

I do. As soon as this mess with Rider is cleared up, I'm going home. I have business in High Tor."

Kevin's eyebrows rose. "Well, give my greetings to everyone. We won't be visiting the Tors again for a while. Too much going on." He glanced up at the room around us. "We plan on building an inn here as soon as possible, and this Rider business is holding things up."

Tilde leaned forward, her dark curls catching the light. "An inn would be of real use in this area with all the comings and goings," she said to no one in particular. "The sooner we finish this place, the better."

"Exactly," Kevin jumped in. "And that's the reason High Tor might help us set things up."

I nodded in agreement. "It would certainly make this leg of the journey from Olin to Phoenix easier. I'll give my recommendation to the Tor council."

"Thanks." He nodded. "After it's safe to send, I hope to put in a word for myself, and I'll see you in High Tor at some point, Daniel. Foreknowledge."

"True." I felt the foreknowledge also and wondered why Evergreen prompted us in that direction.

During the entire conversation, Dasimbe and Dalia said nothing. Their faces reflected only polite curiosity. How Dasimbe managed this, I could not imagine, although I knew both she and Dalia hoped to learn more about me.

"We'd better join the others outside," I said and rose to my feet. They all followed.

"I'll help set up your campsite," Kevin said.

"And I'll bring food to everyone later," Tilde added.

Outside the door, Dasimbe pulled me aside while Dalia, Kevin, and Tilde went on to the barn.

"Daniel, now would be a good time for one of your stories. What is this talk about the High Tors? How can your home be in those mountains? They can't be reached. They're inaccessible for the most part."

Obviously, she had never believed that part of my tale. I grinned because this Dasimbe, with all her questions, was the one I knew the best. After her patience, she deserved a few answers.

"Come on. We'll find a private place to talk."

We headed into the darkness to the left of the barn where the noisy and boisterous sea sprites introduced themselves to Tilde and Kevin. They also inundated Dalia with a deluge of questions and barely noticed as we walked past.

On the other side of the barn, I noticed a worn wooden bench beyond a small paddock. As we headed toward it, I started to answer Sim's questions. "You're right. The High Tors are inaccessible, and that's the way we like it. If people have no idea where we are, or that we truly exist, they'll not try to find us."

"Who is 'us'? The warlocks?"

"Humans call us that. It's an old name for something people barely remember, a legend from long ago. We don't often call ourselves that."

"But others do. My father labels your kind as warlock, and my mother called you a warlock when she told me not to be upset about your kiss. At one time, you also mentioned warlock talents, back in the marsh. Are you a warlock or not?" She challenged me to deny the label.

I shrugged. "As I said, that's what we're called by those humans, like your father, who know we exist." Then I challenged her. "And you're a warlock also."

"What? I'm not half air fairy, and I'd like some answers that make sense."

We had reached the bench. I could feel her frustration as we sat down. "It's being half breed that counts. We're both half breeds. Whatever I am, you are also, with the same capabilities and talents. The true meaning of warlock is in the talent, not the species or the color of the skin."

"Fine," she said, sounding exasperated. "I'm a warlock, but that still doesn't explain why, or how, you hide yourselves in the Tors. What about your family? Why haven't others seen air fairies and this city of yours?" she challenged me in return.

Now her questions fell closer to home, and I could only answer in part. The full truth must wait until she reached High Tor. "All right." I took a breath and started my explanation. "The air fairies live in the Tors and on the plateau beyond, inaccessible for the most part, as you say. The humans of High Tor live near enough to interbreed and have built up strong half-blood lines over the generations. There are no longer any full-blooded humans in High Tor, and most families breed half blood to half blood. Some, like my father, still mate with air fairies. Thus, my father is a half blood, just like you and me, and my mother is Myia, who comes and goes between her people and those of High Tor. I'm the seventh of nine children—all boys except for the youngest two, Celeste and Silva."

I paused for a moment to let this sink in. When Sim nodded without seeming to register my mention of being the seventh child, I continued. "We half bloods have developed abilities exceeding those of either the fairies or sprites, although they continue to grow in their talent, as do some humans. Mountain sorcerers, like your father, will develop stronger talent over time. Evergreen is seeing to that.

"So my people are not all-powerful beings but half breeds just like yourself, only better trained in our talent. Although they don't see many of us, most species know of our existence, and some, like the marsh folk, help us develop our talent. I was fostered at the age of twelve and went back and forth between the marsh and High Tor for many years. Now the very same people who taught me much of what I know have adopted and trained you. Thus, although you always had a half blood's warlock heritage, you lacked our training until recently. Does that tell you more of what you are and who I am?"

She looked slightly bemused but answered, "Yes, thank you. Now, how do you reach your home in the Tors?"

I shook my head and had to laugh. Although I had tried to ignore the original question of High Tor, Dasimbe had not forgotten it. Then I told her what little I could. "Because it's inaccessible on foot, we fly in and out in shape-change as large birds, much like the one that spied on you in the marsh and above the *Ra Shavel*. Then we transport over the highest peak. Shape-change and transport, as simple as that."

She laughed. "That's it? I can do that."

I grinned at her self-assurance. "Yes. That's how you're going to reach High Tor."

Her eyebrows rose. "I'm going with you?"

"Yes." I nodded. "You and your sister will accompany Celeste and me. Foreknowledge. Once there, you will learn of our heritage. But that's for later, after we deal with Paul Rider."

I took her hands in my own. She flinched at the spark of my touch but did not pull away. The touch alone sent energy coursing back and forth between us, a surge that that could easily be picked up by the enemy. I dropped her hands immediately and could see the questions in her eyes.

"What's happening? What does it mean?" she asked of the growing half-blood bond rather than the obvious sexual tension, although one often led to the other. She did not ask about Lam Po's "bride of the seventh son." It seemed she had forgotten it.

"The bond between us is growing," I said. "What it develops into remains to be seen."

After a moment, she nodded and stood up. "Perhaps we should return to the others before they imagine we meet as lovers."

They already wondered, I could feel it, for they felt our strengthening bond, even from a distance.

We returned to the sweet scent of wood smoke and a merry group who laughed and sang within a large circle ringed by tarp-covered bales of hay set well back from the fire. Kevin and Tilde sang along with the sea sprites, and although several pairs of eyes turned in our direction, no one stopped singing.

A platter of flatbread was ready, and a huge kettle of stew steamed nearby. The warmth of the fire, hot food, blankets, and exuberance kept the cold at bay, and no wind gusted to spoil the ambiance. The night remained clear and fine, with a quarter Silver and an almost-full Copper lighting the sky.

Dasimbe went to join her mother while I sat next to Kevin. Dalia glanced in my direction and put an arm around her daughter's shoulder.

Dasimbe looked surprised at her mother's show of affection, and Dalia stopped singing to whisper in her daughter's ear.

I eavesdropped from a distance.

"You never mentioned meeting another warlock."

"I never saw him," Sim replied. "He and Daniel sat in the shadows, and he had left the house by the time I awoke in the morning."

A harmless conversation, so I turned my attention to Kevin. "When you asked about my family in High Tor, you almost let the cat out of the bag, old man," I said, using an expression from a distant past. We had cats in High Tor, so the expression lingered.

"Which cat, out of which bag? How much do your friends know?" He looked pointedly at Dasimbe.

"Nothing of our true heritage, not yet. When we leave for High Tor, Celeste and I will take Dasimbe and her sister with us. I told Dasimbe just enough that she knows in which direction we'll be heading and how we'll get there, nothing more. She has to see High Tor to believe it."

"You have that right. I fear Tilde will never grow accustomed to High Tor."

"Did I hear my name mentioned?" asked a sleepy-eyed Tilde, who leaned against her husband. She turned long-lashed dark eyes in his direction. A smile hovered around her mouth. Although not typically beautiful, she had strength in her features, and her brown hair and bronzed skin glowed with health. One day I would have to hear the story of how they met.

Kevin turned to whisper in her ear, and I heard her giggle.

"I think we're turning in now," he said and got to his feet, pulling Tilde up with him.

I waved good night and watched them enter the house arm in arm. A sudden longing for something I had never had washed over me. I glanced toward Dasimbe, but she already slept at her mother's side, and I noticed everyone else settling for the night. I smiled as I shook out my bedroll and quickly fell into an easy sleep.

We awoke to a clear day that looked promising for travel despite a brisk wind. It seemed the storm scouring Olin had not followed us inland. We said good-bye to Kevin and Tilde after a hardy breakfast, in part supplied by stores from our packs. Then we resumed our journey. Although Rask and the other sprites never approached me about the conversation I had had with Dasimbe, they asked her numerous questions. She seemed to handle it well, so I let her deal with her friends.

After another two days of riding, we approached Phoenix at sunset, as Sim and I had on our first journey. However, an army encampment now stretched across the plains southwest of the Comber River. Rows of tents, tinted pink by the evening light, looked like a strange new growth.

A small group of riders rode out from the camp, forded the river, and headed in our direction. A brief mental scan revealed Ciervo led the group, which included Stephen. Before they had ridden halfway, Dalia urged her horse forward. Dasimbe followed not far behind. The rest of us (and Ciervo's soldiers) held back to let them have their private reunion.

Ciervo left his horse first, then Dalia, and finally Dasimbe. He embraced his wife before turning to hug his daughter, all three laughing and crying together. Difficult to watch, it brought home the truth of the separation they had endured. I hoped better for them in the future.

Before long, they remounted and turned toward us, Ciervo taking the lead.

"Daniel, you've brought them to me, as you promised," he said when they reached us. "I owe you a debt for this reunion. If Cia arrives safely, I'll be content."

"Cia is on her way from the Northern Forest," Dalia informed him, "and I think she is safe enough in the company of Daniel's sister, Celeste."

"Then I can be patient for a while longer," he said, smiling at his wife. His escort had reached us by this time, and I saw that Stephen had discarded his human guise, revealing his blue skin and glittering eyes. I no longer hid my appearance. Although few of Ciervo's men had seen me without a ward, I found keeping up a disguise under the present circumstances difficult and counterproductive. I planned to focus my energy on defeating the enemy. Stephen nodded to me in greeting as a young woman rode forward toward Dasimbe.

"Dasimbe? You've cut your hair," she said.

"Gloria!" Dasimbe's face lit with a huge smile. "What are you doing here? I didn't expect to see you for a long time."

"I joined the army as a telepathic communicator."

"You two can talk in camp," Ciervo interrupted. "Now introduce the rest of your company, Dasimbe."

Dasimbe introduced our mixed group of sea sprites and half breeds to Ciervo and me to her friend Gloria.

Gloria's eyes widened, and with her mental guards practically nonexistent, I could hear her thoughts as if she screamed. "*Oh my, he's another one.*"

I also felt surprise from Ciervo's men, but nothing like what the girl generated.

Stephen and Dasimbe winced as they caught it, and I felt them raise their guards to block her before I put up one of my own.

Meanwhile, Ciervo addressed us. "You will all stay with us in the camp," he said. "Phoenix is overcrowded with those fleeing the South Halcon army. It's now a long and arduous prospect getting into and out of the city, so using guest rooms in the administrative building is out of the question." His eyes roved over our group for dissent. None was forthcoming. I sensed the sea sprites from Fanil, excited and curious, accepted everything as a great adventure.

Stephen rode up beside me. "That was interesting," he said and rolled his eyes. "She must have a strong send, but I didn't notice it as we headed here with the army."

Then the group headed around to the south of Phoenix and forded the river to the encampment. Banners of Halconnida, a gold hawk against black, and of Phoenix, golden sheaves crossed on a white background, snapped in the breeze above the tents where we dismounted. I had never seen the Phoenix symbol sewn onto a pennant and wondered if a few brave souls had ventured from the city to join the army.

"This is our tent." Ciervo pointed out one of the larger tents to his wife and daughter. "Dasimbe, you have a separate room. There are tents for your friends—one for the men, another for the women. I'm sorry, Daniel.

You'll have to share, either with the sea sprites, or my soldiers and Stephen as you did in the past. Please make yourselves comfortable. We meet in an hour to eat and talk."

I turned aside to follow the others as someone took our horses. I chose to stay with my fellow travelers and asked Stephen to join us. I explained that in working with the sprites on our plans to thwart the enemy, we had formed a bond that needed to grow in strength for optimum talent performance.

Dasimbe caught at her father's sleeve before he and Dalia entered their tent.

"Father, I'd prefer to stay with Jacin and Clea. And I'd like Gloria to join us. Is that all right with you?"

Ciervo paused and then turned toward her with a smile. "I can understand wanting to stay with your friends. Gloria can stay with you for tonight. She may even be useful to your unit in some fashion. Think on it."

He grasped her by the shoulders and studied her silently for a moment. "I see you've cut your hair." His voice sounded gruff, and his eyes shone. "It suits you, and it's more practical for travel. You're all grown up, and I'm told you have far greater skills than when I last saw you. We'll talk later, and you can tell me all about it. Now go and join your friends. Your mother and I need time alone." With that, he turned to enter the tent with Dalia.

Dasimbe joined Jacin, Clea, and Gloria in the women's tent while I joined Stephen, Rask, Dom, and Pacel in ours. We had time to rest and refresh ourselves before we met to discuss the impending battle and what we might do to delay it.

THE DIVERSION
Daniel Scott—Winter 1836 AB

"Thank Evergreen. It's great to be off that horse for a while," Dom muttered as he pulled off his boots to stretch out on a cot.

"Yeah, I know what you mean," Pacel agreed, but Rask teased them.

"Well, you wanted to go places and see things. How did you expect to get here? Transport yourselves?"

"Hey, that's not a bad idea," Dom said, "if I could transport that far, which I can't. Are you going to tell me you enjoyed all that riding?"

"Ha! No, but I'm glad we came on this venture," Rask answered and then added, "What happens next, Daniel?"

I too stretched out on a cot, hands behind my head, wondering how I would survive living in close quarters with the curious and lively sprites. I glanced at Stephen, who raised his eyebrows and said, "Yes, what is next?"

"How much did Dasimbe tell you?" I asked the sprites.

"Only that we will try to delay the battle for a few days until others arrive," Dom answered. "Rask said there will be ten of us for a joining."

I nodded. "It was to be ten, but now Stephen is with us, there will be eleven to join with Evergreen. Until then, we tell Dasimbe's father what little we know and try to dream up some idea to delay the battle, so put your creative minds to work. We don't have much time." My statement added nothing to what they already knew.

Silence reigned for a while. Voices outside the tent, an occasional shout, a horse's whinny, the clang of metal, and the rustling of tents in the evening

174

breeze filtered in from the camped army. I fell asleep as the sprites began to talk quietly among themselves.

Stephen shook me awake about an hour later.

Rask asked, "Dream up any answers, Daniel?"

"No. Did you?"

"Not a glimmer of an idea. We should eat. Maybe food will stimulate the creative process."

Stephen and I smiled at his good humor, and I pulled on my boots.

We joined the women to eat outside around one of the campfires and then entered the large main tent to answer Ciervo's questions and explain what plans we had. I sat with Dasimbe and the sea sprites across a narrow table from Ciervo and four of his men. Dalia sat to one side with Gloria, who held a notepad and pen.

"So what you need is time, and you have no clear idea of how to gain it," he said after we reported what we knew. "What do you propose to do after your joining? That sounds vague as well."

I felt his disquiet. He still rebelled at the idea of his family's involvement in the battle, and I had no concrete information to assuage his fears. "It is vague. Only the joining itself will tell us what to do. I'm not asking you to hold back your troops. I realize Phoenix must be defended."

"Good, I'm glad you understand my situation," he said tersely, "and what exactly is a joining?"

Aside from Ciervo, his four troop commanders, and Gloria, everyone in the tent had experienced a joining with Evergreen. Nonetheless, my companions turned to me for an explanation.

"This may be difficult to explain," I warned him.

"Go ahead. Try me," he ordered.

"Have you all opened between each other?" I asked, looking at him and each of his men.

All five looked at each other and nodded warily.

"We have," Ciervo said.

I continued. "It's no secret that the mountain folk have talent and continue to develop new aspects of it, and you know the sprites have talent skills of their own. One of these is joining, something shared by half breeds and many other species including marsh folk and forest elementals. When joining, we place our hands to Evergreen's surface and open to it as you do to each other. Then Evergreen bonds with us and speaks, not in words, but in ideas, pictures, and feelings. Evergreen is alive—a living, thinking entity who communicates with us. That is joining. We also join in groups and share the experience with each other." I looked Ciervo directly in the eye as I finished. "And with coaching, humans can join with Evergreen."

Aside from Dasimbe's soft gasp, silence reigned for a moment. I felt the confusion of the humans among us, and Ciervo's anger at his wife.

Then Dasimbe asked, eyes wide, "Humans can join?"

Ciervo shook his head as if waking from a dream and frowned, asking, "Is this true? If it is, why haven't I heard of it?" He did not even glance at Dalia.

His men stirred uneasily, and Gloria looked stunned, pale.

Blocking their discomfort, I answered. "Because while other species are born with the knowledge and ability to join, humans aren't and must learn of it from someone who's had the experience. Few humans live among the other species long enough to attempt it. All humans in the Northern Forest, and some along the coast who have mated with sea sprites, join with Evergreen under careful guidance, but initially many find it difficult. I doubt other humans who hear about it would try it."

"Perhaps because we would think it ridiculous, a tale for children," Ciervo muttered, "for who would believe that Evergreen is alive, that it speaks." I felt his disbelief war with the trust he had in my knowledge and honesty—and with what he believed of the warlocks. "Our mistake, if this is true." He looked at me, shrewd eyes glinting in the tent's lantern light. "Thank you for sharing this, Daniel. Although I have my doubts, I hope your joining gives you the answers you seek, for all our sakes."

During this exchange, Dalia said nothing. I knew from Ciervo's reaction that she had never explained joining to her husband, perhaps because sea sprites seldom attempted it. They found the experience overwhelming, almost too pleasurable, and had difficulty pulling out of it, something they disliked discussing even among themselves.

Ciervo searched our faces from across the table, his glance alighting on Dasimbe. "Dasimbe, have you tried this joining? Do you understand it?" he asked.

"Yes, Father, and it's everything he says it is. I believe as Daniel does, that joining will help us protect Phoenix."

He nodded and turned back to me. "All right, Daniel, you believe this joining can stop bloodshed and say you must wait until your sister and Cierva arrive. You'll have your chance if you can create the diversion we need to slow the enemy. Can you come up with something by early tomorrow morning? I'd like to see all of you then with some kind of plan in mind. I want details. I want to know what your skills are and their possible applications."

I looked at Dasimbe, Stephen, and the group of sea sprites from Fanil. Dasimbe and Rask nodded, Rask with a smile, assuring me they believed we could think up something.

I nodded to Ciervo. "We can do it."

"Good night then," Ciervo said, standing up, "We meet early tomorrow, before I work with the troops, so use the time before you sleep wisely."

The rest of us stood to filter from the tent.

Dalia approached me. "Whatever you come up with, I'll help if I'm needed. I trust you and Dasimbe to handle this."

"Thank you," I said, wondering if she had some foreknowledge I lacked. "Sleep well," I added, and I nodded good night to her and Ciervo.

Dasimbe and I met immediately with the rest of the sprites in the men's tent for our own conference. Gloria followed, looking bewildered.

"Are you all right?" Dasimbe asked.

Gloria gave a hesitant nod and then smiled. "I guess you've surprised me again, but I'll be all right. Do you mind if I stay and listen?"

I answered for the others. "You're welcome to stay but try not to interrupt with too many questions. We have serious plans to discuss."

Gloria nodded as she sat down, pulling out a pad of paper and a pen.

"Are you taking notes?" I asked.

She looked up with a jerk, eyes wide, and said yes before glancing down again to her lap. "If you don't mind."

Stephen and I intimidated her. I could feel it. She saw us as strange and powerful creatures, with the allure that all our kind held for humans. Impatient, having no time to assuage her, I turned from her to scan the group.

"Ideas, anyone," I said. "Now is the time to tell me if you have any."

"Actually, I have something," said Pacel after a moment of silence.

I nodded for him to continue.

"Yesterday, Jacin and I were talking about imaging illusions to scare the enemy, but one sprite can't do much with them for very long, not like the marsh folk. But we can sing illusions well enough when we're together in a group."

The others nodded in agreement.

"You're right, Pace. That could be developed," I said, using the shortened version of his name I had heard the others use. Even as I did, an idea began to form in my mind. "Yes," I said, catching their attention again. "Pace, it's your idea and a good one. Here's what we'll do with it."

The others grew excited as I outlined the plan.

"We can do this," Dom said with enthusiasm when I finished, and everyone agreed wholeheartedly. They seemed eager to face the danger ahead. Gloria sat silent, listening and writing.

"Right then, we'll outline the plan for Ciervo tomorrow. Now, I don't know about the rest of you, but I'm for bed. Dasimbe, can I speak to you alone for a moment?"

I stepped outside with Dasimbe, as Jacin, Clea, and Gloria left for the other tent. Although the sky had clouded over, hiding the moons, Sim's eyes almost glowed with the anticipation of using her skills in an assault on the enemy.

"Sim," I said, turning toward her, wanting to touch her. However, I took a deep breath and continued. "There's danger in what we're planning to do. You, Stephen, and I will be responsible for the others' safety. Are you ready for that?"

"Am I ready?" she whispered to herself, eyes closed in thought, and then she smiled and opened her eyes to the night.

"If I'm not ready now, I never will be. I trust Evergreen. It's brought me this far. I'll do whatever it takes to bring my friends back safely." Head tilted to one side, she added, "Are you afraid, Daniel?"

"Yes, enough to be cautious."

"So am I, but I'm ready."

I nodded and then added, "I'm sorry my strangeness worries your friend. I know that you feel it too, and I haven't the time to deal with her. Can you handle it?"

She nodded and then reached up to briefly touch a hand to my cheek, a touch that felt like fire.

"We'll do well, Daniel Scott," she said before turning to enter the women's tent.

I stared into the night, struggling to control the bonding fire that welled within me, fearing it would alert the enemy to my presence in Phoenix. Sim had no idea what she had done with a touch. When the energy finally dissipated, I entered the men's tent.

Stephen, resting on his cot, hands behind his head, glanced up with a half smile.

"It's a difficult time to have found your mate, brother," he said.

I returned his smile with a shrug and found my own cot.

I awoke to a gray dawn and the sweet sound of a marsh pipe. The haunting tune spoke of an early morning's watery mist, and for a moment, the marshlands surrounded me. Then I truly woke, to a day colder than any in the marsh, and Dasimbe's music was a painfully pleasant opening to the day.

The others stirred. Rask swung his feet to the floor, as did Pacel soon after. Dom groaned from his cot, "Evergreen, I hate early rising," and Stephen threw a boot at him.

Before long, we all gathered around the campfire, drinking hot Phoenix tea and eating morning bread. I glanced at Dasimbe, who seemed relaxed and refreshed, as did Jacin and Gloria, but the young one, Clea, looked nervous and excited.

No sooner had we finished eating than we met with Ciervo again, and I outlined our plans to delay Paul Rider's army.

"We'll approach the enemy's camp at night. Rask, Dom, Pace, Jacin, and Clea will first sing the perimeter guards to sleep and then the entire camp. Then Dasimbe, Stephen, and I will cut the horses' tether lines before using our talents to set fire to a few supply tents, creating as much damage and smoke as possible. The others will weave the smoke, a marsh-folk skill, creating the illusion of men with weapons. Dasimbe, Stephen, and I will cast confusion wards on top of the illusions before shape-changing into saor to frighten off the horses. We hope when the men wake up, they'll be too busy fighting the fire and our illusions to interfere with the escaping horses. Then we'll leave. Rounding up their mounts and cleaning up the camp should slow the army's advance for a few days—enough time, I believe, for the others to arrive."

Ciervo looked us over before replying. "I wouldn't ordinarily send civilian personnel that close to enemy lines, but if you can do this, the plan sounds good, although dangerous. I want each of you to understand the risk you take. Especially you, Clea—you're very young for this." He looked for her comment.

Lips pursed in thought, she glanced down toward hands folded on her lap, then returned his gaze. "I'm only a few years younger than Dasimbe, and she bears the weight of Evergreen's purpose on her shoulders," she said, glancing at Dasimbe. "I've learned a lot from her and the others. I can to do this."

She defended her right to accompany us better than any of us could have done. Yet despite Evergreen's leading, like Ciervo, I wrestled with the idea of her involvement.

Then plane-change silenced any question of her participation. Everyone in the tent felt it—human, sea sprite, and half breed alike. Clea's words set in motion her own fate, binding it with ours and with Evergreen's purpose. I think it surprised her as much as the rest of us.

"I see," Ciervo managed in reply. Then he excused everyone from the tent save his wife, Stephen, Dasimbe, and me.

Dalia sat beside Ciervo, watching both husband and child while Ciervo sat with his chin in his hand looking at Dasimbe. Stephen and I watched all of them.

"The weight of Evergreen's purpose on your shoulders. How can that be?"

"Not mine alone," Sim hastened to assure him. "Many of us will be used by Evergreen."

"And what does that mean? How does Evergreen use you? What does it speak to you about?"

"It urges us toward unity and belonging," she answered him simply, "not war and bloodshed."

I stepped in to help with the explanation. "For the moment, Evergreen wants us to prevent more bloodshed. After we deal with Paul Rider…" I paused and looked into his eyes before suggesting, "Perhaps you can join with Evergreen and find out for yourself what it wants."

His eyebrows rose. Then he turned to his wife. "What do you say about all this?"

I felt his agitation with her had diminished.

"That it would be well for humans to share in the joy of knowing Evergreen more fully. Evergreen has a purpose for all the species. Yet I've not been given the vision that these young ones have. It's for their generation and the next to make choices for all of us, with Evergreen's guidance. This is foreknowledge."

"Then so be it," Ciervo said rising. He turned to Stephen, Dasimbe, and me. "When Paul Rider's troops are but a few days out from Phoenix, they will near the dry plains where we could meet in battle with the least harm to surrounding farmlands. You must slow them before they reach that point. That gives you only three days to prepare. I leave it in your hands," he said before excusing us.

Over the next few days, we prepared for our encounter with the enemy while Gloria wrote notes of our progress. Under the cover of wards, we half breeds practiced using our fire-making skills on a few well-worn tents and discovered that the oily substances used to waterproof tent fabric caught fire readily and created the necessary smoke. The sprites sang and managed to put half of Phoenix to sleep at one point. They practiced developing direction and focus for their song before working on their imaging skills.

Dasimbe and I showed them the marsh folk's smoke-imaging, a skill they picked up naturally as an extension of their own imaging. Time passed swiftly. We spent every moment honing our skills, and as the day of the confrontation grew closer, I wished that we could join with Evergreen before it occurred rather than after, but I knew that we would reveal ourselves to the enemy in the process. Despite my misgivings, the sprites believed in themselves and their talent. I put my trust in Evergreen.

During this time, Ciervo worked with his army and further prepared the city for a possible siege. Although I had little time to explain to him exactly what we accomplished, he appeared impressed with the results he saw.

On the day we were to ride out, I again awoke to the sound of reed-pipe music. We were up and out of our tents before dawn, and a heavy mist greeted us as we gathered for breakfast around the fire. I clutched a cup of hot tea as I glanced at Dasimbe.

"Sim, I like your music. It reminds me of the marsh."

"Thank you." She smiled. "It relaxes me, and I enjoy playing it. Today it calms me and gives me courage."

"And I also," Clea looked up from her food to add.

"We all enjoy your playing," Stephen added, and Jacin nodded to agree.

Gloria smiled over her tea. "And it helps me imagine your life in the marsh."

Ciervo appeared from out of the mist leading a horse. "Dasimbe, an old friend has come to join you. She arrived late last night. The marsh folk thought you might need her."

"Neh Hah!" Sim exclaimed, jumping up to take the bridle and rub her horse's nose. "I'd forgotten the marsh folk's promise. Did they bring her?"

"No. She arrived with farmers seeking shelter. Are you prepared for your foray?" he asked.

"We're ready." I spoke for all of us.

"Will you need any weapons? A rifle or guns to protect yourselves?" he asked.

I looked at the sea sprites, Stephen, and Sim before answering. I felt their surprise at the question, and Rask's added curiosity as he asked, "Will we need them?"

Stephen and I knew how to use a weapon but had never needed that aid to supplement our talent, and the sea sprites had never handled guns.

"Our talent and stealth should be sufficient," I answered.

Rask flashed a hint of a smile with his nod of approval.

Then we finished our food and rose to gather our gear as the rest of our horses were brought around.

Dalia approached as we prepared to mount up.

"Keep in mind touch," I requested. "It's prudent that someone knows what's happening to us."

"I had already planned to," she replied. Then she, Ciervo, and Gloria watched as we rode off into the mist, a hint of pink heralding the dawn.

In the two long days it took to reach Leda Springs, Dasimbe ranged ahead, using the nekka to seek out scout patrols that grew more numerous as we drew closer to Rider's army camped on the far side of town. We added confusion wards to our caution.

We approached as near the enemy camp as we dared before true nightfall and dismounted to wait until the troops settled. Stephen cautioned the sprites to be quiet as Dasimbe kept watch from above through the nekka, and I opened to receive thoughts from anyone who drew near.

When the time came for us to try our gambit, the moons had not yet risen. We crept forward using night vision, taking the horses only a little closer, their hooves muffled and quiet placed upon them. Halting before we reached the camp perimeter, Sim, Stephen, and I waited, breath misting in the cold while Rask, Dom, Pace, Jacin, and Clea began to hum, a barely audible sound that soon grew into haunting whispers. We half breeds, prepared and guarded against their song, remained alert while the nearby sentries soon slept soundly. The sprites' song wove into a complex dream, growing stronger and louder until it spread in cascading waves over the entire army, and the faint smell of apple cider permeated air that felt heavy and warm.

Meanwhile, Sim, Stephen, and I mentally searched for the enemy's horses. When the entire army slept, we crept to the horses and swiftly cut individual tethers along with the main tether line. Then we agitated the substance coating several unoccupied supply tents until the fabric caught fire. Before long, thick smoke wreathed through the camp, forming the cloaking fog we needed. The singing stopped, but the scent of cider remained as the sprites imaged figures in the smoke. I sent a signal to Stephen and Sim, and setting ourselves to the north of the horses, we changed into saor. Flexing scaly limbs, I growled. Catching the sound and our scent, the horses snorted and reared, tugging at the severed lines. Discovering themselves free, they stampeded, running from our large cat forms toward the south, in the direction the army had come from. I heard shouts from the tents, and soldiers erupted to fight the spreading flames and smoke army. Even while running as a saor, I set a confusion ward to replace the sprites' illusion.

"Sim. Stephen." I braved a send after we had chased the horses well beyond the camp. Then I changed into my own form. The others had already shape-changed, ready to find Rask and Jacin who had raced to wait with our horses beyond the southern edge of the army. I spotted the sprites, both mounted and ready to flee as soon as we arrived. The other sprites already headed toward Phoenix.

As soon as we grabbed the reins, Rask and Jacin set their horses into a gallop and raced to circle the enemy army. Dasimbe, Stephen, and I hastily mounted and followed.

After passing the army, I sensed a stirring in the use of talent and glanced back. Dasimbe also turned in the saddle even as she urged her horse forward, and Stephen shouted, "Curses on them!" as he too pushed on. Amid the smoke, flames, and confusion of the camp, two black forms rose into the air on huge wings.

I put up a cloaking ward, as did the others, but we trailed too far behind the sprites to cover them and could only send a warning.

"Danger follows from behind, in the air."

I felt the large shapes overhead and pushed my horse to greater effort. I could see each of the sprites look up to see what followed them, and then they too urged their horses onward in the vain hope of a clean escape. Grouped too far apart to use their ward skills in unison, they were easy prey.

One of the large birds swooped toward Pacel while the other began to dive toward Clea. I flashed a mental image to Sim and Stephen, hoping they understood what I intended. As I drew near Pacel, I leaped off my running horse, shape-changing in midair into a larger than normal saor. I sensed that Sim did likewise near Clea, and Stephen raced to aid her.

I heard Pacel scream as the bird dropped to grasp him by the shoulders. In one mighty leap, I landed on the giant bird's back and sank my teeth into its neck, almost snapping it in two. The bird screamed and let go of Pacel. Too badly hurt to easily throw me off, it thrashed on the ground wildly. I hung on until Pacel staggered to his horse, caught it, remounted, and took off again at a gallop. Then I let go of the bird and looked around to see Stephen lifting Clea's body across the front of his saddle. Then he too remounted and raced off. Dasimbe caught her horse and mounted, a black bird lying nearby.

"He's dead. I killed him with one snap of the neck," she sent and disappeared into the night.

The one near me still thrashed as I called Bad Boy to me, mounted, and followed the others. After that, we rode closer together, warding ourselves for protection.

Even from a distance, we felt Paul Rider's broadcast of rage when he discovered his dead and wounded minions. Now, all our earlier precautions seemed more than justified. Although the enemy now knew we existed, he did not know how many or what we were.

We stopped only briefly on our return to Phoenix, to rest the horses and to minister to Clea's wounds, deep punctures in which Dasimbe found buroot poison. The bird's talons had been coated with the noxious substance and only a thick leather jacket from Phoenix had saved Pacel from the same fate. During our short breaks, Dasimbe did what she could, as she had more skill in healing than I, but a badly injured Clea needed deep-healing and a healing tent's sanctuary as soon as possible. We neither ate nor slept but pushed on through to Phoenix in a day and a night. Clea did not regain consciousness during that ride, but she lived because of Dasimbe's ministrations.

Tired and despondent, we arrived outside Phoenix near dawn. A tent filled with the pungent scent of healing herbs waited. Sim had sent on ahead to her mother for these preparations.

As we dismounted, Dasimbe muttered, "Live Clea, for the life I took." I felt the guilt she felt. It distressed her that she had inadvertently killed even a man bent on evil.

Then she and her mother disappeared into the tent after Stephen, who carried Clea. I followed as a backup healer.

Since Sim was exhausted from the ride, Dalia, Stephen, and I fed her our combined energy as she worked to save Clea's life. The other sea sprites fed us support from outside the tent. Eventually, our efforts countered the effects of the poison and healed the deep wounds. Before long, Clea rested naturally, no longer unconscious, merely asleep.

"I'll stay with her," Dalia offered, and I smiled my thanks. Dasimbe needed immediate rest. We arose and exited the tent.

Ciervo waited with Gloria and the sprites, his face worn with concern. "How is she?" he asked.

"She's alive and now sleeps naturally," Dasimbe said, leaning into her father's embrace. She instantly fell asleep.

He hefted her into his arms, his concern now for his daughter. He took her into the women's tent, the other women following. I headed for my own rest.

Most of us met again around the evening fire, but Sim and Clea still slept. Somewhat refreshed, I ate and felt even better, well enough to listen to Ciervo's assessment of our venture.

"You did well, although I'm concerned about Clea's part in it. My scouts tell me that the enemy has spent all day searching for their horses and will still be searching tomorrow. Their camp is a smoking wreck, and they lost supplies in the fire. You have gained at least three days for all of us, perhaps more."

High praise, although it did little to raise our spirits, and the sea sprites remained unusually subdued. We retired early, still drained from the healing and the long ride back to the camp. Yet until Clea recovered, none of us would rest easy.

THE BATTLE OF PHOENIX
Daniel Scott—Winter 1836 AB

I woke later than usual the next morning and, peeking out the tent flap, found that the fog plaguing us for a week had vanished. Now brilliant sunlight sparkled off the Comber River and lit the roofs of Phoenix as if with fire. Despite the sun, the temperature remained bitterly cold. A biting breeze scoured the encampment, and the tents rustled, sharp, slapping sounds that mingled with shouts from the army practicing drills beyond the camp. Shivering in the icy air, I nudged Stephen with my boot before leaving the tent. I heard him grunt before I adjusted my body temperature and hastened to the fire. Frost crunched under my feet, and my breath steamed.

Dasimbe sat sipping tea, elbows on knees, as she leaned in toward the flames, eyes alight with excitement despite worry over Clea's condition.

"They're coming, Daniel. Cia and Celeste are near Phoenix," she said.

I felt what she felt, their anxiousness to reach Phoenix. I poured myself tea and settled beside her, leaning in toward the fire as it crackled and spat sparks when a gust fanned its embers.

I detected movement from the corner of my eye and turned to see a grinning Rask in the entrance of the healing tent. He cradled a smiling Clea in his arms. But she grimaced slightly and shivered when he stepped forward toward the fire. I felt her adjust for the cold, and then she smiled again.

"Have I slept long?" she asked. "I don't remember the ride back. I must have been exhausted." She laughed. "And now my legs are so weak I can barely walk."

Dasimbe smiled and shook her head. "You slept no longer than the rest of us. See? The others haven't even stirred yet."

Rask deposited Clea next to Dasimbe.

"Thank you, Rask," Clea said before giving Sim a hug. Rask folded his legs, sitting next to her as Dasimbe poured their tea.

"Hello, Daniel," she greeted me.

"Good morning, Clea. How do you feel?"

"All right, just tired and a little stiff from riding."

I nodded as Sim handed Clea her cup. "Thank you," Clea said.

Gloria appeared. "Clea! Are you all right? Should you be up yet?" she asked, gaping at her, with Dom, Pacel and Stephen following close on her heels. Then Jacin came out of the women's tent, and they all clustered around Clea, full of questions. She looked slightly puzzled at their concern until she caught the gist of what they said.

"Was I hurt? I lost a whole day? I don't remember anything after that horrible black bird grabbed me."

"Thank Evergreen for that," Dom said, and everyone agreed. Then they sorted themselves out to settle down with their own tea and breakfast.

Following this reunion, we spent the morning and early afternoon lazing together, the respite from work our reward for a job well done—and a chance for Clea to recuperate. Meanwhile, Ciervo and his army drilled, raising great clouds of dust into the winter sky.

About midafternoon, Dasimbe jumped to her feet. "Celeste and Cierva are almost here. I'm going to meet them."

"You're not going alone," I said, as Dalia and Ciervo approached with horses—their mounts along with Sim's and my own. The reunion would be a family affair with Stephen, Gloria, and the sprites from Fanil remaining in camp.

I saw Sim give her horse's nose a rub before she mounted. Then she looked up, seeking the nekka. The bird answered with a screech and flew to circle above us as we rode around Phoenix and headed north.

We kept well to the east side of the busier than normal North Road, avoiding the noise and chaos of the produce-laden carts and wagons as they continued pouring into the city, churning the road into splintered ice and mush.

Ciervo waved toward the melee. "We're fortunate to receive as much food as we do, considering it's winter," he said. "As long as this influx of supplies continues, the army and refugees should be well fed."

Sim and I nodded in reply, and then she grinned in my direction and gestured toward the nekka. I grinned in return before she closed her eyes and joined the bird in mind-share.

Ciervo looked up in alarm. "What was that?" He could feel the use of power but had no idea who wielded it, or for what.

"I believe Dasimbe has joined with the bird ahead," Dalia offered, "but Daniel knows more about that than I do."

He remained silent for a moment and then, nodding toward the nekka, said, "So someone can join with an animal as well? Daniel, tell me what, exactly, Sim is doing."

I grabbed Neh Hah's bridle, leading her forward with Sim as I rode up beside Ciervo. He looked at his daughter and then at me.

"It's called mind-share. The marsh folk use it as a tool for scouting and hunting," I explained. "She looks for Celeste and Cierva."

Ciervo turned to watch the bird. "A useful skill," he muttered.

Wheeling high in the cold, clear air, Sim searched for the two mounted figures heading in our direction.

Then her eyes snapped open. "There're here!" she shouted, urging her horse forward. Ciervo, Dalia, and I followed suit. The two distant riders also set their horses to a gallop.

We pulled up just short of each other. Sim and Cia, first off their horses, ran toward each other and fell into each other's arms, laughing and crying.

Celeste and I had a more sedate reunion, having experienced separation throughout our lives. Nonetheless, we greeted each other with huge smiles and a hug.

Then she censured me. "Daniel, it's been too long since you last visited me. I almost think you avoid the forest. Nevertheless, you're looking well."

"And you look great, as always. The Northern Forest suits you."

Meanwhile, Cierva and Sim had separated, and Cierva hugged her father. Ciervo's eyes shone with unshed tears, and Cierva wept through her smile.

"It's good to see you, child," Ciervo said, his voice husky as he released her from the hug. "I've missed you in the past year. Your mother informed me of your marriage and my granddaughter."

"And I've missed you, Father. But now I'm here, and I can tell you all about Serena, my marriage, and the Northern Forest," she replied. Then she paused, her smile fading as she added, "It was hard to leave Selena and the others, but strong foreknowledge bombarded me, almost a directive, and I felt we're needed here. I hope we've arrived in time."

Then she turned to Celeste. "Celeste, I would like you to meet my father, Ciervo, my mother, Dalia, and my sister, Dasimbe."

As Celeste stood beside Cierva, it was easy to see they were almost the same height, and with their long, dark hair and slim statures, they looked enough alike to be sisters—if one discounted Celeste's glittering black irises and blue skin. Indeed, they were sister-wives in the forest fashion.

Immediately after the introductions, Sim stepped forward to give Celeste a hug. "Thank you for taking care of my sister," she said.

Celeste looked surprised but accepted the hug gracefully and answered with a smile, "She's fun to take care of."

I grinned at Celeste's response.

Sim chuckled. "Thank Evergreen, you've finally arrived," she said. "What with Paul Rider breathing down our necks."

Celeste frowned. "Curse his warped soul," she said and spat on the ground in a most unladylike fashion.

"Yes, and I hate to rush things," Ciervo added, "but we should head back to the camp where you can get off your horses and rest properly."

We all mounted up, and as we started toward Phoenix, Ciervo asked Celeste, "You arrived before we expected you. Did you ride short on sleep?"

She nodded. "Yes. We felt an urge to push forward and slept as little as we dared, sometimes taking turns to sleep in the saddle. Were we correct about the need to rush?"

"Unfortunately, yes. The sooner you arrived, the better, if anything is going to come from this joining Daniel insists is so important." His good-humored smile at seeing Cierva again dissolved, his forehead creasing in a frown as he turned to her. "Have you also experienced joining with Evergreen?"

"Yes. It was wonderful." She flashed him a smile. "And I hope you will join before long."

His answering grin seemed forced. "I have a battle to fight first."

As we rode around Phoenix to the encampment, Ciervo, Dalia, and Dasimbe clustered around Cierva asking questions about her child and the Northern Forest. Meanwhile, Celeste and I lagged behind to catch up on each other's lives.

Celeste laughed when I told her about my initial travels with Dasimbe and nodded when I told her about Sim's training. On hearing something of our reunion in Olin, she asked, "So something is brewing between you?"

I nodded. "Yes, although little can come of it until this battle is over with."

"That's true," she said and then laughed. "My wandering brother has finally found a mate. I hope she likes to travel as much as you do."

I grinned at her reply before turning serious. "And how have you progressed with Cierva's training?"

"I've followed Evergreen's leading, and Cia's done very well although her heart's not in this venture. It's too soon after the birth of her child. Do you know what Evergreen needs of us?" Her eyebrows rose over dark eyes swirling with flashes of light like my own.

"Only that her skills, as well as your own, will be needed in battle. Beyond that, I know little more than you."

She looked at me thoughtfully before responding. "I hoped that Cia and I wouldn't be engaged in the actual battle, but I've felt more leading from Evergreen than usual and suspected more involvement than I would like. Nevertheless, I trust Evergreen and your judgment."

I nodded. "Then you've done what you can. I hope we have enough talent to succeed. When we join with Evergreen, we'll know for sure."

Then we rejoined the others, enjoying their chatter on the return ride.

We reached the encampment as Ciervo's army prepared for the evening meal under a red-blooming, late-afternoon sky. The sea sprites from Fanil greeted us with enthusiasm, even Clea hobbling forward as they gathered around the newcomers to introduce themselves en masse.

Stephen edged through the crowd toward Celeste. "Hello, sis," he said with a grin, and she grinned in return.

"I felt your presence," she said. "Good to see you, brother, although I heard your story from Halcon Rider, and I'm sorry about your foster family."

Her grin, and his, had disappeared.

Gloria stepped from behind and approached Cierva. "Hello, Cia," she said above the din of the sprites and the suppertime camp.

Cierva gaped and then said, "Gloria? What are you doing here?"

After Gloria explained her presence, they hugged, and Cierva introduced her to Celeste. Then Cia and Celeste excused themselves and entered the women's tent to rest and refresh themselves.

Except for Dalia and Ciervo, we all met later around the evening fire, first to eat and then to discuss the upcoming joining. We also updated Celeste and Cierva on our recent activities. Cia had told us a little about her life and developing talent in the Northern Forest as we rode back toward the camp, but Cia had known nothing of Dasimbe's training in the marshlands before I recounted our adventure.

"What you did sounds dangerous, and I've never heard of shape-change or of lighting a fire by manipulation," Cia said. She sat with Celeste on one side and Dasimbe on the other. "Although I suspect that's how Celeste lights the fire in her tree house. After what I've learned in the forest, I assume I can do these things also." She looked at Celeste, eyebrows raised in question.

Celeste grinned. "You're right. Anything Dasimbe and I can do, you can, although some have more skill in one area than another. As the need arises, Evergreen will guide you in what you need to know."

Cierva nodded. "I'm finding that out."

"Well, I've never heard of aura vision before," said Sim. "I change my eyes to see like a cat for night vision. Seeing auras sounds intriguing. I plan to try it."

Gloria, clutching a mug of tea, said, "I wish I had half the talent you all do although I expect we sorcerers are capable of more than we know." She dropped her eyes, staring into the flames. "I may never shape-change, but perhaps I can learn to mind-share or at least learn one form of night vision or the other."

Celeste nodded. "Exactly. You should experiment with what you can do, but you will find it easier to grow in talent if you join with Evergreen first."

Then Ciervo and Dalia joined us at the fire, but Ciervo remained standing.

"Early tomorrow morning, our troops move out. In three days, we reach the open plains where we'll meet with Rider's army. He hopes to celebrate his conquest in Phoenix on the night of the double moons. So plan what you intend to do quickly," he told us before returning to his men. Dalia stayed with us by the fire.

Dasimbe leaned forward to catch our attention. "Even though the enemy hasn't retrieved all their horses, they prepare to move out. I can feel them." This heralded her growing skill of knowing the enemy by the energy they used.

"Yes, I feel their movement too," added Celeste, and Stephen nodded.

I also felt the enemy stir and quickly brought the group's attention back to the subject of joining. Everyone had questions about where and when the join should take place and what the results might be. It turned into a noisy babble.

"Now is not the time for conjecture but action," I reminded them, and they quieted to think.

Before long, Cierva leaned forward tentatively. "I have a leading," she said, and everyone listened in expectation.

"Sim, Gloria, I'm thinking of our training room in the administration building."

Sim's face brightened. "Yes, I feel it. That's where we should go. That room has everything we need for our join."

Then Cierva turned toward me. "Daniel, I don't know why, but we should go to the talent-training room in Phoenix."

"Then it's time to get on with it," I said, rising to my feet. I too felt drawn toward Phoenix.

"Should I come too?" asked Gloria.

I hesitated and then nodded. "I feel it is the will of Evergreen that you become one of our group, at least in some things. Yet the choice is yours, and I warn you—you may find some of what we do uncomfortable, difficult, even dangerous."

Gloria nodded and said, "I understand," and Sim smiled, seeming glad of the arrangement, but I frowned, disliking the idea of Gloria's involvement as much as I had Clea's.

We found our horses and mounted up, Rask helping Clea onto his horse and settling behind her before we rode into the city as a group of six sea sprites, two human–sea sprite half breeds, one full human, and we three human–air fairy half breeds. None of us were cloaked, reserving our energy for what lay ahead.

Phoenix's streets teemed with people, every possible corner of the city overflowing with the tents of the displaced and their stacks of provisions, livestock, and bales of hay. A palpable tension hung in the air, but less fear and dismay than I expected. Rumors about our previous encounter with the enemy had taken root and spread. The people of Phoenix now had confidence in the army camped outside its walls.

During the short ride from the river to the portico of the brightly lit administration building, we received stares, whispers, and some cheers. Nevertheless, we managed to reach our goal before too many people realized we were in the city. As it was, we could hardly go completely unobserved.

We dismounted, tethered our horses, and entered the building, Rask supporting Clea as she limped beside him. Despite the evening hour, crowds of people swarmed the halls. Fortunately, the hall attendants immediately recognized Dalia, Cia, and Sim, and we were allowed to make our way through the building with little trouble.

Although electric lights lit the main halls, we used glow lights in the lower, unlit levels. At the base of a huge octagonal tower, Dalia pulled a key from a pouch at her waist and inserted it into the lock of a heavy wooden door.

"This room probably hasn't been opened since we left Phoenix over a year and a half ago," she said as the door swung inward.

Pungent and musty odors assailed us as we followed her into a large and echoing octagonal chamber that followed the shape of the tower above. We spread our glow lights as we entered, yet the upper reaches of the room remained lost in a chilly gloom. Despite the tables, chairs, shelves, worn carpet, and the tapestries and maps on the walls, the space seemed sparsely furnished.

"I can feel the power in this place," Rask commented, his breath misting as his voice reverberated into the shadows above. I felt strong cloaking wards drop into place as he closed the door behind us.

Then we began our search, moving aside manuscripts, looking into jars, and inspecting the rocks, stones, and artifacts littering the shelves above the tables. We had no idea yet what we looked for.

"I've never been in this room at night," Dasimbe said, her voice hushed. "It feels different, like something from a dream. I can hardly see the tapestries, and it's colder than I remember. How about you, Cia?"

Cierva looked around before answering, her eyes glimmering faintly in the dim light. "It hasn't been heated in a long time, and like you, I remember it in daylight. But for now, I think we should forget the past and do a mental search."

Dasimbe must have agreed, for they sat for a search while the rest of us stood watching in curiosity. Some instinct stirred, and all but Gloria felt it. She asked no questions but watched intently.

They began to hum, much as the sprites did in their imaging, and faint vibrations filled the room. Again, all but Gloria understood what Sim and Cia were doing, and we added our humming to their search into air, floor, and walls. We listened for a response of some sort, and Cierva felt it first. She stood and walked toward one wall, bare except for a large tapestry. Arms to her sides, she held her hands with fingers spread wide, palms parallel to the floor. Dasimbe accompanied her. By this time, we all felt the existence of a lower, hidden room, even Gloria, who had now opened to our search.

"Here is the entrance," Cierva said well before she reached the wall, "but how do we open it?"

Dasimbe, still in search, stepped over to press a flower woven into the tapestry, pushing hard against the wall behind it. She had found the key to opening the entrance.

A sharp pinging sound preceded a louder grating noise, and in front of Cierva's feet, a slab in the stone floor slid down and away. I heard a few gasps and breathed a sigh of relief that none of us had been standing on that spot. Dasimbe snapped out of her search, and with the rest of us, she stared into the gaping, black hole. A stone staircase disappeared into the darkness below.

Celeste urged a few glow lights forward and down the stairs.

I turned from Dalia to Cierva to Gloria to Dasimbe and back again. "Do you know anything about this hidden room?" I asked. They looked at each other.

"I've never seen or heard of it," Gloria said.

Sim shook her head. "Neither have I."

"Nor have I," said Cia, and they turned to Dalia with questioning eyes.

She stared at the staircase. "I believe I've heard of it although I've never seen it," she informed us. "I remember Ciervo talking of a place under the tower where someone had hidden an empty room with a dirt floor. He never learned why it was hidden, and I never heard of it being used. I believe that's what lies below us," she finished.

I felt Evergreen's mental touch and unexpected thoughts flowed. "Did any of you feel the touch of joining?" I asked, and all nodded, even Gloria, her eyes wide in wonder.

"Some human in Phoenix's past discovered an ability to join with Evergreen and kept it to himself." I said and carefully started down the stone steps. The others followed. We found an empty earthen-floored room, just as Dalia had described.

"Here we join," I stated, savoring the feel of strong cloaking wards shielding us from the enemy's attention. Then I turned to Gloria. "We'll tell you what to do. Follow our example. You must join with Evergreen to continue with us," I instructed.

She nodded and copied us as we sat cross-legged on the floor, forming a circle.

"Wait," said Cierva, jumping to her feet again. "There's something we're missing, and I know what it is." She disappeared up the staircase.

Before long, she returned with a wooden casket and rejoined the circle. Then she opened the box. Nestled in a bed of soft fabric, an Evergreen Stone glimmered, the essence of Evergreen snaking through its pale, smoky depths. I heard several gasps, including my own.

"Father wouldn't touch it," Dasimbe said. "He said no human could, for it burns where it touches flesh."

Dalia grimaced with a slight shiver. "Touching an Evergreen Stone draws sea sprites into a joining not easily broken," she said. "The temptation for us to stay in joining is great enough without it."

"You have that right," Rask added.

The other sprites and Gloria said they had never seen one. "I thought it was a myth," Gloria added.

Celeste, Stephen, and I looked at each other. We had all used Evergreen Stones and knew their affect on the different species. Sim and Cia obviously didn't know that as half breeds, they could safely handle and use the stone.

"Then none of you need touch it," I assured them. "But despite past experiences and the Evergreen Stone, you all must join," I said, indicating the sea sprites.

Rask grinned and said, "We know what we have to do." Dalia only nodded.

I carefully lifted the glimmering stone out of its box and felt its pull as warmth caressed my fingers. Kneeling in the center of our circle, I dug a small pit in the soil with one hand and placed the stone to rest half in, half out of the pit.

"It's not at its most powerful here, with no sunlight touching it, but it will do for our purpose," I said and returned to my place in the circle.

Then I turned to Gloria. "I've felt you opening to everything we do. Are you ready to open to Evergreen?"

She nodded. "I've picked up the threads of feeling from Evergreen from my openings with this group. But I'm a little nervous."

"Sim, will you stay with her?" I asked.

"I'd be glad to," she said, flashing a smile at Gloria.

"It's time," I said and leaned forward to place my hands flat to the surface of Evergreen. The others did the same. The sea sprites began to sing softly, and as the rest of us joined them, I felt Sim draw Gloria into the song's weave. Before long, the air swirled and whispered around us, and the stone began to glow. Then Evergreen pulled us into itself.

I had no idea what Evergreen intended or where the join would lead us but found myself swept along with the group, not to the depths of the planet, but under the surface of the plains. Then we stopped, hovering under the enemy's encampment before emerging within a tree in the camp itself, mentally seeing and hearing what went on around us as if the tree had ears and eyes. Our own identities merged without losing a sense of self, but I had no time to wonder at this similarity to the Northern Forest before Evergreen directed our thoughts to what surrounded us.

Dark silhouettes moved against crackling campfires. The shouts of men, whinnying horses, a snatch of song, and a dog's bark carried in the smoke-scented air as the enemy troops prepared for their move at dawn. Four men stood by a nearby fire, their faces revealed in its flickering light. Evergreen next directed our attention to one man, and though I had never seen the face of the enemy before, I instantly knew him as Paul Rider.

Clothed in black and tan leather, his tall frame dominated the group with the stance of a leader, similar in bearing to Ciervo. Blond hair pulled back in a braided tail framed a broad face that spoke of determination. His eyes held a glint of impatience and a fire that led people to follow him and his cause. At that moment, his eyes also held unease. Two of the three men with him, half bloods like himself, also looked uneasy while the third man, fully human, had only enough skill to see that something disturbed his comrades.

Paul Rider's nostrils flared. I knew he sensed us. I could feel him questing for mental intrusion or danger. He turned toward the direction in which Evergreen held our group within the tree. Rider's eyes narrowed into glowing slits, and an answering gleam leaped in a stone set in gold at his neck—an Evergreen Stone.

Within an instant, Evergreen pulled us back down from the tree and rushed us under the ground toward Phoenix. We reached the underground room quickly, and in a snap, rather than in the usual ascending levels, I found myself back in my body.

My eyes flew open, just as the sprites from Fanil started talking at once, expressing amazement at their easy release from Evergreen.

"There's a first time for everything," Rask said as their conversation slowed.

"The unusual circumstances warranted it," I suggested. "Evergreen spat us all out in a hurry, except for Dasimbe," I said, nodding in her direction. She alone remained in join. "I feel Evergreen still working with her."

"Is she all right?" Gloria asked, frowning.

"She's fine," Dalia responded. "Evergreen takes care of its own. I see you have felt no ill effects from the joining."

"No, I feel fine, and I felt Sim's presence the whole time. It was quite an adventure."

I smiled at that and then said, "OK, everyone, about what we saw. Any comments?"

"I was surprised to see an Evergreen Stone around Rider's neck," Rask responded, his excitement diminishing as the effect of the join wore off.

"Yes. A danger or a help?" added Stephen.

I shook my head. "I don't know, but it's what Evergreen wanted us to see. Perhaps Sim will know the answer."

She came back to us with a broad smile. "We have him, or rather him and his whole army," she said, chuckling.

"Well, share it with us," I scolded just before her mother added, "Don't tease us, Sim."

"Yes, tell us," added Cierva.

Sim reached forward, showing no fear as she scooped the Evergreen Stone up out of its indentation to hold it before us. "The answer lies here but out in the sunlight with the army leaving tomorrow, not under the building. We take the stone with us. Come on. Let's return to camp, and I'll tell you about it around the fire."

"Oh my! I can walk again," Clea said, as we rose from the circle. She beamed a smile, and the group expressed their joy at her recovery.

"Was it the join?" Dom asked.

"I guess so," she said as she headed for the staircase.

As we left the underground room, I thought about how Evergreen gave us each different tasks and different times to lead or be led. Cierva had led us to the hidden room in Phoenix and the Evergreen Stone, and now Dasimbe would lead us in its use. Although I had led our group for most of our venture, now I followed.

On our way through the talent-training room, Dasimbe found a soft pouch for the Evergreen Stone and strung it on a cord to wear around her neck. Then we left the administrative building and Phoenix as easily as we had entered, and we returned to the army encampment and our own dwindling campfire. We added wood to the fire and settled around it, eager to hear what Dasimbe had learned about the Evergreen Stone.

"OK, this is how Evergreen intends to use the stone," she said, green eyes aglow with mischief as she leaned in toward the flames. "We travel with the army tomorrow, getting as close to the enemy as we can. When we near their position, we join again and use the stone to gather and focus Evergreen's energy on Paul Rider's stone." She chuckled. "He believes his stone is only a talisman strengthening his talent, not realizing the stone actually absorbs Evergreen's energy, adding it to his, and nor does he grasp that this energy can destroy him. He holds the key to the destruction of his own army around his neck."

Someone in the circle gasped, but Sim continued. "Well, Evergreen doesn't intend to actually harm the men, but the soldiers of South Halcon

will be unable to remain here, even to do battle. They will no longer survive outside their own land for long but will be as bound to it as the sea
sprites are to the sea, losing their strength and health if they venture too far
from home. Whenever they leave South Halcon, they will have to return
quickly. That is what Evergreen intends for them, and Evergreen has the
strength to enforce it," she finished.

"Bravo," said Rask, and the others from Fanil agreed wholeheartedly.
The rest of us, more circumspect in our approval, smiled at Rask's enthusiasm and made little comment, but I wondered if deeper ramifications
would arise from what Evergreen intended to do. Regardless of the consequences, I would do what was necessary to avoid more bloodshed and deal
with any ramifications later.

"We're all tired and need our energy for tomorrow," Dalia noted as the
circle grew quiet.

Dasimbe nodded and stood up. "I'm going to get some sleep."

We roused ourselves from the comfort of the fire, Dom and Pace dousing the flames as the rest of us went to our tents.

The next morning we rose before dawn, awakened by soldiers ready to
take down our tents and pack them into wagons. Ciervo and Dalia joined
us by a newly laid fire for a hasty breakfast.

"Good morning," Ciervo said as they sat down. "Dalia tells me I have
to hear the news from Dasimbe. I saw you all ride into the city last night.
What happened?"

Sim answered him between mouthfuls of morning bread. "We found
an Evergreen Stone and had a joining that took us to the enemy camp.
Evergreen gave us an answer there, for Paul Rider wears an Evergreen Stone
around his neck. That is what we use to defeat him."

Ciervo nodded. "The stone I found in a box and never could touch.
How will you use it?"

Dasimbe told him what Evergreen had planned, and Ciervo's reaction
seemed subdued.

"If what you say is true, it will be an easily won battle, or rather, no
battle at all. However, we're prepared to fight, and we plan to ride out

shortly. Be ready to go." Then he stood and left to rejoin his men. Dalia remained with us.

Ciervo rode at the head of the army while we followed further back amid the noise and dust stirred by men on the move. A small but select group of soldiers surrounded us. These men, the best of North Halcon's troops, protected our group and guarded Ciervo's wife. Because they came from a land of sorcerers and had heard rumors of our last encounter with the enemy, they held our group in awe. We had given the army of North Halcon confidence in something they believed in but few knew much about.

We rode three days before we neared the army of Paul Rider, and each night, Copper and Silver drew closer to conjunction, their mingled glow growing in brightness. I felt a rising tension in the troops, and our group grew restless at the army's slow pace. Dasimbe scouted ahead through the eyes of the nekka and saw only the enemy's expected forward scouts who kept clear of our men.

As we left our encampment on the fourth day, a haze of dust arose from Paul Rider's troops in the distance. We rode just behind Ciervo and his commanders, but before long, Ciervo rode back to us.

"Are you close enough yet? You had better do what you've planned soon, or you'll be in join with his men all around you."

I nodded. I had already felt Paul Rider's search for some presence like ours and had set up a minor ward shield to cover our presence. Once the joining began, it no longer mattered what he saw. I also felt a stir of talent from his direction and wondered what he and his half breeds might try.

At her father's comment, Dasimbe headed off through the thorny bushes and sparse grass at the road's verge. The rest of our group, including Gloria, followed, leaving the main body of the army as it slowly came to a halt.

In a relatively thorn-free patch, we dismounted and sat to form a circle for our join. Dasimbe drew the stone from its pouch and placed it, as I had, in a small hollow of earth, only now it caught the morning sun's rays.

The wind suddenly gusted, and I heard shouts. I turned to see whirlwinds forming before our troops. The small funnels quickly grew in size and picked up speed along with dirt and debris as they sped toward our front line.

"Gloria, are you ready to do this with us?" I asked.

"Yes," she said and nodded, so we placed our hands to Evergreen's surface, and the sea sprites began to sing.

Soon we sat in the midst of a whirlwind as horses whinnied and men shouted around us. Yet the stone began to glow, and as we wove the tune, the stone grew brighter—until it blazed like a miniature sun. Then I dropped the wards, and we descended into Evergreen. Energy flowed with us, gathering strength as we went. Arriving under the enemy's army, we directed the gathered energy upward, focusing the flow into the stone Paul Rider wore around his neck. His stone flared, and the ground shifted. Too late, he realized it was an attack. He had no time to shield himself as the energy of Evergreen poured into his body and out into the men around him. It spread in waves, a raging flood covering the entire army. I felt my own being within them and knew their fear. I cried out as they did and cowered within them on the shaking earth. Then, gradually, I felt myself withdraw, along with the energy of Evergreen, returning the soil to recede deep into the planet's interior. Much later, I felt myself rise again, slowly, in levels, until at last I felt an awareness of my own body, my own mind.

I came back to a night lit by two moons and a blazing campfire. The fire outshone the now dim glow of the stone in front of us. A tent had been erected nearby, and a blanket covered all of me but my head. I took a deep breath, moving stiff limbs as I looked around to see Dasimbe, Celeste, Cierva, Stephen, and Gloria also stirring beneath blankets, working to ease their muscles.

"Thank Evergreen some of you are back," Ciervo said from outside our circle. "It happened as you said, and now Rider's army is leaving, and my troops are still stiff with fear."

I felt his agitation and fear for his wife, and I saw Dalia and the other sea sprites still held in join with Evergreen.

"The others should return shortly," I tried to reassure him, as he sat down near his wife to wait.

Although exhausted, I managed to get to my feet. I grabbed my blanket and stumbled to Sim's side.

"How are you?" I asked, as I sat cross-legged beside her.

She looked up and smiled. "I'm fine," she said and turned to Gloria, "How about you, Gloria?"

"I'm all right but tired." She sat staring into the flames.

Sim nodded, and as she turned back to me, I reached for her hands within the folds of blanket. No energy sparked from our touch. We were too spent for that—at least for a while. A different kind of fire flared now, that which existed naturally between a man and a woman and had little to do with Evergreen's power. Without a word or a thought for who saw us, I leaned over to kiss her, a kiss she returned. I welcomed her response. As the kiss deepened, her pulse quickened, and I felt myself grow hot.

All too soon, I sensed the sea sprites stirring and reluctantly pulled away from the kiss, but I kept hold of Sim's hands. We smiled at each other before turning to watch the emerging sprites.

"How long have we been gone?" Rask asked as he stretched stiff muscles.

"Since you started your join this morning, and it's nearly midnight," Ciervo answered and pulled his wife close.

Then he and Dalia stood up to enter the tent. "If you huddle together, there's enough room in the tent for everyone" he said.

One by one, we rose to follow.

Unobtrusively, Sim reached down to pick up the Evergreen Stone and returned it to its pouch around her neck.

Celeste turned to me, eyes widening slightly. "Daniel, you didn't pick up the stone. Sim is the Stone Keeper," she whispered.

Sim heard her and asked, "What is that?"

Stephen answered, "Stone Keepers are often great healers chosen by Evergreen to carry the stones. Or sometimes the Keeper is a lonely traveler with great talent to aid people in need."

"But I'm neither of those," Sim protested.

Celeste smiled and said quietly as we entered the tent, "Maybe not yet, but apparently you will be. Tell her, Daniel."

"It's true," I whispered and pulled her down beside me to sleep. I could feel questions war with her weariness, but she slept. The next morning, as we turned back toward Phoenix, Dasimbe remained quiet about the stone.

We returned to the plains outside Phoenix by midmorning on the day of Copper and Silver's conjunction. Ciervo ordered his commanders to care for the troops while he went to meet with Phoenix's city council. When he returned from reassuring the city's leaders that Phoenix was safe, he requested that we all meet again with his troop commanders. When we gathered in his tent, his men reported the growing restlessness of the army.

"Those who wanted a fight didn't get one, and the others just want to go home. We should give them that much, or there may be trouble. Is there any reason to stay around Phoenix?" one commander asked.

Ciervo paced back and forth. "No, Phoenix is fine as she is, but we aren't. I think some of what hit South Halcon's army hit us. I feel the urge to go racing back to North Halcon as fast as my horse can carry me."

Sim and Cia stared at him, looking horrified as the ramifications of our join with Evergreen became clear.

"Evergreen worked better than we hoped, Daniel," he continued. "Everyone in both armies has been affected, except, perhaps, for those of you who joined with Evergreen. How do you feel, and what do you have planned for yourselves?"

Shaking off my concern for him and Dalia, I answered, "I don't think we've been affected. Celeste, Stephen, and I will return to our home for a while, and we hope Cia and Sim will accompany us. I'm not sure about Gloria or those from Fanil. Rask, what are your plans?" I turned to Rask.

Rask looked at his friends, and they nodded for him to speak for them. "I intend to take everyone home via Olin. After that, personally, I feel a need to visit my home in Meral. I think some of Evergreen's leading rubbed off on me too."

"I can't wait to see my family again," Clea added. "I've had enough adventure for a while."

Rask grinned and said, "We should be home in time for your seventeenth birthday."

No one asked Dalia about her plans. She faced a potentially permanent separation from her husband.

"So be it," Ciervo said. "The troops will leave tomorrow. There's still a war going on and a border to defend." Ciervo dismissed his commanders to ready the troops for a hasty departure and then turned to me. "I've managed to secure an apartment in the Phoenix administration building for one night. I'd like you, your brother and sister, and Gloria to accompany my family. I want to hear about this home of yours you're planning to take my daughters to. Go ahead with Dalia to see that we have food and that the rooms are prepared."

He included the group from Fanil by offering them separate guest rooms, but they declined, preferring to stay away from the city and in their tents for one last night. Although they had started preparing for their journey home, they assured us they would wait to see us before they left.

As it was already late afternoon, we parted ways, Ciervo heading to the troops, and our group of sprites, half breeds, and one human packing up our gear. Then Dalia, Cia, Sim, Gloria, Celeste, Stephen, and I left the camp for the city and the apartment.

Fortunately, the administration building sat at the edge of the city, for crowds celebrating the midwinter moon conjunction and the victory over South Halcon clogged the streets. This time I used a confusion ward to screen myself, as did Stephen and Celeste. When we reached the building, we dropped the wards.

While the women settled in, I went on an errand of my own. My appearance drew stares, but within the building, I remained safe even without a ward. Eventually I found the administrator I wanted, and when I told him what I needed, he happily obliged.

Ciervo arrived just after sundown, and we all met in the apartment's living area where food, wine, and a blazing hearth fire awaited us. Ciervo stretched and relaxed in a large chair as he broached the subject of my home.

"Now, perhaps you can tell me where it is you plan on taking my daughters and why." I noticed Dalia listened as intently for the answer as Ciervo.

I repeated what I had told Dasimbe of my home in High Tor. Celeste and Stephen, who of course knew as much as I did, let me handle the delicate explanation.

"That explains where you're taking them," he said, "and how you plan on getting there, as unbelievable as it is. It still doesn't explain why," he reminded me.

Celeste leaned forward now, stopping me from answering with a touch on my sleeve, and then she gave an answer that concerned her and Cia.

"My reason for wanting Cia to come with me to High Tor is that she is my sister-wife, and I want her to see my home and meet my family before we return to the Northern Forest. When we return to the forest, we'll seldom leave it, and this is too good an opportunity to miss."

Ciervo nodded. "I understand." Then he turned to me. "But why should Dasimbe go?"

Dasimbe jumped in before I could say a word. "Father, I want to go. I want to see High Tor for myself."

He looked at her for a moment and then smiled. "I imagine that you do." He again turned to me. "Daniel?" he said, and I knew he asked my intentions.

I nodded my understanding and turned to Dasimbe. "With Dasimbe's permission, and that of her family, I would like her to become my wife. Then I will take her home to meet my family."

No one said a word for a moment, but Gloria gasped, and while Dalia and Celeste smiled knowingly, Stephen grinned. Ciervo finally turned to Sim.

"Dasimbe?" he questioned.

Sim looked at me, smiled, and nodded. "Yes, permission granted." And for once her emotions remained well screened. Where had her sudden control come from?

"Well then, this may take some planning, and I'll miss everything," Ciervo added in mock dismay, for he seemed as happy for Dasimbe as any father could be.

"Not at all," I informed him. "The ceremony is arranged for tonight, at the twenty-seventh hour. An administrator has agreed to perform the ceremony. I wanted all your family to be present."

"You must have been very sure of her answer," Ciervo said, laughing.

"Very sure," I said, smiling at Sim.

She grinned. "You know me far too well, Daniel. But I'll surprise you yet," she teased.

Ciervo looked thoughtful. "Both my daughters have surprised me—Cia with her marriage and a child, Dasimbe with her new skills and being all grown up." He chuckled then. "Dalia, did you know about Daniel and Sim?"

"I had my hopes, yes, but could never be sure what his intentions were," she answered. "And with everything else going on, it was hard to read the situation."

Celeste stood up, holding out her hand toward Dasimbe. "Come on, Sim. We'll help you get ready for your marriage. We of the Northern Forest love a good marriage ceremony. Ask Cia." Cierva smiled, and then all the women retreated toward their rooms.

Ciervo's eyes sparkled in the firelight. "One daughter already married, and now the other will be wed. Not bad, considering the reason we came here in the first place."

"And if you had never had to leave Phoenix because of the war?" I asked.

He looked at me for a moment before answering. "There is both good and bad in that answer, as you well know. The cruelty lies in our family being separated, with no surety of seeing each other again. On the other hand"—and here he smiled—"I have my daughter's happiness to be thankful for, although I must admit, I would like to know more about your family." Looking at Stephen and me, he gave us a lead we had to follow.

Although I would have liked to reveal more, we told him only what I had told Dasimbe of my half-blood line. I assured him that she would be united with a proud, prosperous, and prominent family of High Tor. He nodded, seeming satisfied with what we could tell him.

At the appointed hour, we gathered in the apartment's living area. Ciervo and Dalia looked pleased with the situation, yet their impending separation, and memories of their own marriage in Phoenix, must have intruded in a pleasant and painful mixture.

The sea sprites from Fanil appeared, at first curious and then eager to congratulate us when they realized they had been called to attend our wedding.

"A wedding on the night of the moons' conjunction—how appropriate," Rask said, grinning as usual.

Then Dasimbe entered the room, and time seemed to stop for a moment. A white gown of human fashion emphasized her red-gold hair, flawless skin, and brilliant, flashing green eyes, so like her father's. The tightly laced bodice hugged her from beneath cupped breasts to her waist. From there, a skirt covered with tiny pearls billowed out in glittering splendor. Pearls also gleamed in her hair. She glowed, an apparition, as the double moons' light blazed through a large, arched window. I took her hand and flinched at the pulsing energy that again flashed between us.

The administrator performed the ceremony in the simple time-honored fashion that ended at the record book. After I had signed my name, Dasimbe did the same. I heard her gasp as she saw what I had written.

"'Daniel Scott, seventh son of Terrence Scott.' So you knew all along what 'bride of the seventh son' meant?"

"Yes, but I was as surprised as you when Lam Po spoke of it."

She smiled in mischief and traced fingers across the back of my hand, spreading fire at her touch. She knew now what her touch could do, for I had the same effect on her.

"How many secrets do you hide, Daniel? Will I ever learn them all?" she asked.

"No." I grinned, teasing her.

"We'll see about that," she said, and we turned from the record book to join family and friends.

A small marriage feast took place after the ceremony. The administrator had even managed to find a few musicians despite the late hour. Then we celebrated the double-moon conjunction with all those in our small group: Rask, Dom, Pacel, Jacin, Clea, Stephen, Celeste, Cierva, Gloria, Ciervo, Dalia, and Dasimbe and I. Nevertheless, the hour was late, and the gathering ended before long. We soon said our good-nights and departed to our rooms.

The administrator had given me the keys to a room set apart for newly-weds. I led Dasimbe there, and as soon as the door closed behind us, I took her in my arms. I could feel her trembling slightly.

I laughed, and then I kissed her, and as before, the deepening kiss ignited a fire in both of us. One arm pulled her closer as my other trailed fingers down her cheek to her neck and to the tops of her breasts above the gown. Her pulse increased, and her breathing became ragged. I broke the kiss and kissed her neck and the flesh above the bodice. Then I pushed her away gently, trembling a little myself.

"We have to get you out of that gown," I said, voice husky with emotion. As her hands went to the laces in her dress, I pushed them away. "No, let me do that," I said and tugged at the laces and undressed her.

My breath caught as everything I had imagined—sweet curves and flawless skin begging to be touched—gave promise of delight and release from a growing and almost painful need. I gestured toward the bed, already turned down and waiting. She climbed onto it and lay back to watch as I removed my own clothing. I grew harder as she watched me.

Then I slid onto the bed and reached to tangle a hand in her hair, not otherwise touching her as I looked into her eyes. She smiled and then gazed down at my body.

"You're beautiful," she said.

"So are you," I said, "and you had best watch where you put your hands, or I won't have anything left to work with."

She laughed, low and quiet, and I reached for her, her skin like fire beneath my touch. Without thought, my mind shields dropped, and I opened to her, energy flowing between us in increasing cycles as she caressed me, and I caressed her. I kissed her again, my hunger for her growing until a bonding join started. I felt the pleasure she felt, and she felt the release I soon needed from the pleasure she gave me. Then, while in join, I pressed into her warmth and fell, lost somewhere in the fire and pleasure she felt as intensely as I did, until an explosion of sensation completed our melding of body and mind.

Fully bonded, we remained in join, savoring the contentment and sensations from our first union, but the fire had barely receded before we felt it rise again. Every touch during the night awakened us to the same need and the same fire.

I awoke late, immediately feeling Evergreen's presence and a spark of new life stirring within Sim.

She opened her eyes, green jewels in the morning light, and smiled, snuggling closer. I ran a finger down her cheek, to her neck, and across her breasts to her stomach. "Sim, can you feel it? It's barely begun, but a new life is forming."

"Yes," she whispered, her eyes opening wide. Strong eddies of plane-change whirled around us, and the presence of Evergreen grew stronger.

"This must be important to Evergreen," she added, wonder in her voice.

We remained in each other's arms awhile longer, not entirely sure we were finished with lovemaking, but farewells awaited, and reluctantly, we left the bed.

After bathing, we dressed and went to the apartment. We found Stephen, Gloria, and our sisters eating in the dining area.

"Finally," Celeste said, after she downed a mouthful of morning bread. She chuckled. "Although I'm not surprised you're late. I woke up several times to splashes of energy bouncing about all over the place."

"Your guards were completely down, and no wards were in place," Stephen added.

"I had no thought and little energy for guards or wards," I told them.

Cia laughed. "Well, now you had better hurry. Mother and Father left ages ago. I spoke to them this morning, and I know we'll have to leave soon."

We finished eating and left Phoenix within the hour with all our belongings. As we approached the camp, we became more subdued. The camp itself no longer existed but had turned into a moving mass of humanity, horses, and wagons, all cloaked in clouds of dust.

Our friends from Fanil waited near where our tents had stood. Nothing remained but the blackened ring of soil where the campfire had blazed. Everything else had been packed up onto packhorses and into supply wagons. In fact, troops already moved out onto the road to North Halcon.

Ciervo and Dalia rode up and dismounted.

"This is where we part, my friends," Ciervo shouted above the din, "but I expect I'll see some of you in North Halcon in the future," he added, referring to those of us who could visit him there.

Rask stepped forward to shake Ciervo's hand. "I'll certainly never forget my experiences here. I'm only sorry I'll not be able to visit you."

Ciervo nodded. "Thank you all for your help. It prevented a great deal of bloodshed."

Then Rask turned in my direction. "Congratulations on your marriage," he said, thumping my shoulder before shaking my hand. "I expect I might see you in Meral undersea someday. Just a hunch." Then he turned to hug Dasimbe. All the sprites from Fanil hugged Dasimbe in turn.

As we said our good-byes, Ciervo and Dalia said theirs. At last, Dalia turned from her husband and led her horse to join the group of sea sprites.

Dasimbe and Cierva hugged their mother.

"Will you be all right without us in Olin?" Dasimbe asked. Although she managed to control her broadcast of emotion, I felt it.

"I've been in Olin without you before, remember?" she assured her daughters. "Besides, I have my friends, and Olin is my home."

Good-byes said, we mounted up and sat for a moment, silently looking at each other. Then Ciervo gestured to Gloria as he addressed me. "If possible, I want Gloria to go with your group. I would like a representative of North Halcon in High Tor."

I felt the question and an appeal born out of frustrated curiosity. He would have gone himself if he could.

I nodded. "She is welcome as your envoy."

He turned to Gloria. "Will you go? Or have you something unique to offer the army in Halconnida? I can't let you join your family on the war front."

She seemed stunned and, as usual, had no shield on her thoughts or emotions. She wanted to go, but fear held back her reply.

"If you come with us, we can get you over the mountains," I said and added, "I'm sure Cia and Sim will enjoy your company."

She nodded. "I'll go."

Ciervo nodded in return and gave a brief salute before he turned away. Dust spurted under his horse's hooves as he rode to join his departing army. Dalia's face remained blank, showing nothing as her husband rode away.

Then Rask broke the silence. "We'd best be on our way. Good-bye and good fortune in your travels," he said to those of us going into the Tors.

"Thank you, Rask, and you in yours. We'll meet again, as you say," I replied. Then the group of sea sprites turned to ride out.

"*I'll see you and your children in Olin,*" Dalia said, a final parting mental thread of farewell to her daughters before turning to follow the others.

We watched as they rode away while the plains around us emptied of the army.

As the sprites disappeared into the east, the last of the army reached the Halcon Road. I shoved aside uncomfortable emotions stirred by this parting, preferring instead to focus on the satisfaction of a battle won without bloodshed and the excitement of the journey ahead.

Bad Boy snorted and tossed his head as I looked toward the west, thinking of the mountains and High Tor. I glanced at Stephen, who nodded, feeling and understanding my emotions. Then I glanced toward Dasimbe. The Evergreen Stone still rested in its pouch around her neck, a symbol of her unity with this planet. She caught my look and smiled.

"Well, Daniel, what lies ahead?"

What lies ahead? More than she could ever guess.

I felt her roil of emotions through our mate-bond. Anticipation overpowered sadness at parting from friends. It was mixed with a little thrill of fear at facing the unknown—much the same mix she had broadcast when leaving Olin on our first journey together.

I felt a touch of unease myself. How would she and Cia and Gloria respond to High Tor, a world so different from anything they knew? And would they accept the real answer to the question of why humans found it difficult to bond with Evergreen?

I shrugged off my concern and smiled as I nodded toward the Comber road. The real answer would have to wait just a little longer.

"The journey to High Tor lies ahead," I answered, "and it's time to leave."

"Finally," I heard Stephen mutter as my eyes returned to the west, and I urged Bad Boy forward, letting him break into a run as the others followed. Exhilaration flooded through me, and I warded by habit, but the fire in my blood surged as we headed away from Phoenix toward the distant mountains.

Made in the USA
Monee, IL
07 July 2026

56551694R00128